Mark Antony Lower

The Lives of William Cavendishe, Duke of Newcastle, and of his Wife, Margaret, Duchess of Newcastle

Mark Antony Lower

The Lives of William Cavendishe, Duke of Newcastle, and of his Wife, Margaret, Duchess of Newcastle

ISBN/EAN: 9783744714891

Printed in Europe, USA, Canada, Australia, Japan

Cover: Foto ©Raphael Reischuk / pixelio.de

More available books at **www.hansebooks.com**

MARGARET CAVENDISH,

THE LIVES OF
WILLIAM CAVENDISHE,
DUKE OF NEWCASTLE,

AND OF HIS WIFE,

MARGARET DUCHESS OF NEWCASTLE.

WRITTEN BY THE THRICE NOBLE AND

ILLUSTRIOUS PRINCESS,

MARGARET, DUCHESS OF NEWCASTLE.

EDITED WITH A PREFACE AND OCCASIONAL

NOTES BY

MARK ANTONY LOWER, M.A., Etc.

LONDON:

JOHN RUSSELL SMITH,

36, SOHO SQUARE.

1872.

Preface.

AMONG the curiofities of biographical and autobiographical literature of the feventeenth century, there are but few which exceed in intereft the two mentioned in the title-page of this book. By way of introduction, it is neceffary to quote their titles in full. The firft is—

"The Life of the Thrice Noble, High, and puiffant Prince, WILLIAM CAVENDISHE, Duke, Marquefs, and Earl of NEWCASTLE, Earl of Ogle; Vifcount Mansfield; and Baron of *Bolfover*, of *Ogle*, *Bothal*, and *Hepple*: Gentleman of His Majefties Bed-Chamber; one of His Majefties moft Honourable Privy Council; Knight of the Moft Noble Order of the Garter; His Majefties Lieutenant of the County and Town of *Nottingham;* and Juſtice in Ayre, *Trent North:* who had the honour to be Governour to our moſt Glorious King, and Gracious Soveraign, in his Youth, when He was Prince of *Wales;* and ſoon after was made Captain General of all the Provinces beyond the River of *Trent,* and other Parts of the Kingdom of *England,* with Power, by a ſpecial Commiſſion to make Knights.—Written by the thrice Noble, Illuſtrious, and Excellent Princeſs, MARGARET, Duchefs of Newcaſtle, His [ſecond] Wife.— London, Printed by *A. Maxwell* in the year 1667."

The title of the ſecond work is—

"A True Relation of the Birth, Breeding, and Life of MARGARET CAVENDISH, Duchefs of Newcaſtle." [Written by herſelf.]

The latter was not publiſhed in a ſeparate form, but it appears in a ſcarce and curious folio, called "𝕹atures 𝕻ictures drawn by FANCIES PENCIL to the Life. Written by the thrice Noble, Illuſtrious, and Excellent Princeſs, THE LADY MARCHIONESS OF NEW-CASTLE.—*In this Volume there are ſeveral feigned ſtories of Natural Deſcriptions, as Comi-*

cal, *Tragical, and Tragi-comical, Poetical, Ro-*
mantical, Philofophical, and Hiftorical, both in
Profe and Verfe, fome all Profe, fome mixt, partly
Profe and partly Verfe. Alfo there are fome
Morals, and fome Dialogues, but they are as
the advantage Loaves of Bread as a Baker's
Dozen; and a true Story at the latter End,
wherein there is no feinins."—London: Printed
by J. Martin, and J. Alleftrye at the Bell in
Saint Pauls Church-yard, 1656.[1]

The latter work (or rather part of a work)
was printed as a brochure by Sir Egerton
Brydges at his private prefs at Lee Priory,
with a " critical preface," &c., in 1814.
This reprint is one of the worft ever given
to the world, the typography being fhamefully
incorrect. In the prefent re-impreffion the
punctuation and capital letters have been
carefully attended to, fo that I truft it will
be found a faithful copy of the quaint original.

It is fcarcely neceffary to add to thefe
remarks any biographical notices of the Duke
and Duchefs. The hufband was undoubtedly

---

[1] *Nature's Pictures*, p. 368.

a true Nobleman, and whatever opinion the prefent age may hold concerning his political views, there can be no doubt that loyalty to his pupil, afterwards Charles II., influenced him in a direction which, but for that, might have been different. We forgive errors in our own children and friends which we fhould not excufe in other people—the errors, I mean, of *partiality*.

As to MARGARET, the Duchefs, and authorefs of thefe two biographies, Sir Egerton Brydges makes fome excellent remarks. "That the Duchefs was deficient in a cultivated judgment," he fays; "that her knowledge was more multifarious than exact; and that her powers of fancy and fentiment were more active than her powers of reafoning, I will admit; but that her productions, mingled as they are with great abfurdities, are wanting either in talent or virtue, or even in genius, I cannot concede. . . . . 'I fear my ambi-tion,' fays the Duchefs, 'inclines to vain-glory; for I am very ambitious; yet 'tis neither for beauty, wit, titles, wealth, or power, but as they are Steps to raife me to Fancies Tower, which is to live by Remem-

brance in after Ages. . . . . I was addicted
from **my Childhood** to Contemplation, rather
then Converfation; **to** Solitarinefs rather then
Society; **to** Melancholy rather **then Mirth;
to write with** the Pen then to work with my
Needle."

She further adds: " My Difpofition is **more**
inclining to Melancholy **than** Merry; **but**
not crabbed or peevifh **Melancholy,** but foft,
melting, folitary, **and** contemplating Melancholy, and **I** am **apt to weep** rather **than**
laugh." **For** other features of her character
the reader muft feek **in** the body of her auto-
biography, and I feel certain that no modern
reader, on a candid perufal of her writings,
will concur in attributing to her the nickname
which **her** jealous (female?) contemporaries
gave her—" *Mad Madge of Newcaftle!* "

" **The** labours of **no** modern authorefs,"
fays Dyce, in his *Britifh Poeteffes,* " can be
compared **as to** quantity with thofe of the
indefatigable Duchefs of Newcaftle, who filled
nearly twelve volumes **folio** with plays, poems,
orations, philofophical difcourfes, &c. Her
writings fhow that fhe poffeffed a mind of
confiderable power and activity, with much

imagination, but not one particle of judgment
or tafte." But this is by far too fweeping a
criticifm—eccentric fhe doubtlefs was, and
perhaps John Evelyn's dictum will not be
difputed when he fays, in a few brief words,
after he had paid the Duke and Duchefs a
vifit at their town-houfe in Clerkenwell Clofe;
" I was much pleafed with the extraordinary
fanciful habit, garb and difcourfe of the
Duchefs."

When in the country, the Duke and
Duchefs refided chiefly at Welbeck Abbey
in Nottinghamfhire, and at Bolfover Caftle
in Derbyfhire, feats about fix or feven miles
apart. There is a portrait of her Grace, in
a kind of theatrical coftume, now at Welbeck
Abbey, and another (a very fine one) at
Wentworth Caftle, Yorkfhire, which has
been engraved, after a painting by Abraham
Van Diepenbach of Antwerp, a pupil of
Rubens. This picture has been attributed
by miftake to Sir Peter Lely.

The Duchefs died in London, and was
buried near the Duke in Weftminfter Abbey,
January 7th, 1674. A fine monument in the
north tranfept bears the following infcrip-
tion :—

HERE LYES THE LOYALL DUKE OF NEWCASTLE, AND HIS DUTCHESS HIS SECOND WIFE, BY WHOM HE HAD NO ISSUE : HER NAME WAS MARGARETT LUCAS, YONGEST SISTER TO THE LORD LUCAS, OF COLCHESTER; A NOBLE FAMILIE, FOR ALL THE BROTHERS WERE VALIANT, AND ALL THE SISTERS VIRTUOUS. THIS DUTCHESS WAS A WISE, WITTIE, AND LEARNED LADY, WHICH HER MANY BOOKES DO WELL TESTIFIE; SHE WAS A MOST VIRTUOUS AND A LOVEING AND CAREFULL WIFE, AND WAS WITH HER LORD ALL THE TIME OF HIS BANISHMENT AND MISERIES, AND WHEN HE CAME HOME NEVER PARTED FROM HIM IN HIS SOLITARY RETIREMENTS.

I have not enlarged this preface as I might have done, becaufe all the main incidents of the lives of the Duke and Duchefs will be found in the text of the two biographies included in this volume, and in the occafional notes which I have added in the courfe of my editorfhip. M. A. L.

POSTSCRIPT.

MR. HALLIWELL, in his "Letters of the Kings of England," prints feveral from Charles the Firft to the Duke of Newcaftle. The firft is dated from Shrewfbury, 23rd September, 1642. "This is to tell you that this rebellion is grown to that height, that I

muſt not look what opinion **men are of who**
at the time [are] willing and able to **ſerve** me.
Therefore, I **do** not **only** permit, but command you to make uſe **of all** my loving ſub-
jeƈts' ſervices, **without examining** their con-
ſciences (more than **their loyalty to me)** as
you ſhall find moſt **to** conduce to the uphold-
ing **of my juſt** regal **power.**—So I reſt, Your
moſt **aſſured** faithful friend,

" CHARLES **R.**"

The next letter is dated from Oxford,
November 2, 1642, in which he ſays : " Newcaſtle.   Your letters are ſo really faithful and
lucky in my **ſervice,** that though **I pretend**
not **to** thank you in words, yet **I cannot** but
tell **you** . . . . of the ſenſe I have of **them.**"
The king goes on to ſtate that he has ſent
the Duke £4,000 for war expenſes, and concludes with " **Your** moſt aſſured conſtant
friend, CHARLES R."
In the third letter **the** King thanks Newcaſtle (then Earl) **for** his eminent ſervices,
and avers that he ſhall look upon him as " a
principal inſtrument in keeping the crown on
my head."   In this letter the King informs

the Earl that he has given orders for a commiffion "to command all the countries beyond Trent." This letter is dated from
Oxford, December 15, 1642.

The next is alfo dated from Oxford, a few
days later, December 29, 1642. The King
thanks the Earl for fending for the Queen
with "earneftnefs," and regrets that he cannot fend him more arms, at the fame time
wondering that as there were 12,000 of the
trained bands in the Earl's diftrict, he fhould
find any lack of weapons. It concludes with:
"I pray you let me hear from you as oft as
you may."

The fifth letter bears date Oxford, April 5,
1644, and contains ftrong expreffions refpecting the Scots. The King fays: "Remember
all courage is not in fighting: conftancy in a
good caufe being the chief, and the defpifing
of flanderous tongues and pens being not the
leaft ingredient."

The next is of little importance. It is
dated from Oxford, April 11, 1644, and refers
to the Scots' invafion.

The feventh letter is addreffed to Newcaftle under his new title of Marquis, in final

teftimony of his great fervices after the dif-
comfiture of the royal forces in the North. It
is dated from " Our court at Oxford 28. Nov.
1644," and is full of praifes and gratitude, and
addreffed : " To our right trufty and entirely
beloved councillor, William, Marquis of Newcaftle."

THE
LIFE

OF THE

Thrice Noble, High and Puiſſant PRINCE,

William Cavendiſhe,

Duke, Marqueſs, and Earl of *Newcaſtle;* Earl of *Ogle;* Viſcount *Mansfield;* and Baron of *Bolſover,* of *Ogle, Bothal* and *Hepple:* Gentleman of His Majeſties Bed-chamber; one of His Majeſties moſt Honourable Privy-Councel; Knight of the moſt Noble Order of the Garter; His Majeſties Lieutenant of the County and Town of *Nottingham;* and Juſtice in Ayre *Trent-North:* who had the honour to be Governour to our moſt Glorious King, and Gracious Soveraign, in his Youth, when He was Prince of *Wales;* and ſoon after was made Captain General of all the Provinces beyond the River of *Trent,* and other Parts of the Kingdom of *England,* with Power, by a ſpecial Commiſſion, to make Knights.

WRITTEN

By the thrice Noble, Illuſtrious, and Excellent Princeſs,
MARGARET, *Ducheſs of* Newcaſtle,
His 2d *Wife.*

LONDON,

Printed by *A. Maxwell,* in the Year 1667.

To His moſt Sacred Majeſty
Charles the Second,

By the Grace of God, of *England, Scotland, France* and *Ireland* King, Defender of the Faith, *&c.*

May it pleaſe Your Majeſty,

 HAVE, in confidence of your Gracious acceptance, taken the boldneſs, or rather the preſumption, to dedicate to Your Majeſty this ſhort Hiſtory (which is as full of Truths, as words) of the Actions and Sufferings of Your moſt Loyal Subject, my Lord and Huſband (by Your Majeſties late favour) Duke of *Newcaſtle;* who when Your Majeſty was Prince of *Wales,* was Your moſt careful Governour, and honeſt Servant. Give me therefore leave to relate here, that I have

heard him often fay, He loves Your Royal
Perfon fo dearly, that He would moft willingly,
upon all occafions, facrifice his **Life and Pof-**
terity **for Your** Majefty : whom that Heaven
will ever blefs, **is the Prayer of**

Your moft Obedient, **Loyal,**

humble Subject

and Servant,

Margaret Newcaftle.

To His Grace the Duke of Newcaſtle.

My Noble Lord,

*IT hath always been my hearty Prayer to God, ſince I have been your Wife, That firſt I might prove an honeſt and good **Wife**, whereof your Grace muſt **be** the onely Judg: **Next,** That God would be pleaſed to enable me **to** ſet forth **and** declare **to** after-ages, **the** truth **of** your loyal actions and endeavours, for the ſervice of your King **and** Country; For the accompliſh-ing of which deſign, I have followed the beſt and trueſt Obſervations of your **Secretary** John Rol-leſton, and your Lordſhips **own** Relations, and have accordingly writ the Hiſtory of your Lord-ſhips Life, which although I have endeavoured to render as perſpicuous as **ever** I could, yet one* *thing I find hath much darkned it; which is, that your* **Grace** *commanded* **me not** *to mention any thing or passage to the prejudice or disgrace of any Family or particular* **person** *(although they might be of great truth, and would* **illustrate** *much the actions of your* **Life**) *which* **I have** *dutifully* **performed** *to* **satisfie** *your* **Lordship**, *whose* **Nature is so Generous,** *that you* **are as well pleased to** *obscure* **the** *faults of your* **Enemies,** *as you* **are to** *divulge the* **vertues** *of your* **Friends** ; *And certainly,* **My Lord,** *you have had as many* **Enemies,** *and as many* **Friends,** *as ever any one particular person had; and* **I** *pray God* **to** *forgive* **the** *one, and prosper the other:* **Nor do I** *so much wonder at it,* **since I, a** *Woman,* **cannot** *be ex-* **empt from** *the* **malice and** *aspersions of spightful tongues, which they cast upon* **my poor** *Writings, some denying me to be* **the true Authoress of them ;** **for your** *Grace remembers well, that those Books* **I put out first, to the** *judgment* **of** *this censorious Age, were accounted not to be written* **by a** *Woman, but that some body else had* **writ** *and* **publish'd** *them in my Name; by* **which your** **Lordship was** *moved* **to** *prefix* **an** *Epistle before* **one of them in my** *vindication, wherein you assure* **the** *world* **upon** *your honour,* *That what* **was** *written* and *printed in my name, was my own;* and *I have also made known, that your Lordship* was *my onely* Tutor, *in declaring to me what* you *had found and observed by your own experi-* rience; *for I being young when your Lordship* married me, *could not have much knowledg of the world; But it pleased God to command his Servant Nature to indue me with a Poetical and Philosophical Genius, even from my Birth; for I did write some Books in that kind, before I was twelve years of Age, which for want of good method and order, I would never divulge. But though the world would not believe that those Conceptions and Fancies which I writ, were my own, but transcended my capacity, yet they found fault, that they were defective for want of Learning; and on the other side, they said I had pluckt Feathers out of the Universities; which was a very preposterous judgment. Truly, My Lord, I confess that for want of Scholarship, I could not express my self so well as otherwise I might have done, in those Philosophical Writings I publish'd first; but after I was returned with your Lordship into my Native Country, and led a retired Country life, I applied my self to the reading of Philosophical Authors,*

*of purpose to learn those names and words of Art
that are used in Schools; which at first were so
hard to me, that I could not understand them, but
was fain to guess at the sense of them by the whole
context, and so writ them down as I found them
in those Authors, at which my Readers did wonder,
and thought it impossible that a Woman could
have so much Learning and Understanding in
Terms of Art, and Scholastical Expressions; so
that I and my Books are like the old Apologue
mention'd in Æsop, of a Father, and his Son,
who rid on an Ass through a Town when his
Father went on Foot, at which sight the People
shouted and cried shame, that a young Boy should
ride, and let his Father, an old man, go on Foot:
whereupon the old Man got upon the Ass, and
let his Son go by; but when they came to the
next Town, the People exclaimed against the
Father, that he a lusty man should ride, and
have no more pity of his young and tender child,
but let him go on foot: Then both the Father and
his Son got upon the Ass, and coming to the third
Town, the People blamed them both for being so
unconscionable as to over-burden the poor Ass with
their heavy weight: After this both Father and
Son went on foot, and led the Ass; and when*

they came to the fourth Town, the People railed as much at them as ever the former had done, and called them both Fools, for going on foot, when they had a Beaſt able to carry them. The old Man, ſeeing he could not pleaſe Mankind in any manner, and having received ſo many ble-miſhes and aſperſions, for the ſake of his Aſs, was at laſt reſolved to drown him when he came to the next bridg. But I am not ſo paſſionate to burn my Writings for the various humours of Mankind, and for their finding fault, ſince there is nothing in this world, be it the nobleſt and moſt commendable action whatſoever, that ſhall eſcape blameleſs. As for my being the true and onely Authoreſs of them, your Lordſhip knows beſt, and my attending Servants are witneſs that I have had none but my own Thoughts, Fancies and Speculations to aſſiſt me; and as ſoon as I have ſet them down, I ſend them to thoſe that are to tranſcribe them, and fit them for the Preſs; whereof ſince there have been ſeveral, and amongſt them ſuch as onely could write a good hand, but neither underſtood Orthography, nor had any Learning (I being then in baniſhment with your Lordſhip, and not able to maintain learned Secre-taries) which hath been a great diſadvantage to *my poor works, and the cause that they **have been** printed so false, and so full of Errors ; for besides that, I want also the skill of Scholarship and **true** writing, I did many times not peruse the Copies that were transcribed, lest they should disturb my following Conceptions ; by which neglect, as **I** said, many Errors are slipt into my Works, which yet I hope Learned and Impartial Readers will soon rectifie, and look more upon **the** sense, **then** carp at words. I have been a Student even from my Childhood; and since I have been your Lordships **Wife, I** have lived for the most part a strict and retired Life, as is best known to your Lordship, and therefore my Censurers cannot **know** much **of me, since** they have little or no acquaintance with **me :** 'Tis true, **I** have been a Traveller both before and after **I** was married **to** your Lordship, and sometimes shew my self at your Lordships Command in Publick places **or** Assemblies ; but yet I converse with few. Indeed, **My Lord,** I matter not the Censures of this Age, **but** am rather proud of **them ; for** it shews **that my Actions are** more then ordinary, **and** according to the old **Proverb, It** is better to be Envied, then **Pitied :** for I know well, **that** it is meerly out of spight and malice, whereof this* *preſent Age is ſo full, that none can eſcape them, and they'l make no doubt to ſtain even Your Lordſhips Loyal, Noble and Heroick Actions, as well as they do mine, though yours have been of War and Fighting, mine of Contemplating and Writing: Yours were performed publickly in the Field, mine privately in my Cloſet: Yours had many thouſand Eye-witneſſes, mine none but my Waiting-maids.   But the Great God that hath hitherto bleſs'd both Your Grace and me, will, I queſtion not, preſerve both our Fames to after Ages, for which we ſhall be bound moſt humbly to acknowledg his great Mercy; and I my ſelf, as long as I live, be*

Your Graces Honeſt Wife,

and Humble Servant

M. NEWCASTLE.

The Preface.

HEN I firſt Intended to write this Hiſtory, knowing my ſelf to be no Scholar, and as ignorant of the Rules of writing Hiſtories, as I have in my other Works acknowledg'd my ſelf to be of the Names and Terms of Art; I deſired my Lord, That he would be pleaſed to let me have ſome Elegant and Learned Hiſtorian to aſſiſt me; which requeſt his Grace would not grant me ; ſaying, That having never had any Aſſiſtance in the writing of my former Books, I ſhould have no other in the writing of his Life, but the Informations from himſelf, and his Secretary, of the chief Tranſactions and Fortunes occurring in it, to the time he married me. I humbly anſwer'd, That without a learned Aſſiſtant,

the History would be defective: But he replied, That Truth could not be defective. I
said again, That Rhetorick did adorn Truth:
And he answer'd, That Rhetorick was fitter
for Falshoods then Truths. Thus I was
forced by his Graces Commands, to write
this History in my own plain Style, without
elegant Flourishings, or exquisit Method, re-
lying intirely upon Truth, in the expressing
whereof, I have been very circumspect ; as
knowing well, that his Graces Actions have
so much Glory of their own, that they need
borrow none from any bodies Industry.

Many Learned Men, I know, have pub-
lished Rules and Directions concerning the
Method and Style of Histories, and do with
great noise, to little purpose, make loud exclamations against those Historians, that keeping close to the Truth of their Narrations,
cannot think it necessary to follow slavishly
such Instructions ; and there is some Men of
good Understandings, as I have heard, that
applaud very much several Histories, meerly
for their Elegant Style, and well-observ'd
Method ; setting a high value upon feigned
Orations, mystical Designs, and fancied

Policies, which **are, at the** beft, but pleafant
Romances. **Others approve,** in the Relations
of Wars, and **of** Military Actions, fuch tedious
Defcriptions, **that the Reader, tired** with
them, will imagine that **there was more** time
fpent in Affaulting, Defending, and taking of
a **Fort, or a** petty Garifon, then *Alexander* **did**
employ in conquering the greateft part **of the**
World : **which proves, That fuch** Hiftorians
regard **more** their own **Eloquence, Wit** and
Induftry, **and the knowledg** they believe to
have of the Actions of **War,** and **of all** manner of **Governments, than** of the truth of the
Hiftory, which is the main thing, and wherein
confifts the hardeft tafk, very few Hiftorians
knowing **the** Tranfactions they write of, and
much lefs the Counfels, and fecret Defigns of
many different Parties, which they confidently
mention.

Although there be many forts of Hiftories,
yet thefe three are the chiefeft : 1. a General
Hiftory.   2. **A** National Hiftory.   3. **A Par-**
ticular Hiftory.   Which three forts may, not
unfitly, be **compared to** the three forts of
Governments, Democracy, Ariftocracy, and
Monarchy.   The firft **is the** Hiftory **of the**

known parts and people of the World; The fecond is the Hiftory of a particular **Nation, Kingdom or Commonwealth.** The third is the Hiftory of the **life** and actions **of** fome particular Perfon. The firft is profitable for Travellers, **Navigators and** Merchants; **the** fecond is pernicious, by **reafon** it teaches fubtil Policies, begets **Factions, not** onely between particular **Families and Perfons, but alfo** between **whole** Nations, and **great** Princes, rubbing old fores, **and** renewing old Quarrels, that **would otherwife have** been forgotten. The laft **is the moft** fecure; becaufe it goes **not out of its** own Circle, but turns on its **own Axis, and for the moft** part, keeps within the **Circumference of Truth.** The firft is **Mechanical, the** fecond Political, and the third Heroical. The firft fhould onely **be** written by **Travellers, and** Navigators; The fecond by Statefmen; The third by the Prime Actors, **or the** Spectators of thofe Affairs and Actions of which they write, **as** *Cæfars* Commentaries are, which **no Pen but of** fuch an Author, **who was alfo Actor** in the particular Occurrences, private Intrigues, fecret Counfels, clofe Defigns, and rare **Exploits of War** he relates, could ever have brought to fo high Perfection.

This Hiftory is of the Third fort, as that is ; and being of the Life and Actions of my Noble Lord and Hufband, who hath informed me of all the particular paffages I have recorded, I cannot, though neither Actor, nor Spectator, be thought ignorant of the Truth of what I write ; Nor is it inconfiftent with my being a Woman, to write of Wars, that was neither between *Medes* and *Perfians*, *Greeks* and *Trojans*, *Chriftians* and *Turks;* but among my own Countreymen, whofe Cuftoms and Inclinations, and moft of the Perfons that held any confiderable Place in the Armies, was well known to me ; and befides all that (which is above all) my Noble and Loyal Lord did act a chief Part in that fatal Tragedy, to have defended (if humane power could have done it) his moft Gracious Soveraign, from the fury of his Rebellious Subjects.

This Hiftory being (as I have faid) of a particular Perfon, his Actions, and Fortunes ; it cannot be expected, that I fhould here Preach of the beginning of the World; nor feem to exprefs underftanding in the Politicks, by

tedious moral Difcourfes, with long Obfervations **upon the** feveral **forts** of Government
that have **been in** *Greece* & *Rome*, and upon
others more modern ; I will neither endeavour
to make fhow of Eloquence, making Speeches
that never **was fpoken, nor pretend** to great
fkill **in War,** by making Mountains of Mole-
hills, and telling Romanfical Falfhoods for
Hiftorical Truths ; and much lefs will **I** write
to amufe my Readers, in a myftical and alle-
gorical Style, of the difloyal Actions of the
oppofite Party, of the Treacherous Cowardife,
Envy and Malice of fome Perfons, my Lords
Enemies, and of the ingratitude of fome of his
feeming Friends ; wherein **I** cannot better
obey his Lordfhips Commands **to** conceal
thofe things, then in leaving them quite out,
as I do, with fubmiffion to his Lordfhips defire, from whom I have learn'd Patience to
overcome my Paffions, and Difcretion **to** yield
to his Prudence.

Thus am I refolved to write, in a natural
plain ftyle, without Latin Sentences, moral
Inftructions, **politick** Defigns, feigned Ora-
tions, or envious and malicious Exclamations,
this fhort Hiftory **of** the Loyal, Heroick and

Prudent Actions of **my Noble Lord, as alſo of** his Sufferings, Loſſes, and ill-Fortunes, which in honour and Conſcience **I** could not ſuffer **to be buried in** ſilence; **nor could I** have undertaken ſo hard a taſk, had not my love to his Perſon, and to Truth, been my Encourager **and** Supporter.

I might have made this Book larger, in tranſcribing (as is ordinary **in** Hiſtories) **the** ſeveral Letters, full **of** Affection, and **kind** promiſes he received from **His** Gracious Soveraign, *Charles* the **Firſt,** and **from** his Royal Conſort, **in** the time he was in the Actions of War, **as** alſo ſince the War, from his dear Soveraign and Maſter, *Charles* the Second; But many of the former Letters having been loſt, when all was loſt; I thought it beſt, ſeeing I had not them all, to print none. As for Orations, which is another way **of** ſwelling the bulk of Hiſtories; it is certain, that My Lord made not many; chuſing rather **to** fight, then **to** talk; and his Declarations having been printed already, it had been ſuperfluous to inſert them in theſe Narrations.

This Book would **however,** have been a great Volume, if **his** Grace would have given me leave to publish his Enemies Actions ; But being to write of his own onely, I do it briefly and truly ; and not as many have done, who have written of the late Civil War, with but few fprinklings of Truth, like as Heat-drops upon a dry barren Ground ; knowing no more of the Tranfactions of thofe Times, then what they learned in the Gazets, which, for the moft part, (out of Policy to amufe and deceive the People) contain nothing but Falf-hoods and Chimeraes ; and were fuch Para-fites, that after the Kings Party was over-powred, the Government among the Rebels changing from one Faction to another, they never mifs'd to exalt highly the Merits of the chief Commanders of the then prevailing fide, comparing fome of them to *Mofes*, and fome others to all the great and moft famous Heroes, both Greeks and Romans ; wherein, unawares, they exceedingly commended my Noble Lord ; for if thofe Ring-leaders of Factions were fo great men as they are reported to be, by thofe Time-fervers, How much greater muft his Lordfhip be, who beat moft of them, except the Earl of *Effex*, whofe employment was never in the Northern parts, where all the reſt of the greateſt ſtrength of the Parliament was ſent, to oppoſe my Lord's Forces, which was the greateſt the Kings Party had any where.

Good Fortune is ſuch an Idol of the World, and is ſo like the golden Calf worſhipped by the Iſraelites, that thoſe Arch-Rebels never wanted Aſtrologers to foretel them good ſucceſs in all their Enterpriſes, nor Poets to ſing their Praiſes, nor Orators for Panegyricks; nay, which is worſe, nor Hiſtorians neither, to record their Valour in fighting, and Wiſdom in Governing. But being, ſo much as I am, above baſe Profit, or any Preferment whatſoever, I cannot fear to be ſuſpected of Flattery, in declaring to the World the Merits, Wealth, Power, Loyalty, and Fortunes of My Noble Lord, who hath done great Actions, ſuffered great Loſſes, endured a long Baniſhment, for his Loyalty to his King and Countrey; and leads now, like another *Scipio,* a quiet Countrey-life. If notwithſtanding all this, any ſhould ſay, That thoſe who write Hiſtories of themſelves, and their own actions, or of their own Party, or inſtruct and inform thoſe that write them, are partial to them-

felves; I anfwer, That it is very improbable,
Worthy Perfons, who having done Great,
Noble and Heroick Exploits, deferving to be
recorded, fhould be fo vain, as to write falfe
Hiftories; **but** if they do, it proves but their
Folly; **for** Truth can never **be** concealed,
and **fo it will be more for** their difgrace, then
for their Honour **or** Fame. **I fear not** any
fuch blemifhes in this prefent Hiftory, **for I am**
not confcious of any fuch Crime **as** Partiality
or Falfhood, but write it whileft My Noble
Lord is yet alive, and at fuch a time where
Truth may be declared, and Falfhood con-
tradicted; and **I** challenge any one (although
I be a Woman) to contradict any thing that I
have fet down, **or** prove **it to** be otherwife
then Truth; for be **there never** fo many Con-
tradictions, Truth will conquer all at laft.

    Concerning My Lords Actions in War,
which are comprehended in the firft Book,
the relation of them I have chiefly from my
Lords Secretary Mr. *Rollefton*, a Perfon that
has been an Eye-witnefs thereof, and accompanied My **Lord as** Secretary in his Army,
and gave out **all** his Commiffions; his honefty
and worth is unqueftionable by all that know

him. And as for the Second Book, which contains My Lords Actions and Sufferings, during the time of his Exile, I have set down so much as I could possibly call to mind, without any particular Expression of time, onely from the time of his Banishment, or rather (what I can remember) from the time of my Marriage, till our return into *England.* To the end of which I have joined a Computation of My Lord's Losses, which he hath suffered by those unfortunate Warres. In the third Book I have set down some particular Chapters concerning the Description of his Person, his Natural Faculties, and Personal Vertues, *&c.* And in the last, some Essayes and Discourses of My Lords, together with some Notes and Remarques of mine own; which I thought most convenient to place by themselves at the end of this Work, rather then to intermingle them with the Body of the History.

It might be some prejudice to my Lord's Glory, and the credit of this History, not to take notice of a very considerable thing I have heard, which is, That when his Lordship's Army had got so much Strength and Reputation, that the Rebellious Parliament finding themfelves overpower'd with it, rather then to be utterly ruin'd, (as was unavoidable) did call the *Scots* to their Affiftance, with a promife to reward fo great a Service, with the Four Northern Counties of *Northumberland*, *Cumberland*, *Weftmerland*, and the Bifhoprick of *Durham*, which I have not mention'd in the Book.

And it is moft certain, That the Parliaments Forces were never Powerful, nor their Commanders or Officers Famous, until fuch time as my Lord was overpower'd; neither could Loyalty have been overpower'd by Rebellion, had not Treachery had better Fortune then Prudence.

When I fpeak of my Lord's Pedigree, where *Thomas* Earl of *Arundel*, Grandfather to the now Duke of *Norfolk*, is mention'd, they have left out *William* Vifcount *Stafford*, one of his Sons, who did marry the Heir of the laft Baron *Stafford*, defcended from the Dukes of *Buckingham*; which was fet down in my Original Manufcript.

Some of thofe Omiffions, and very probably others, are happened, partly for want of timely Information, **and** chiefly **by** the death of my **Secretary, who did copy** my Writings for **the** Prefs, and dy'd in *London,* **attending that** Service, afore the Printing **of** the Book was quite finifh'd. And as **I** hope of your Favour to be excus'd for omitting thofe things in the Book; fo I expect **of your** Juftice to be approv'd in putting them here, though fomewhat unfeafonably.

Before I end this Preface, **I do** befeech my Readers not **to** miftake me when I fpeak of my Lord's Banifhment, as if I would conceal that he **went** voluntarily out of his Native Country; for it is moft true, that his Lord-fhip prudently perceiving all the King's Party loft, not onely in *England,* but alfo in *Scotland* **and** *Ireland;* and that it was impoffible **to** withftand the Rebels, after the fatal overthrow of his Army; his Lordfhip, in **a poor and mean** condition quitted his own Countrey, and went beyond Sea; **foon** after **which,** the Rebels having got an **Abfolute** Power, and granted a general Pardon **to** all thofe that would come in to them, **upon** compofition, at the Rates they had fet down, his Lordfhip, with but few others, was excepted from it, both for Life **and** Eftate, and did remain thus banifh'd till His Majefties happy Reftauration.

I muft alfo acknowledg, That I have committed great **Errors** in taking no notice of Times as I fhould have done in many places of this Hiftory: I mention in **one** place the Queen Mothers being in *France*, when **my Lord** went thither, but do not fay in what year that was: Nor do **I** exprefs when **His** Majefty (our now Gracious Soveraign) came in, and went out again feveral times from that Kingdom, which has happen'd for want of Memory, and I defire my Readers to excufe me **for it.**

No body can certainly be more ready to find faults in this Work, then I am to confefs them; being very confcious that I have, as I told my Lord **I** fhould, committed many for want of Learning, and chiefly of fkill in writing Hiftories: **But** having, according to his Lordfhips Commands, written his Actions and Fortunes truly and plainly, I have reafon to expect, that whatfoever elfe fhall be found amifs, **will** be favourably pardoned by the candid Readers, to whom I wifh all manner **of happinefs.**

An Epiſtle to Her Grace the Duchefs of Newcaſtle.

May it pleaſe your Grace,

I HAVE been *taught, and do be-lieve, That Obedience is better then Sacrifice; and know, that both are due from me to your Grace; and ſince I have been ſo long in obeying your Commands, I ſhall not preſume to uſe any Arguments for my excuſe, but rather chuſe inge-niouſly to confeſs my fault, and beg your Graces Pardon. And becauſe forgiveneſs is a Glory to the ſupreameſt Powers, I will hope that your Grace by that great example will make it yours. And now I humbly take leave to repreſent to your Grace, as faithfully and truly as my memory will ſerve me, all my Obſervations of the moſt memo-rable Actions, and honourable Deportments of*

His Grace, my *moſt Noble* **Lord** *and Maſter*, William *Duke of* Newcaſtle, *in the* **Execution** *and Performance* **of** *the* **Truſts** *and high* **Employments** *committed and commended to his* **care** *and charge by three* **Kings of** *England*; *that is to ſay,* **King** James, *King* **Charles** *the* **Firſt**, *of ever bleſſed* **Memory**; *and our Gracious King,* Charles **the Second**; **under** *whom* **he hath** *had the happineſs* **to live**, *and the honour* **to ſerve** **them** *in ſeveral* **capacities :** *And becauſe* **I humbly** *conceive,* **that it** *is not within the intention* **of** *your Graces Commands, that I ſhould give you* **a** *particular Relation of His* **Graces High Birth,** *his* **Noble** *and* **Princely Education and Breeding,** **both at home and abroad;** *his Natural* **Faculties, and Perſonal Vertues;** *his* **Juſtice,** *Bounty, Charity, Friendſhip;* **his** *Right Approved* **Courage, and** *True* **Valour,** *not grounded upon,* **or** **govern'd by** *Paſſion,* **but** *Reaſon;* **his** *Magnificent manner of living and ſupporting his Dignity,* **teſtified by his** *great* **Entertainments** **of their** *Majeſties,* **and** *his private Friends, upon all* **fit** *occaſions,* **beſides his** *ordinary and conſtant* **Houſekeeping and Attendants;** *ſome for Honour, and ſome for buſineſs, wherein* **he exceeded** *moſt* **of** *his* **Quality; and** *that he was, and is an incom-*

parable *Master to his Servants, is sufficiently
testified by all or most of the chiefest of them,
living and dying in His Graces Service, which
is an Argument that they thought themselves as
happy therein, as the World could make them;
nor of his well-chosen Pleasures, which were
principally Horses of all sorts, but more particularly Horses of Mannage;*[1] *His Study and Art
of the true use of the Sword; His Magnificent
Buildings. These are his chiefest Delights,
wherein his Grace spared for no cost nor charge,
which are sufficiently manifested to the World;
for other Delights, as those of running Horses,
Hawking, Hunting,* &c. *His Grace used them
meerly for societies sake, and out of a generous and
obliging Nature to please others, though his know
ledg in them excelled, as well as in the other.
And yet notwithstanding these his large and vast*

---

[1] *Mannage,* from the Fr. *menager,* to carry on, to
conduct; hence a careful housewife is called " a good
manager," and a careless one " a bad manager."
Manage, as applied to horses, signifies the graceful
government of a horse. Shakespeare has—

" Speak terms of *manage* to the bounding steed,"
and Young has—

" They vault from hunters to the *managed* steed."

expences, before his Grace **was called to the**
Court, he encreaſed his Revenue by way **of Pur-**
chaſe to a great value; and when he was called
to the Court, he was then free from Debts, and,
as I have heard, ſome Thouſands of Pounds **in**
his Purſe. Theſe Particulars, and as **many**
more of this kind as would ſwell a Volume, I
could enumerate to your Grace; but that they
are ſo well known to your Grace, **it** would be a
Preſumption in me, rather then a Service, to
give your Grace that trouble; and therefore **I**
humbly forbear, and proceed, according to my
Intention, **to** give your Grace a faithful account
of Your Graces Commands, as becomes

   May it pleaſe your Grace,

      Your Graces moſt humble,

         and moſt obedient Servant,

            John Rolleſton.

The

Life of the Moſt Illuſtrious
Prince, William Duke of
Newcaſtle.

THE FIRST BOOK.

SINCE my chief intent in this preſent Work, is to deſcribe the Life and Actions of My Noble Lord and Huſband, *William, Duke of Newcaſtle*, I ſhall do it with as much Brevity, Perſpicuity and Truth, as is required of an Impartial Hiſtorian. The Hiſtory of his Pedigree I ſhall refer to the Heralds, and partly give you an account thereof at the latter end of this work; onely thus much I ſhall now mention, as will be requiſite for the better underſtanding of the following diſcourſe.

His Grandfather by his Fathers ſide was

Sir *William Cavendish*, **Privy** Counsellour and Treasurer of the Chamber to King *Henry* the Eighth, *Edward* the Sixth, and Queen *Mary*. His Grandfather **by his** Mother was *Cuthbert* Lord *Ogle*, **an** ancient Baron. His Father Sir *Charles Cavendish* was **the** youngest son **to** Sir *William*, and had **no other** Children but three **Sons**, whereof My **Lord was** the Second; **but** his elder Brother dying **in** his Infancy, left both his Title and Birth-right **to My** Lord, so that My Lord had then but one onely Brother left, whose name was *Charles* after **his** Father, whereas My Lord had the name **of** his Grandfather.

These **two** Brothers **were** partly bred with *Gilbert* Earl **of** *Shrewsbury* **their** Uncle in Law, and their **Aunt** *Mary*, Countess of *Shrewsbury*, *Gilbert's* Wife, and Sister to their Father; **for** there interceded an intire **and** constant Friendship between the said *Gilbert*, Earl of *Shrewsbury*, and My Lord's Father, Sir *Charles Cavendish*, caused not onely by the marriage **of** My Lord's Aunt, his Fathers Sister, **to** the aforesaid *Gilbert*, Earl of *Shrews-bury*, and **by the** marriage of *George*, Earl of *Shrewsbury*, *Gilbert's* Father, with My **Lord's**

Grandmother, by his Fathers fide; but Sir *Charles Cavendiſh*, My Lord's Father, and *Gilbert*, Earl of *Shrewſbury*, being brought up and bred together in one Family, and grown up as parts of one body, after they came to be beyond Children, and travelled together into foreign Countries, to obſerve the Faſhions, Laws, and Cuſtoms of other Nations, con- tracted ſuch an intire Friendſhip which laſted to their death: neither did they out-live each other long, for My Lord's Father, Sir *Charles Cavendiſh*, lived but one year after *Gilbert* Earl of *Shrewſbury*.

But both My Lords Parents, and his Aunt and Uncle in Law, ſhewed always a great and fond love to My Lord, endeavouring, when He was but a Child, to pleaſe him with what he moſt delighted in. When He was grown to the Age of fifteen or ſixteen, he was made Knight of the *Bath*, an ancient and honour- able Order, at the time when *Henry*, King *James*, of bleſſed Memory, His eldeſt Son was created Prince of *Wales*: and ſoon after he went to travel with Sir *Henry Wotton*,[1]

---

[1] Sir Henry Wotton. See the Biographical Dic- tionaries for accounts of this diſtinguiſhed perſon, and alſo his " Life " by Walton.

who was fent as Ambaffador Extraordinary to
the then *Duke* of *Savoy;* which Duke made
very much of My Lord, and when he would
be free in Feafting, placed Him next to himfelf. Before My **Lord did** return with the
Ambaffador into *England,* **the** faid Duke profer'd My Lord, **that if he would** ftay with
him, he would not onely confer upon **him** the
beft Titles of Honour he could, but alfo give
him an honourable Command in War, although
My Lord was but young, for the Duke had
then **fome** defigns of War. But the Ambaffador, who **had** taken the care **of** My Lord,
would not **leave** Him behind without his
Parents confent.

At laft, when My Lord took **his** leave of the
Duke, the Duke being a very generous perfon,
prefented Him with **a** *Spanifh* Horfe, a Saddle
very richly embroidered, and with a rich Jewel
of Diamonds.

Some time after **My** Lord's return into
England, Gilbert Earl of *Shrewfbury* died, and
left My Lord, though he was then but young,
and about Twenty two years of age, his
Executor ; a year after, his Father Sir *Charles
Cavendifh,* died alfo. His Mother, being then

a Widow, was defirous that My Lord fhould marry: in obedience to whofe Commands, he chofe a Wife both to his own good liking, and his Mothers approving; who was Daughter and Heir to *William Baffet* of *Blore* Efq. ; a very honourable and ancient Family in *Stafford-fhire*, by whom was added a great part to His Eftate, as hereafter fhall be mentioned. **After My Lord was married, he lived, for** the moft **part,** in the Country, **and pleafed Himfelf** and his neighbours **with Hofpitality,** and fuch delights as **the Country afforded;** onely now and **then** he **would go up to** *London* for fome fhort time to wait on **the King.**

About this time King *James*, **of** bleffed memory, having **a** purpofe to confer fome Honour upon My Lord, made him Vifcount *Mansfield*, and Baron **of** *Bolfover;* **and** after the deceafe **of** King *James*, King *Charles* **the Firft,** of bleffed Memory, conftituted him **Lord** Warden of the Forreft of *Sherewood*, **and** Lieutenant of *Nottingham-fhire*, and reftored his Mother *Catharine*, **the** fecond Daughter of *Cuthbert* Lord *Ogle*, to her Fathers Dignity, after the death of her onely Sifter *Jane* Countefs of *Shrewfbury*, publickly declaring, that it was her Right; which Title after the death of his Mother, defcended alfo upon My Lord, and his Heirs General, together with a large Inheritance of 3,000 l. a year, in *Northumberland.*

About the fame **time,** after the deceafe of *William,* late **Earl of** *Devonfhire,* his Noble Coufin German, **My Lord was by** his faid Majefty made Lord Lieutenant of *Derbyfhire;* which **truft** and honour, after **he had** enjoyed for feveral years, and managed it, like **as** all other offices put to his Truft, with all poffible care, faithfulnefs and dexterity, during **the** time **of the** faid Earls Son, *William,* the now Earl of *Devonfhire,* his Minority, as foon **as** this fame **Earl was** come **to** age, and by Law made capable **of** that truft, he willingly and freely refign'd it into his hands, he having hitherto kept it onely for him, that he and no body elfe might fucceed his Father **in** that **dignity.**

In thefe, and all other both publick and private imployments, My Lord hath ever been careful to keep up the Kings Rights to **the** uttermoft **of** his power, to ftrengthen **thofe mentioned** Counties with Ammunition, and to adminifter **Juftice** to every one; for he refufed no **man's Petition,** but fent all that came to him, either for relief or juftice, away from him fully fatisfied.

Not long after his being made Lieutenant of *Nottingham-fhire*, there was found fo **great** a **defeft** of Armes and Ammunition **in that** County, that the Lords of the Council **being** advertifed thereof, **as the manner then was,** His Majefty **commanded a levy to be made** upon the whole County for the fupply thereof; whereupon **the** fum **of 500 l. or** thereabout, was accordingly levied for that purpofe, and three Perfons o^c Quality, then Deputy Lieu-tenants, were defired by My Lord to receive the money, and fee it difpofed; which being done accordingly, and **a** certain account ren-**dred to** My Lord, **he** voluntarily ordered **the** then Clerk of the Peace **of** that County, **That** the fame account fhould **be** recorded amongft the Seffions Roles, and **be** publifhed in open Seffions, to the end that the Country might **take** notice how their monies were difpofed **of,** for which **aft** of Juftice My Lord was highly commended.

Within fome few years after, King *Charles*

the Firſt, of bleſſed Memory, His **Gracious** Soveraign, in regard of His true and faithful ſervice to his King and Country, was pleaſed to honour him with the Title of *Earl of New-caſtle*, and *Baron of Bothal* and *Heple*; which Title he graced ſo much **by** His Noble Ac-tions and Deportments, that **ſome** ſeven years after, which was in the Year 1638, His Ma-jeſty called him up to Court, and thought Him the fitteſt Perſon whom He might intruſt with the Government **of** His Son *Charles*, then Prince of *Wales*, now our moſt Gracious King, and made him withal a Member of the Lords of His Majeſties moſt honourable Privy Council; **which,** as it was **a** great Honour and Truſt, ſo He ſpared no care and induſtry to diſcharge His Duty accordingly; and to that end, left all the care of governing his own Family and Eſtate, with all Fidelity attending His Maſter not without conſiderable Charges, **and** vaſt Expences of his own.

In this preſent Employment He continued for the ſpace of three Years, during which time there happened an Inſurrection and Re-bellion of His Majeſties diſcontented Subjects in *Scotland*, which forced **His** Majeſty **to** raiſe an Army, to reduce them to their Obedience, and His **Treaſury** being at that time exhauſted he was neceſſitated to deſire ſome ſupply and aſſiſtance of the Nobleſt and Richeſt of his Loyal Subjects; amongſt the reſt, My Lord lent His Majeſty 10000 l. and raiſed Himſelf a Voluntier-Troop of Horſe, which conſiſted of 120 Knights and Gentlemen **of** Quality, who marched to *Berwick* by **His** Majeſties Command, where it **pleaſed His** Majeſty **to** ſet this mark **of** Honour **upon** that Troop, that it ſhould **be** Independent, and not commanded **by any** General Officer, but onely by his Majeſty Himſelf;[1] The reaſon thereof was upon this following occaſion.

His Majeſties whole body of Horſe, being commanded to march into *Scotland* againſt **the** Rebels, a place **was** appointed **for their** Rendezvous; Immediately upon their meeting, My Lord ſent a Gentleman of Quality of

---

[1] We have **ſeveral** King's **or** Queen's "Own Regiments." Query, **if** this troop **was** not the origin **of** that title? Loyal **men,** if rich enough, frequently raiſed troops or regiments of ſoldiers and preſented them to the ſovereign.

his Troop[1] to His Majesties then General of the Horse, to know where his Troop should march; who returned this answer, That it was to march next after the Troops of the General Officers of the Field. My Lord conceiving that his Troop ought to march in the Van, and not in the Rear, sent the same Messenger back again to the General, to inform him, That he had the honour to march with the Princes Colours, and therefore he thought it not fit to march under any of the Officers of the Field; yet neverthelefs the General ordered that Troop as he had formerly directed. Whereupon, My Lord thinking it unfit at that time to difpute the bufinefs, immediately commanded his Cornet[2] to take off the Princes Colours from his staff, and so marched in the place appointed, choofing rather to march without his Colours flying, then to leffen his Mafters dignity by the command of any fubject.

Immediately after the return from that expedition to his Majesties Leaguer, the General

---

[1] Sir *William Carnaby*, Kt.
[2] Mr. *Gray*, Brother to the Lord *Gray* of the North.

made a complaint thereof to his Majefty; who being truly informed of the bufinefs, commended my Lords difcretion for it, and from that time ordered that Troop to be commanded by none but himfelf. Thus they remain'd upon duty, *without receiving any payment or allowance from His Majefty,*[1] until His Majefty had reduced his Rebellious Subjects, and then My Lord returned with honour to his Charge, *viz.* The Government of the Prince.

At laft when the whole Army was difbanded, then, and not before, my Lord thought it a fit Time to exact an account from the faid General for the affront he pafs'd upon him, and fent him a Challenge; the place and hour being appointed by both their Confents, where and when to meet, My Lord appear'd there with his Second,[2] but found not his Oppofite: After fome while his Oppofite's Second came all alone, by whom my Lord perceiv'd that their Defign had been difcover'd to the King by

---

[1] In both the copies now before me the words in italic have been carefully obliterated with ink. Why?

[2] Francis Palmes.

fome of his Oppofite's Friends, who prefently caufed them both to be confined until he had made their Peace.

My Lord having hitherto attended the Prince, his Mafter, with all faithfulnefs and duty befitting fo great an Employment, for the fpace of three years, in the beginning of that Rebellious and unhappy Parliament, which was the caufe of all the ruines and misfortunes that afterwards befell this Kingdom, was privately advertifed, that the Parliaments Defign was to take the Government of the Prince from Him, which he apprehending as a difgrace to Himfelf, wifely prevented, and obtained the Confent of His late Majefty, with His Favour, to deliver up the Charge of being Governor to the Prince, and retire into the Countrey ; which he did in the beginning of the Year 1641, and fetled himfelf, with his Lady, Children and Family, to his great fatisfaction, with an intent to have continued there, and refted under his own Vine, and managed his own Eftate ; but he had not enjoyed himfelf long, but an Exprefs came to him from His Majefty, who was then unjuftly and unmannerly treated by the faid Parliament, to repair with all poffible fpeed and privacy to *Kingfton* upon **Hull,** where the greateft part of His Majefties Ammunition and Arms then remained in that Magazine, it being the moft confiderable place for ftrength in the Northern parts of the Kingdom.

Immediately upon the receipt of thefe His Majefties Orders and Commands, my Lord prepared for their execution, and about Twelve of the Clock at night, haftned from his own houfe when his Familie were all at their reft, fave two or three Servants which he appointed to attend him. The next day early in the morning he arrived at *Hull*, in the quality of a private Gentleman, which place was diftant from his houfe forty miles; and none of his Family that were at home, knew what was become of him, till he fent an Exprefs to his Lady to inform her where he was.

Thus being admitted into the Town, he fell upon his intended Defign, and brought it to fo hopeful an iffue for His Majefties Service, that he wanted nothing but His Majefties further Commiffion and Pleafure to have fecured both the Town and Magazine for

His Majefties ufe : and to that end by a fpeedy Exprefs[1] gave His Majefty, who was then at *Windfor*, an account of all his Tranfactions therein, together with his Opinion of them, hoping His Majefty would have been pleafed either to come thither in Perfon, which He might have done with much fecurity, or at leaft have fent him a Commiffion and Orders how he fhould do His Majefty further Service.

But inftead thereof he received Orders from His Majefty to obferve fuch Directions as he fhould receive from the Parliament then fitting : Whereupon he was fummoned perfonally to appear at the Houfe of Lords, and a Committee chofen to examine the Grounds and Reafons of his undertaking that Defign ; but my Lord fhewed them his Commiffion, and that it was done in obedience to His Majefties Commands, and fo was cleared of that Action.

Not long after, my Lord obtained the freedom from His Majefty to retire again to his Countrey Life, which he did with much

---

[1] Capt. Mazine.

alacrity: He had not remained many months there, but His Majesty was forced by the fury of the said Parliament, to repair in Person to *York*, and to send the Queen beyond the Seas for her safety.

No sooner was His Majesty arrived at *York* but he sent his Commands to my Lord to come thither to him; which, according to his wonted custom and loyalty, he readily obeyed, and after a few days spent there in Consultation, His Majesty was pleased to Command him to *Newcastle* upon *Tyne*, to take upon him the Government of that Town, and the four Counties next adjoining; that is to say, *Northumberland, Cumberland, Westmerland*, and the Bishoprick of *Durham*; which my Lord did accordingly, although he wanted Men, Money and Ammunition, for the performance of that design; for when he came thither he neither found any Military provision considerable for the undertaking that work, nor generally any great encouragement from the people in those parts, more then what his own interest created in them: Neverthelefs, he thought it his duty rather to hazard all, then to neglect the Commands of His Soveraign; and refolved to fhew his Fidelity, by nobly fetting all at ftake, as he did, though he well knew how to have fecured himfelf, as too many others did, either by Neutrality or adhering to the Rebellious Party ; but his Honour and Loyalty was too great to be ftained with fuch foul adherencies.

As foon as my Lord came to *Newcaftle*, in the firft place he fent for all his Tenants and Friends in thofe parts, and prefently raifed a Troop of Horfe confifting of 120, and a Regiment of Foot, and put them under Command, and upon duty and exercife in the Town of *Newcaftle;* and with this fmall beginning took the Government of that place upon him ; where with the affiftance of the Towns-men, particularly the Mayor,[1] (whom by the power of his Forces, he continued Mayor for the year following, he being a perfon of much truft and fidelity, as he approved himfelf) and the reft of his Brethren, within few days he fortified the Town, and raifed men daily, and put a Garrifon of Soldiers into *Tinmouth*-Caftle, ftanding upon the River *Tyne*, betwixt *New-*

---

[1] Sir *John Marlay*, Kt.

caſtle and the Sea, to ſecure that Port, and armed the Soldiers as well as he could: And thus he ſtood upon his Guard, and continued them upon Duty; playing his weak Game with much Prudence, and giving the Town and Country very great ſatisfaction by his noble and honourable Deportment.

In the mean time, there happend a great mutiny of the Trainband Souldiers of the Biſhoprick at *Durham*, ſo that my Lord was forced to remove thither in Perſon, attended with ſome forces to appeaſe them; where at his arrival (I mention it by the way, and as a merry paſſage) a jovial Fellow uſed this ex-preſſion, That he liked my Lord very well, but not his Company (meaning his Soldiers.)

After my Lord had reduced them to their obedience and duty, he took great care of the Church Government in the ſaid Biſhoprick (as he did no leſs in all other places committed to his Care and Protection, well knowing that Schiſm and Faction in Religion is the Mother of all or moſt Rebellions, Wars and Diſtur-bances in a State or Government) and con-ſtituted that Learned and Eminent Divine the then Dean of *Peterborough*, now Lord-Biſhop of *Durham*,[1] to view all Sermons that were to be Preached, and fuffer nothing in them that in the leaft reflected againft His Majefties Perfon and Government, but to put forth and add whatfoever he thought convenient, and punifh thofe that fhould trefpafs againft it. In which that worthy Perfon ufed fo much care and induftry, that never the Church could be more happily govern'd then it was at that prefent.

Some fhort time after, my Lord received from Her Majefty the Queen, out of *Holland* a fmall fupply of Money, *viz.* a little barrel of Ducatoons, which amounted to about 500 l. *Sterling;* which my Lord diftributed amongft the Officers of his new raifed Army, to encourage them the better in their fervice ; as alfo fome Armes, the moft part whereof were configned to his late Majefty ; and thofe that were ordered to be conveyed to his Majefty, were fent accordingly, conducted by that onely Troop of Horfe, which my Lord had newly raifed, with orders to return again to him ; but it feems His Majefty liked the Troop fo

---

[1] **Dr.** Coofens.

well, that he was pleafed to command their ftay to recruit his own Army.

About the fame time the King of *Denmark* was likewife pleafed to fend His Majefty a Ship, which arrived at *Newcaftle*, laden with fome Ammunition, Armes, Regiment Pieces, and *Danifh* Clubs ;[1] which my Lord kept for the furnifhing of fome Forces which he intended to raife for His Majefties fervice ; for he perceiving the flames increafe more and more in both the Houfes of Parliament then fitting at *Weftminfter*, againft his Majefties Perfon and Government ; upon Confultation with his Friends and Allies, and the intereft he had in thofe Northern parts, took a refolution to raife an Army for His Majefties fervice, and by an exprefs acquainted His Majefty with his defign ; who was fo well pleafed with it, that he fent him Commiffions for that purpofe, to conftitute him General of all the Forces raifed and to be raifed in all the parts of the Kingdom, *Trent-North*, and moreover in the feveral Counties of *Lincoln, Nottingham,*

---

[1] Danifh Clubs were war-maces originally ufed by the Danes inftead of fwords.

Derby, Lancaſhire, Cheſhire, Leiceſter, Rutland, Cambridg, Huntington, Norfolk, Suffolk, **and** *Eſſex*, and Commander in Chief for the ſame ; as alſo to impower and authorize him to confer **the** honour of Knighthood **upon** ſuch Perſons as he ſhould conceive deſerved it, and to coin Money and Print[1] **whenſoever** he ſaw occaſion for it. **Which as** it **was** not **onely a** great Honour, but a great Truſt and **Power ;** ſo he uſed **it** with **much** diſcretion and wiſdom, onely in ſuch occurrencies, where he found it tending to the advancement of His Majeſties Service, and conferr'd the honour of Knight-hood ſparingly, and but on ſuch perſons whoſe Valiant and **Loyal** Actions did juſtly deſerve it, ſo that he Knighted in **all** to **the** number of Twelve.

Within a ſhort **time,** my Lord formed an

---

[1] **This is an early** inſtance **of** making **Knights** by Deputy. **I am not aware** that the **power** ſtill exiſts, **except in the** caſe **of the Lord** Lieutenant **of** Ireland. **As to the** coining of money, not of royal mintage, we **have many** inſtances **during the** Civil Wars; **and the** ſo-called " ſiege **pieces," for the** payment of ſoldiers, **and** other uſes, are **not uncommon.** They are generally of ſilver, and very rudely executed.

Army of 8000 Foot, Horfe and Dragoons, and put them into a condition to march in the beginning of *November*, 1642. No fooner was this effected, but the Infurrection grew high in *York-fhire*, in fo much, that moft of His Majefties good fubjects of that County, as well the Nobility as Gentry, were forced for the prefervation of their perfons, to retire to the City of *York*, a walled Town, but of no great ftrength; and hearing that my Lord had not onely kept thofe Counties in the Northen parts generally faithful to his Majefty, but raifed an Army for His Majefties Intereft, and the protection of his good fubjects; thought it convenient to employ and authorife fome perfons of Quality to attend upon my Lord, and treat with him on their behalf, that he would be pleafed to give them the affiftance of his Army, which my Lord granted them upon fuch Terms as did highly advance His Majefties Service, which was my Lords chief and onely aim.

Thus my Lord being with his Army invited into *York-fhire*, He prepared for it with all the fpeed that the nature of that bufinefs could poffibly permit; and after he had fortified the

Town of *Newcastle*, *Tynmouthcastle*, **Hartle-pool** (a Haven Town) and some other necessary Garisons in those parts, and Mann'd, Victuall'd and order'd their constant supply, He thought it fit in the first place, before he did march, to manifest to the World by a Declaration in Print, the reasons and grounds of his undertaking that design; which were in General, for the preservation of His Majesties Person and Government, and the defence of the Orthodox Church of *England*; where He also satisfied those that murmur'd for my Lords receiving into his Army such as were of the Catholick Religion, and then he presently marched with his Army into *York-shire* to their assistance, and within the time agreed upon, came to *York*, notwithstanding the Enemies Forces gave him all the interruption they possibly could, at several passes; whereof the chief was at *Pierce-bridg*, at the entering into *York-shire*, where 1500 of the Enemies Forces, Commanded in chief by Col. *Hotham*, were ready to interrupt my Lord's Forces, sent thither to secure that passe, consisting of a Regiment of Dragoons, commanded by Colonel *Thomas* **Howard**, and a Regiment of Foot,

Commanded by Sir *William Lambton*, which they performed with fo much Courage, that they routed the Enemy, and put them to flight, although the faid Col. *Howard* in that Charge loft his life by an unfortunate fhot.

The Enemy thus miffing of their defign, fled until they met with a conjunction of their whole Forces at *Tadcafter*, fome eight miles diftant from *York*, and my Lord went on without any other confiderable Interruption. Being come to *York*, he drew up his whole Army before the Town, both Horfe and Foot, where the Commander in Chief, the then Earl of *Cumberland*, together with the Gentry of the Country, came to wait on my Lord, and the then Governor of *York*, Sir *Thomas Glemham*, prefented him with the Keys of the City.

Thus my Lord marched into the Town with great joy, and to the general fatisfaction both of the Nobility and Gentry, and moft of the Citizens; and immediately without any delay, in the later end of *December* 1642, fell upon Confultations how he might beft proceed to ferve his King and Country; and particularly, how his Army fhould be maintained and paid, (as he did alſo afterwards in every Country whereſoever he marched) well knowing, that no Army can be governed without being conſtantly and regularly ſupported by proviſion and pay. Whereupon it was agreed, That the Nobility and Gentry of the ſeveral Counties, ſhould ſelect a certain number of themſelves to raiſe money by a regular Tax, for the making proviſions for the ſupport and maintenance of the Army, rather than to leave them to free-quarter, and to carve for themſelves; and if any of the Soldiers were exorbitant and diſorderly, and that it did appear ſo to thoſe that were authoriſed to examine their deportment, that preſently order ſhould be given to repair thoſe injuries out of the moneys levied for the Soldiery; by which means the Country was preſerved from many inconveniences, which otherwiſe would doubtleſs have followed.

And though the ſeaſon of the year might well have invited my Lord to take up his Winter-quarters, it being about *Chriſtmas*; yet after he had put a good Gariſon into the City of *York*, and fortified it, upon intelligence that the Enemy was ſtill at *Tadcaſter*, and had fortified that place, he refolved to march thither. The greateft part of the Town ftands on the Weft fide of a River not fordable in any place near thereabout, nor allowing any paffage into the Town from *York*, but over a Stone-bridge, which the Enemy had made impaffable by breaking down part of the Bridg, and planting their Ordnance upon it, and by raifing a very large and ftrong Fort upon the top of a Hill, leading Eaftward from that Bridg towards *York*, upon defign of commanding the Bridg and all other places fit to draw up an Army in, or to plant Cannon againft them.

But notwithftanding all thefe Difcouragements, my Lord after he had refrefh'd his Army at *York*, and recruited his provifions, ordered a march before the faid Town in this manner : That the greateft part of his Horfe and Dragoons fhould in the night march to a Pafs at *Weatherby*, five miles diftant from *Tadcafter*, towards North-weft, from thence under the Command of his then Lieutenant General of the Army, to appear on the Weft fide of *Tadcafter* early the next morning, by which time my Lord with the reft of his

Army refolved to appear at the Eaft-fide of
the faid Town ; which intention was well defign’d, but ill executed ; for though my Lord
with that part of the Army which he commanded in perfon, that is to fay, his Foot and
Cannon, attended by fome Troops of Horfe,
did march that night, and early in the morning
appear’d before the Town on the Eaft fide
thereof, and there drew up his Army, planted
his Cannon, and clofely and orderly befieged
that fide of the Town, and from ten in the
morning till four a Clock in the afternoon,
battered the Enemies Forts and Works, as
being in continual expectation of the appearance of the Troops on the other fide, according
to his order; yet (whether it was out of
Neglect or Treachery that my Lords Orders
were not obeyed) that days Work was rendred ineffectual as to the whole Defign.

However the vigilancy of My Lord did
put the Enemy into fuch a Terror, that they
forfook that Fort, and fecretly fled away with
all their Train that very night to another
ftrong hold not far diftant from *Tadcafter*,
called *Cawood*-Caftle, to which, by reafon of
its low and boggy Scituation, and foul and

narrow Lanes and paffages, it was not poffible for my **Lord to purfue them** without too great an hazard **to his** Army ; **whereas had** the Lieutenant General **performed his Duty, in** all probability the greateft part **of the prin-** cipal Rebels in *York-fhire* would **that day** have been taken in their own **trap, and their** further mifchief prevented. **My Lord, the** next morning, inftead **of ftorming** the Town (as he had intended), entred without interrup- tion, and **there** ftayed **fome** few days **to refrefh** his Army, **and order** that part of the Country.

In *December*, 1642, **My** Lord thought it fit to march to *Pomfret*,[1] and to quarter his Army in that part of the Country which was betwixt *Cawood* and fome Garifons of **the** Enemy, in the weft part of *York-fhire*, *viz.* *Hallifax*, *Bradford*, *Leeds*, *Wakefield*, *&c.*, where **he remained fome** time **to** recruit **and** enlarge **his** Army, which was **much** leffened by erecting **of** Garifons, and **to keep thofe** parts in order and obedience to His **Majefty;** And after **he had** thus **ordered his Affairs, He** was enabled **to** give **Protection** to thofe **parts**

---

[1] Pontefract.

of the Country that were moſt willing to embrace it, and quarter'd his Army for a time in ſuch places which he had reduced. *Tadcaſter*, which ſtood upon a Paſs, he made a Gariſon, or rather a ſtrong Quarter, and put alſo a Gariſon into *Pomfret* Caſtle, not above eight Miles diſtant from *Tadcaſter*, which commanded that Town, and a great part of the Country.

During the time that his Army remained at *Pomfret*, My Lord ſetled a Gariſon at *Newark* in *Nottingham-ſhire*, ſtanding upon the River *Trent*, a very conſiderable paſs, which kept the greateſt part of *Nottingham-ſhire*, and part of *Lincoln-ſhire*, in obedience ; and after that he returned, in the beginning of *January*, 1642, back to *York*, with an intention to ſupply Himſelf with ſome Ammunition, which He had ordered to be brought from *Newcaſtle :* A Convoy of Horſe that were imployed to conduct it from thence, under the Command of the Lieutenant General of the Army, the Lord *Ethyn*, was by the Enemy at a paſs, called *Yarum-bridg*, in *York-ſhire*, fiercely encountred ; in which encounter My Lord's Forces totally routed them, flew many, and took many Prifoners, and moft of their Horfe Colours, confifting of Seventeen Cornets; and fo march'd on to *York* with their Ammunition, without any other Interruption.

My Lord, after he had received this Ammunition, put his Army into a condition to march, and having intelligence that the Queen was at Sea, with intention to land in fome part of the Eaftriding of *York-fhire*, he directed his March in *February*, 1642, into thofe parts, to be ready to attend Her Majefties landing, who was then daily expected from *Holland.* Within a fhort time, after it had pleafed God to protect Her Majefty both from the fury of Wind and Waves, there being for feveral days fuch a Tempeft at Sea that Her Majefty, with all her Attendance, was in danger to be caft away every minute; as alfo from the fury of the Rebels, which had the whole Naval Power of the Kingdom then in their Hands, fhe arrived fafely at a fmall Port in the Eaft riding of *York-fhire* called *Burlington* Key, where Her Majefty was no fooner landed, but the Enemy at Sea made continual fhot againft her Ships in the Port, which reached not onely Her Majesties landing, but even the House where she lay (though without the least hurt to any), so that she her self, and her Attendants, were forced to leave the same, and to seek Protection from a Hill near that place, under which they retired; and all that while it was observed that Her Majesty shewed as much Courage as ever any person could do; for Her undaunted and Generous spirit was like her Royal Birth, deriving it self from that unparrallell'd King, Her Father, whose Heroick Actions will be in perpetual Memory whilest the World hath a being.

My Lord finding Her Majesty in this condition, drew his Army near the place where she was, ready to attend and protect Her Majesties Person, who was pleased to take a view of the Army as it was drawn up in order; and immediately after, which was in *March*, 1643, took Her journey towards *York*, whither the whole Army conducted Her Majesty, and brought her safe into the City. About this time, Her Majesty having some present occasion for Money, My Lord presented Her with 3000 l. *Sterling*, which she graciously accepted of, and having spent fome time **there** in Confultation **about the** prefent affairs, fhe was pleafed to fend fome **Armes and** Ammunition to the King, who **was** then in *Oxford;* to which **end,** my **Lord** ordered **a** Party, confifting of **1**500, well Commanded, to conduct the fame, with whom the Lord *Percy,* who then had waited upon Her Majefty from the King, **returned to** *Oxford;* which Party His **Majefty was** pleafed to **keep with him for** his own Service.

Not long after, **My Lord,** who always en-deavoured **to** win any **place** or perfons **by** fair means, rather **then by** ufing of force, reduced **to** His Majefties obedience a ftrong Fort and Caftle upon the Sea, and a very good Haven, call'd *Scarborough*-Caftle, perfwading the Go-vernour thereof, who heretofore **had** oppofed his Forces **at** *Yarum*-bridg, with **fuch rational** and convincible Arguments, that he willingly **rendred** himfelf, and **all** the Garifon, unto His Majefties Devotion; **By** which prudent Action My Lord highly advanced His Majef-ties Intereft ; **for** by **that** means the Enemy **was much** annoyed **and** prejudiced **at** Sea, **and a great part** in the Eaft-riding **of** *York-fhire* kept in **due** obedience.

After this, My Lord having received Intelligence that the Enemies General of the Horfe[1] had defigned to march with a Party from *Cawood* Caftle, whither they were fled from *Tadcafter*, as before is mentioned to fome Garifons which they had in the Weft of *York-fhire* ; prefently order'd a party of Horfe, Commanded by the General of the Horfe, the Lord *George Goring*,[2] to attend the Enemy in their March, who overtook them on a Moor, call'd *Seacroft-Moor*, and fell upon their Rear, which caufed the Enemy to draw up their Forces into a Body ; to whom they gave a Total rout (although their number was much greater) and took about 800 Prifoners, and 10 or 12 Colours of Horfe, befides many that were flain in the charge ; which Prifoners were brought to *York*, about 10 or 12 miles diftant from that fame place.

Immediately after, in purfuit of that Victory, My Lord fent a confiderable Party into the

---

[1] Sir *Thomas Fairfax.*

[2] Created Earl of Norwich, 1644. His fon General George Goring, who died before him, was alfo an eminent leader in the loyalift caufe.

Weſt of *York-ſhire*, where they met with about 2000 of the Enemies Forces, taken out of their ſeveral Gariſons in thoſe parts, to execute ſome deſign upon a Moor called *Tankerly-Moor*, and there fought them, and routed them ; many were ſlain, and ſome taken Priſoners.

Not long after, the Remainder of the Army that were left at *York*, marched to *Leeds*, in the Weſt of *York-ſhire*, and from thence to *Wakefield*, being both the Enemies Quarters, to reduce and ſettle that part of the Country : My Lord having poſſeſſed himſelf of the Town of *Wakefield*, it being large, and of great compaſs, and able to make a ſtrong quarter, order'd it accordingly ; and receiving Intelligence that in two Market-Towns Southweſt from *Wakefield, viz. Rotherham* and *Sheffield*, the Enemy was very buſie to raiſe Forces againſt his Majeſty, and had fortified them both about four miles diſtant from each other, hoping thereby to give protection and encouragement to all thoſe parts of the Country which were populous, rich and rebellious, he thought it neceſſary to uſe his beſt endeavours to blaſt thoſe their wicked deſigns in the bud ; and thereupon took a reſolution in *April* 1643, to march with part of his Army from *Wakefield* into the mentioned parts, attended with a convenient Train of Artillery and Ammunition, leaving the greateſt part of it at *Wakefield* with the remainder of his Army, under the Care and Conduct of his General of the Horſe, and Major General of the Army,[1] which was ſo conſiderable, both in reſpect of their number and proviſion, that they did, as they might well, conceive themſelves Maſter of the Field in thoſe parts, and ſecure in that quarter, although in the end it proved not ſo, as ſhall hereafter be declared, which muſt neceſſarily be imputed to their invigilancy and carelefsnefs.

My Lord firſt marched to *Rotheram*, and finding that the Enemy had placed a Gariſon of Soldiers in that Town, and fortified it, he drew up his Army in the morning againſt the Town, and ſummon'd it; but they refuſing to yield, my Lord fell to work with his Can-

---

[1] In both the copies which I have before me a sidenote to explain the * has been ſmudged with ink for the purpoſe of obliteration; but I can make out the words "The Lord Goring and Sir Francis Mackworth, Knight."

non and Mufket, and within a fhort time took
it by ftorm, and enter'd the Town that very
night; fome Enemies of note that were
found therein, were taken Prifoners; and as
for the common Soldiers, which were by the
Enemy forced from their Allegiance, he
fhew'd fuch Clemency to them, that very
many willingly took up Arms for his Majefties
Service, and proved very faithful and loyal
Subjects, and good Soldiers.

After my Lord had ftayed two or three
dayes there, and order'd thofe parts, he
march'd with his Army to *Sheffield,* another
Market-Town of large extent, in which there
was an ancient Caftle; which when the Enemies Forces that kept the Town, came to
hear of, being terrified with the fame of my
Lords hitherto Victorious Army, they fled
away from thence into *Derbyfhire,* and left
both Town and Caftle (without any blow) to
my Lords Mercy; and though the people in
the Town were moft of them rebellioufly
affected, yet my Lord fo prudently ordered the
bufinefs, that within a fhort time he reduced
moft of them to their Allegiance by love, and
the reft by fear, and recruited his Army daily;

he put a Garifon of Soldiers into the Caftle,
and fortified it in all refpects, and conftituted
a Gentleman of Quality[1] Governour both of
the Caftle, **Town and Country**; and finding
near that place fome Iron Works, he gave
prefent order for the cafting of Iron Cannon
for his Garifons, and for the making of other
Inftruments and Engines of War.

Within a fhort time after, my **Lord** receiving Intelligence that the Enemy **in the**
Garifons near *Wakefield* had united themfelves,
and being drawn into a body in the night time,
had furprifed **and enter'd the Town of** *Wakefield*, **and taken all** or moft of the Officers and
Soldiers, left there, Prifoners, (amongft whom
was alfo the **General of the Horfe, the** Lord
Goring, whom **my Lord** afterwards redeem'd
by Exchange) and poffeffed themfelves of the
whole Magazine, which **was a** very great lofs
and hinderance to my Lords defigns, it being
the Moity of his Army, **and** moft of his Ammunition, he fell upon new Counfels, **and** refolved
without any delay to march from thence back
towards *York*, which was in *May* 1643, where

---

[1] Sir *Will. Savil* Kt. and Bar.

after he had rested some time, Her Majesty being resolved to take Her Journey towards the Southern parts of the Kingdom, where the King was, designed first to go from *York* to *Pomfret*, whither my Lord ordered the whole Marching Army to be in readiness to conduct Her Majesty, which they did, he himself attending Her Majesty in person. And after Her Majesty had rested there some small time, she being desirous to proceed in Her intended Journey, no less then a formed Army was able to secure Her Person: Wherefore my Lord was resolved out of his fidelity and duty to supply Her with an Army of 7000 Horse and Foot, besides a convenient Train of Artillery, for Her safer Conduct; chusing rather to leave himself in a weak condition (though he was even then very near the Enemies Garisons in that part of the Country) then suffer Her Majesties Person to be exposed to danger. Which Army of 7000 men, when Her Majesty was safely arrived to the King, He was pleased to keep with him for His own Service.

After Her Majesties departure out of *York-shire*, my Lord was forced to recruit again his Army, and within a short time, *viz.* in *June*,

1643, took a refolution to **march** into the Enemies Quarters, in the Weftern parts; **in** which march he met with **a** ftrong ftone houfe well fortified, call'd *Howley*-Houfe, wherein **was a** Garifon **of** Soldiers, which my Lord fummon'd; **but** the **Governour** difobeying **the** fummons, he batter'd **it** with his Cannon, and **fo** took it by force; the Governour having quarter given him contrary **to** my Lord's Orders, was brought before my Lord by a Perfon of Quality, for which the Officer that brought **him** received a check; and though he refolved then **to** kill him, yet my **Lord** would not fuffer him to **do** it, faying, It was inhumane **to kill** any man **in** cold blood. Hereupon the Governour kiff'd the Key of the Houfe door, and prefented it to my Lord; to which my Lord return'd this anfwer: *I need **it** not*, faid he, *for I brought **a** Key along with me, which yet I was unwilling to ufe, until you forced me to it.*

At this Houfe my Lord remained five or fix days, till he had refrefhed his Soldiers; and then **a** refolution was taken to march againft **a** Garifon of the Enemies call'd *Bradford*, a little **but a** ftrong **Town**; in the way he met with a ftrong interruption by the Enemy drawing forth a vaft number of Mufquetiers, which they had very privately gotten out of *Lancafhire*, the next adjoining County to thofe parts of *York-fhire*, which had fo eafie an accefs to them at *Bradford*, by reafon the whole Country was of their Party, that my Lord could not poffibly have any conftant intelligence of their defigns and motions; for in their Army there were near 5000 Mufquetiers, and 18 Troops of Horfe, drawn up in a place full of hedges, called *Atherton-moor*, near to their Garifon at *Bradford*, ready to encounter my Lords Forces, which then contained not above half fo many Mufquetiers as the Enemy had; their chiefeft ftrength confifting in Horfe, and thefe made ufelefs for a long time together by the Enemies Horfe poffeffing all the plain ground upon that Field; fo that no place was left to draw up my Lords Horfe, but amongft old Coal-pits: Neither could they charge the Enemy, by reafon of a great ditch and high bank betwixt my Lord's and the Enemies Troops, but by two on a breaft, and that within Mufquet fhot; the Enemy being drawn up in hedges, and continually playing upon them, which rendred the service exceeding difficult and hazardous.

In the mean while the **Foot of** both sides on the right and **left** Wings encounter'd each other, who fought from Hedg **to** Hedg, and for **a long time** together overpower'd and got **ground of my** Lords **Foot, almost to the** invironing **of his** Cannon; my Lords **Horse** (wherein consisted his greatest strength) all this while being made, by reason **of** the ground, incapable of charging; at last the Pikes of my Lords Army having had no employment all the day, were **drawn** against the Enemies left wing, and particularly **those of my Lords** own Regiment, **which were** all stout and valiant **men, who fell so** furiously **upon the** Enemy, **that** they forsook their hedges, and fell to their heels : At which very instant **my Lord caused a** shot **or two to be made by his** Cannon against the Body **of the** Enemies Horse, drawn up within Cannon shot, which took so good effect, that it disordered **the** Enemies Troops; Hereupon my Lord's Horse got over the Hedg, not in a body (for that they could not), but dispersedly two on a breast ; and **as** soon as some considerable number **was gotten** over, and **drawn** up, they **charged the** Enemy, and routed them; fo that in **an inftant there** was **a** ftrange change of **Fortune,** and **the Field** totally **won** by my Lord, notwithftanding he had quitted 7000 Men, **to conduct Her Ma-** jefty, befides a good **Train of Artillery, which** in fuch a Conjuncture would have weakned *Cæfars* Army. In this Victory **the** Enemy loft moft **of** their **Foot,** about **3000 were** taken Prifoners, and **700** Horfe **and F**oot flain, and **thofe** that efcaped **fled into** their Garifon at *Bradford,* amongft whom was alfo their General **of** the Horfe [Sir Thos. Fairfax.]

After this My Lord caufed his Army to **be**. rallied, and marched in order that night before *Bradford,* with an intention **to ftorm** it **the** next morning; but **the** Enemy that were **in** the Town, it feems, **were** fo difcomfited, that the fame night they efcaped all **various ways,** and amongft them **the faid General of the** Horfe, whofe Lady being behind a Servant on Horfe-back, **was taken by** fome of My Lord's Soldiers, and brought **to his Quarters, where** fhe was treated and attended with all **civility**

and refpect, and within few days fent **to** *York*
in my Lords own Coach, and from thence
very fhortly after to *Kingftone* upon *Hull*,
where fhe defired to be, attended by my
Lords Coach and Servants.

Thus my Lord, after the Enemy was gone,
entred the Town and Garifon **of** *Bradford*,
by which Victory the Enemy was fo daunted,
that they forfook the reft of their Garifons,
that is to fay, *Hallifax*, *Leeds* and *Wakefield*,
and difperfed themfelves feverally, the chief
Officers retiring to *Hull*, a ftrong Garifon of
the Enemy; **and** though my Lord, knowing
they would make their efcape thither, as
having **no other place of** refuge **to** refort to,
fent **a** Letter **to** *York* to the Governour of
that City, **to ftop** them **in** their paffage; yet
by neglect of the Poft, it coming not timely
enough to his hands, his Defign was fruftrated.

The whole County of *York*, fave onely
Hull, being now cleared and fetled by my
Lords Care and Conduct, he marched to the
City of *York*, **and** having **a** competent num-
ber **of** Horfe well armed and commanded, he
quarter'd them in the Eaft-riding, **near** *Hull*,

there being no vifible **Enemy** then to oppofe them : In the mean while my Lord receiving News that the Enemy had made an Invafion **into the** next adjoining County of *Lincoln,* where he had fome Forces, he prefently dif-patched[1] his Lieutenant General of the Army away with fome Horfe and Dragoons, and foon after marched thither himfelf with **the** body of the Army, being earneftly defired by his Majefties Party there. The Forces which my Lord **had** in the fame County, commanded **by** the then Lieutenant General **of the** Horfe, Mr. *Charles Cavendifh,* fecond Brother to the now Earl of *Devonfhire,* though they had timely notice, and Orders from my Lord to make their retreat to the Lieutenant-General of the Army, and not to fight the Enemy ; yet the faid Lieutenant-General of the Horfe being tranfported by his Courage (he being a Perfon **of great** Valour and Conduct), **and having charged the** Enemy, unfortunately **loft the** field, and himfelf was **flain** in the Charge, his Horfe lighting in a bogg : Which news being brought to **my** Lord when he was on his

---

[1] The Lord *Ethyn.*

March, he made all the haft he could, and was no fooner joined with his Lieutenant General, but fell upon the Enemy, and put them to flight.

The firft Garifon my Lord took in *Lincoln-fhire* was *Gainfborrough*, a Town ftanding upon the River *Trent,* wherein (not long before), had been a Garifon of Soldiers for His Majefty, under the Command of the then Earl of *Kingftone,* but furprifed, and the Town Taken by the Enemies Forces, who having an intention to conveigh the faid Earl of *Kingftone* from thence to *Hull* in a little Pinnace, met with fome of my Lords Forces by the way, commanded by the Lieutenant of the Army, who being defirous to refcue the Earl of *Kingftone,* and making fome fhots with their Regiment Pieces, to ftop the Pinnace, unfortunately flew him and one of his Servants.

My Lord drawing near the mentioned Town of *Gainfborrough,* there appear'd on the top of a Hill above the Town, fome of the Enemies Horfe drawn up in a body; whereupon he immediately fent a party of his Horfe to view them; who no fooner came within their fight, but they retreated fairly fo long as they could well endure; but the purfuit of my Lords Horfe caufed them prefently to break their ranks, and fall to their heels, where moft of them efcaped, and fled to *Lincoln,* another of their Garrifons. Hereupon my Lord fummon'd the Town of *Gainjborough;* but the Governour thereof refufing to yield, caufed my Lord to plant his Cannon, and draw up his Army on the mention'd Hill; and having play'd fome little while upon the Town, put the Enemy into fuch a terror, that the Governour fent out, and offer'd the furrender of the Town upon fair terms, which my Lord thought fit rather to embrace, then take it by force; and though according to the Articles of Agreement made between them, both the Enemies Arms and the Keys of the Town fhould have been fairly delivered to my Lord; yet it being not performed as it was expected, the Arms being in a confufed manner thrown down, and the Gates fet wide open, the Prifoners that had been kept in the Town began firft to plunder; which my Lords Forces feeing, did the fame, although it was againft my Lords will and orders.

After my Lord had thus reduced the **Town,** and put a good Garifon of Soldiers into **it, and** better fortified it, he marched before *Lincoln,* and there he entred with his Army without **great** difficulty, and plac'd **alfo a** Garifon in **it,** and raifed **a** confiderable Army, both **Horfe,** Foot and Dragoons, for the prefervation of that County, and put them under Commanders, and conftituted a Perfon **of** Honour[1] Commander in Chief, with intention to march towards the South, which **if** it had taken effect, would doubtlefs have made an end **of** **that** War; but **he** being daily importuned by the Nobility and Gentry of *York-fhire,* to return into that County, efpecially **upon the** perfwafions of the Commander **in** Chief of **the** Forces left there, who acquainted my Lord **that** the Enemy grew fo ftrong every **day,** **being got** together in *Kingftone* upon *Hull,* **and** annoying that Country, that his **Forces** **were not** able to bear up againft them; alledging withall, that my Lord would **be** fufpected **to** betray the Truft repofed in him, if he came **not to** fuccour and affift them; he went back

---

[1] The *Lord Widdrington.*

with his Army for the protection of that same Country; and when he arrived there, which was in *August*, 1643, he found the Enemy of fo fmall confequence, that they did all flie before him. About this time His Majefty was pleafed to honour my Lord for His true and faithful Service, with the Title of *Marquefs of Newcaftle*.

My Lord being returned into *York-fhire*, forced the Enemy firft from a Town called *Beverly*, wherein they had a Garifon of Soldiers; and from thence, upon the entreaty of the Nobility and Gentry of *York-fhire*, (as before is mentioned) who promifed him Ten thoufand men for that purpofe, though they came fhort of their performance, marched near the Town of *Kingftone* upon *Hull*, and befieged that part of the Garifon that bordered on *York-fhire*, for a certain time; in which time the Enemy took the courage to fally out of the Town with a ftrong party of Horfe and Foot very early in the morning, with purpofe to have forced the Quarters of a Regiment of my Lords Horfe, that were quarter'd next the Town; but by the vigilancy of their Commander Sir *Marmaduke Langdale*, afterwards

Lord *Langdale*, his Forces being prepared for their reception, they received such a **Welcome** as cost many of them their Lives, most of their Foot (but such as were slain) being taken Prisoners; and those of their Horse that escaped, got into their Hold **at** *Hull*.

The Enemy thus seeing **that** they could do my Lords Army **no** further damage on that side of the **River in** *York-shire*, endeavoured by all means (from *Hull*, and other confederate places in the Eastern parts of the Kingdom) **to** form a considerable party to annoy and disturb the Forces raised by my **Lord** in *Lincoln-shire*, and left there for the protection of that **County**; where the Enemy being drawn together in a body, fought my **Lords** Forces in his absence, and got the honour of the day near *Hornby* Castle **in** that County; which loss, caused partly by their own rashness, forced my Lord to leave his design upon *Hull*, and to march back with his Army **to** *York*, which was in *October*, 1643, **where** he remained but a **few** dayes **to refresh** his Army, **and** receiving intelligence that the Enemy **was** got into *Derbyshire*, and **did** grow numerous there, and busie **in seducing the people,**

that Country being under my Lords Command, he refolved to direct his **March thither in** the beginning of *November*, 1643, to fupprefs their further growth ; **and to that end quarter'd his** Army at *Chefterfield*, and in all the parts **there-about,** for a certain time.

Immediately after his departure **from *York*** to *Pomfret*, in his faid March into *Derbyfhire*, the City **of *York*** fent **to** my Lord to **inform** him of their intention to chufe another Mayor for the **year** following, defiring his pleafure about it : **My** Lord, who knew that the Mayor for the year before, **was a** perfon of much Loyalty and Difcretion, declared his mind to them, That he thought it fit to continue him Mayor alfo for the **year** following ; which **it** feems they did not like, but refolved to chufe **one** which they pleafed, contrary **to my Lords** defire. **My** Lord perceiving their intentions, **about the time** of the Election, **fent orders** to **the Governour** of the **City of** *York***, to permit** fuch Forces **to enter** into the City as he fhould fend ; which being done accordingly, **they** upon the Day **of** the Election repaired **to** the Town-Hall, **and** with their Arms ftaid there until they had continued the said Mayor according to my Lords desire.[1]

During the time of my Lords stay at *Chesterfield* in *Derbyshire*, he ordered some part of his Army to march before a strong House and Garison of the Enemies, call'd *Wingfield Mannor*, which in a short time they took by storm. And when my Lord had raised in that County as many Forces, Horse and Foot, as were supposed to be sufficient to preserve it from the fury of the Enemy, he armed them, and constituted an Honourable Person[2] Commander in Chief of all the Forces of that County, and of *Leicestershire*; and so leaving it in that condition, marched in *December* 1643, from *Chesterfield* to *Bolsover* in the same County, and from thence to *Welbeck* in *Nottinghamshire*, to his own House and Garison, in which parts he staid some time, both to

---

[1] Perhaps as notable an instance of intimidation at an election as was ever known! We have still in many free (?) boroughs the objectionable and thoroughly feudal custom, for the steward of the Lord to dictate to the householders what constables they must choose for the year.

[2] The Lord of *Loughborrough*.

refresh his **Army, and to** settle **and** reform
some diforders **he found** there, leaving no
vifible Enemy behind **him** in *Derbyfhire*, fave
onely an inconfiderable party **in the T**own **of**
Derby, which they **had** fortified, not worth
the labour to reduce it.

About **this** time **the** report **came, that a**
great **Army** out of *Scotland,* **was upon their**
march towards the Northern parts of *England,*
to affift the **Enemy** againft **His** Majefty, **which**
forced the Nobility **and Gentry of** *Yorkfhire*
to invite **my** Lord back **again into** thofe parts,
with promife **to raife for his** fervice, an Army
of 10000 **men; My** Lord (not upon this
proffer, which had already heretofore deceived
him, but out of his Loyalty and **duty** to preferve thofe parts which were committed **to**
his **care** and protection) returned **in** the middle
of *January* 1643.   And **when** he came there,
he found **not** one man raifed **to** affift **him**
againft fo powerful an **Army,** nor an **intention**
of raifing any ; Wherefore he was neceffitated
to raife himfelf, out of **the** Countrey, what
forces he could get, and when he had fettled
the affairs in *York-fhire* as well as time and his
prefent **condition would permit, and** confti-

tuted an honourable Perfon[1] Governor of *York* and Commander in chief of a very confiderable party of horfe and foot for the defence of the County (for Sr. *Thomas Glemham* was then made Colonel General, and marched into the Field with the Army) he took his march to *Newcaftle* in the beginning of *February* 1643, to give a ftop to the *Scots* army.

Prefently after his coming thither with fome of his Troups, before his whole army was come up, he received intelligence of the *Scots* Armie's near approach, whereupon he fent forth a party of horfe to view them, who found them very ftrong, to the number of 22000 Horfe and Foot well armed and commanded: They marched up towards the Town with fuch confidence, as if the Gates had been open'd for their reception; and the General of their Army feem'd to take no notice of my Lords being in it, for which afterwards he excufed himfelf; but as they drew near, they found not fuch entertainment as they expected; for though they affaulted a

---

[1] The Lord *Bellafis*.

Work that was not finished, yet they **were** beaten off **with much lofs.**

The Enemy being thus ftopt before the Town, thought fit **to** quarter near it, in that **part** of the Country; and fo foon as my Lords Army was come up, he defigned one night to have fallen into their Quarter; but by **reafon** of fome neglect of his Orders **in not** giving timely **notice** to the party defigned **for it,** it took not an effect anfwerable **to his** expecta-tion. In a word, there were **three Defigns** taken againft the Enemy, whereof if one had but hit, they would doubtlefs have been loft; but there was **fo much** Treachery, Jugling and Falfhood in my Lord's own Army, that it was impoffible for him to be fuccefsful in his Defigns and Undertakings. However, though it failed in the Enemies Foot-Quarters, which **lay** neareft **the** Town; yet **it took** good effect in their Horfe-Quarters, which were more remote; **for** my Lord's **Horfe,** Commanded **by** a very gallant and worthy Gentleman[1] falling upon them, gave them fuch an Alarm, **that** all they could do, was to draw

---

[1] The Lord *Langdale.*

into the Field, where my Lord's Forces charged them, and in a little time routed them totally, and kill'd and took many Prisoners, to the number of 1500.

Upon this the Enemy was forced to draw their whole Army together, and to quarter them a little more remote from the Town, and to seek out inacceffible places for their fecurity, as afterwards appear'd more plainly; for fo foon as my Lord had prepared his Army for a March, he drew them forth againft the *Scots*, which he found quarter'd upon high Hills clofe by the River *Tyne*, where they could not be encounter'd but upon very difadvantagious terms; befides, that day proved very ftormy and tempeftuous, fo that my Lord was neceffitated to withdraw his Forces, and retire into his own Quarters.

The next day after, the *Scots* Army finding ill harbour in thofe quarters, marched from hill to hill into another part of the Bifhoprick of *Durham*, near the Sea coaft, to a Town called *Sunderland;* and thereupon my Lord thought fit to march to *Durham*, to ftop their further progrefs, where he had contrived the bufinefs fo, that they were either forced to fight or ſtarve within a little time. The firſt was offered to them twice, that is to ſay, at *Penſher-hills* one day, and at *Bowden-hills* another day in the Biſhoprick of *Durham:* But my Lord found them at both times drawn up in ſuch places, as he could not poſſibly charge them; wherefore he retired again to *Durham,* with an intention to ſtreighten their Quarters, and to wait upon them, if ever they left their Holds and inacceſſible places. In the mean time it hapned that the Earl of *Montroſs* came to the ſame place, and having ſome deſign for his Majeſties ſervice in *Scotland,* deſired My Lord to give him the aſſiſtance of ſome of his Forces; and although My Lord ſtood then in preſent need of them, and could not coveniently ſpare any, having ſo great an Army to oppoſe; yet out of a deſire to advance His Majeſties ſervice as much as lay in his power, he was willing to part with 200 Horſe and Dragoons to the ſaid Earl.

The *Scots* perceiving My Lords vigilancy and care, contented themſelves with their own quarters, which could not have ſerv'd them long, but that a great misfortune befel My Lords Forces in *York-ſhire;* for the Governour whom he had left behind with fufficient Forces for the defence of that Country, although he had orders not to encounter the Enemy, **but** to keep himfelf in a defenfive pofture ; yet he **being a man of** great valour and courage, it tranfported him fo much that **he** refolved to **face** the Enemy, and offering to **keep a Town** that was not tenable,[1] was utterly routed, and himfelf taken Prifoner, although he **fought** moft gallantly.

So foon as my Lord received this fad Intelligence, **he** upon Confultation, and upon very good Grounds of Reafon, took a refolution not to ftay between the two Armies of the Enemies, **viz.** the *Scots* and the *Englijh*, **that had prevailed** in *York-jhire ;* but immediately to march into *York-jhire* with his **Army, to** preferve (if poffible) **the City of *York* out** of the Enemies hands : which retreat was ordered fo well, and with fuch excellent Conduct, that though the **Army of the** *Scots* marched clofe upon their **Rear, and fought** them **every** day **of their** retreat, **yet they gained** feveral Paffes for their

---

[1] *Selby* in *Yorkjhire.*

fecurity, and entred fafe and well into the City of *York*, in *April* 1643.

My Lord being now at *York*, and finding three Armies againſt him, *viz.* the Army of the *Scots*, the Army of the *Engliſh* that gave the defeat to the Governour of *York*, and an Army that was raiſed out of aſſociate Counties, and but little Ammunition and Proviſion in the Town; was forced to ſend his Horſe away to quarter in ſeveral Counties, *viz. Derbyſhire, Nottinghamſhire, Leiceſterſhire,* for their ſub-ſiſtance, under the Conduct of his Lieutenant-General of the Horſe, My dear Brother Sir *Charles Lucas,* himſelf remaining at *York,* with his Foot and Train for the defence of that City.

In the mean time, the Enemy having cloſely beſiedged the City on all ſides, came to the very Gates thereof, and pull'd out the Earth at one end, as thoſe in the City put it in at the other end; they planted their great Can-nons againſt it, and threw in Granadoes at pleaſure: But thoſe in the City made ſeveral ſallies upon them with good ſuccefs. At laſt, the General of the aſſociate Army of the Enemy, having cloſely beleaguer'd the North

fide of the Town, fprung a Mine under the
wall of the Mannor-yard, and blew part of it
up; and having beaten back the Town-Forces
(although they behaved themfelves very gallantly) enter'd the Mannor-houfe with a great
number of their men, which as foon as my
Lord perceived, he went away in all hafte,
even to the amazement of all that were by,
not knowing what he intended to do; and
drew 80 of his own Regiment of Foot, called
the White-Coats, all ftout and valiant Men, to
that Poft, who fought the Enemy with that
courage, that within a little time they killed
and took 1500 of them; and My Lord gave
prefent order to make up the breach which
they had made in the wall; Whereupon the
Enemy remain'd without any other attempt in
that kind, fo long, till almoft all provifion for
the fupport of the foldiery in the City was
fpent, which neverthelefs was fo well ordered
by my Lords Prudence, that no Famine or
great extremity of want enfued.

My Lord having held out in that manner
above two Months, and withftood the ftrength
of three Armies; and feeing that his Lieutenant-General of the Horfe whom he had

ſent for relief **to His Majeſty, could** not ſo ſoon obtain **it (although** he uſed his beſt endeavour) for **to gain yet ſome little** time, began **to treat** with the Enemy ; ordering **in the** mean while, and upon the Treaty, to double **and** treble his Guards. At laſt after three Months time from the beginning of **the Siege, His** Majeſty was pleaſed **to ſend an Army,** which joining with my **Lords Horſe that were** ſent to **quarter in the aforeſaid Countreys, came to relieve** the City, **under the** Conduct of the moſt Gallant and Heroick Prince *Rupert*, his Nephew ; upon whoſe approach near *York*, **the** Enemy drew from before the City, **into an** entire Body, and marched away on the Weſt-ſide of the River *Owſe*, that runs through **the** City, His Majeſties Forces being **then of the** Eaſt-ſide of that River.

My **Lord** immediately ſent ſome perſons of Quality to **attend His Highneſs,** and to invite him into the City to conſult with **him** about that important Affair, **and to** gain ſo much time as to open a Port **to march** forth with his Cannon and **Foot** which **were** in the Town, to join with **His Highneſs's** Forces; and went himſelf the **next day in perſon** to wait on His

Highnefs; where after fome Conferences, he declared his Mind to the Prince, defiring **His** Highnefs not to attempt any thing as yet **upon** the Enemy; for he had intelligence that there was fome difcontent between them, and that they were refolved **to** divide themfelves, and fo to raife the Siege without fighting: Befides, my Lord expected within two dayes, Collonel *Cleavering*, with above three thoufand **men** out of the North, and two thoufand drawn out of feveral Garifons, (who alfo came at the fame time, though it was then too late). But His Highnefs anfwered my Lord, That he had **a Letter** from His Majefty (then at *Oxford*) **with a** pofitive and abfolute Command to fight the Enemy; which in Obedience, and according to his Duty he was bound to perform. Whereupon my Lord replied, That he was ready and willing for his part, to obey his Highnefs in all things, no otherwife then if His Majefty was there in Perfon Himfelf; **and** though feveral of my Lords Friends advifed him not to engage in Battel, becaufe the Command (as they faid) was taken from Him: Yet **my** Lord anfwer'd them, That happen what would, he would not fhun to fight, for

he had no other ambition but **to live and dye**
a Loyal Subject to His Majesty.

Then the Prince **and my** Lord conferr'd
with several of their Officers, amongst whom
there were several Disputes concerning **the**
advantages which the Enemy had **of Sun,**
Wind and Ground. The Horse **of His Ma-**
jesties Forces, was drawn **up in** both **Wings**
upon that fatal Moor call'd *Heſſom-Moor;* **and**
my Lord aſk'd His **Highneſs what Service he**
would be pleas'd to **command** him ; **who re-**
turn'd this Anſwer, That he **would** begin no
action upon the Enemy, till early in the morning; deſiring my Lord to repoſe himſelf till
then. Which my Lord did, and went to reſt
in his own Coach that was cloſe by in the
Field, until the time appointed.

Not long had My Lord been there, but he
heard a great noiſe and thunder of ſhooting,
which gave him notice **of** the Armies being
engaged : Whereupon **he** immediately put on
his Arms, **and** was no ſooner got **on** Horſe-
back, but he beheld a diſmal ſight of **the Horſe**
of His Majeſties right Wing, which out of a
panick fear had left the Field, and run away
with all **the** ſpeed they could ; and though my

Lord made them ſtand once, yet they immediately betook themſelves to their heels again,
and killed even thoſe of their own party that
endeavoured to ſtop them ; the Left Wing in
the mean time, Commanded by thoſe two
Valiant Perſons, the Lord *Goring*, and Sir
Charles Lucas, having the better of the Enemies Right Wing, which they beat back moſt
valiantly three times, and made their General
retreat, in ſo much that they ſounded Victory.

In this Confuſion my Lord (accompanied
onely with his Brother Sir *Charles Cavendiſh*,
Major *Scot*, Capt. *Mazine*, and his Page)
haſtning to ſee in what poſture his own Regiment was, met with a Troop of Gentlemen-
Voluntiers, who formerly had choſen him their
Captain, notwithſtanding he was General of
an Army ; to whom my Lord ſpake after this
manner : *Gentlemen*, ſaid he, *You have done
me the* Honour *to chuſe me your Captain, and
now is the fitteſt time that I may do you ſervice ;
wherefore if you'l follow me, I ſhall lead you on
the beſt I can, and ſhew you the way to your own
Honour.* They being as glad of my Lords
Profer, as my Lord was of their Readineſs,
went on with the greateſt Courage; and paſſing

through Two Bodies of Foot, engaged with each other not at forty yards diftance, received not the leaft hurt, although they fired quick upon each other; but marched towards a *Scots* Regiment of Foot, which they charged and routed; in which Encounter my Lord himfelf kill'd Three with his Pages half-leaden Sword, for he had no other left him; and though all the Gentlemen in particular, offer'd him their Swords, yet my Lord refufed to take a Sword of any of them. At laft, after they had pafs'd through this Regiment of Foot, a Pike-man made a ftand to the whole Troop; and though my Lord charg'd him twice or thrice, yet he could not enter him; but the Troop difpatched him foon.

In all thefe Encounters my Lord got not the leaft hurt, though feveral were flain about him; and his White-Coats fhew'd fuch an extraordinary Valour and Courage in that Action, that they were kill'd in Rank and File: And here I cannot but mention by the way, That it is remarkable, that in all actions and undertakings where My Lord was in Perfon himfelf, he was always Victorious, and profpered in the execution of his defigns; but whatfoever was loft or fucceeded ill, happen'd in his abfence, and was caufed either by the Treachery, or Negligence and Carelefnefs of his Officers.

My Lord being the laft in the Field, and feeing that all was loft, and that every one of His Majefties Party made their efcapes in the beft manner they could ; he being moreover inquired after by feveral of his Friends, who had all a great love and refpect for my Lord, efpecially by the then Earl of *Craford* (who lov'd my Lord fo well that he gave 20*s.* to one that affured him of his being alive and fafe, telling him, that that was all he had) went towards *York* late at night, accompanied onely with his Brother, and one or two of his fer-vants ; and coming near the Town, met His Highnefs Prince *Rupert*, with the Lieutenant General of the Army, the Lord *Ethyn* ; His Highnefs afked My Lord how the bufinefs went ? To whom he anfwered, That all was loft and gone on their fide.

That night my Lord remained in *York* ; and having nothing left in his power to do his Majefty any further fervice in that kind ; for he had neither Ammunition, nor Money to

raise more Forces, to keep either *York*, or any
other Towns that were yet in His Majesties
Devotion, well knowing that those which were
left could not hold out long, and being also
loath to have aspersions cast upon him, that he
did sell them to the Enemy, in case he could
not keep them, he took a Resolution, and that
justly and honourably, to forsake the Kingdom ; and to that end, went the next morning
to the Prince, and acquainted him with his
Design, desiring His Highness would be pleased
to give this true and just report of him to his
Majesty, that he had behaved himself like an
honest man, a Gentleman, and a Loyal subject.
Which request the Prince having granted, my
Lord took his leave ; and being conducted by
a Troop of Horse, and a Troop of Dragoons
to *Scarborough*, went to Sea, and took shipping
for *Hamborough* ; the Gentry of the Country,
who also came to take their leaves of My
Lord, being much troubled at his departure,
and speaking very honourably of him, as surely
they had no reason to the contrary.

The
Life of the Moſt Illuſtrious
Prince, William Duke of Newcaſtle.

THE SECOND BOOK.

HAVING hitherto faithfully related the life of My Noble Lord and Huſband, and the chief Actions which He performed during the time of his being employed in His Majeſties Service for the Good and Intereſt of his King and Country, until the time of his going out of *England*, I ſhall now give you a juſt account of all that paſſed during the time of his baniſhment, till the return into his native Country.

My Lord being a Wiſe Man, and foreſeeing well what the loſs of that fatal Battle upon *Heſſom-moor*, near *York*, would produce, by which not onely thofe of His Majefties Party in the Northern **parts of the** Kingdom, but in all other parts of **His Majefties Dominions** both in *England, Scotland,* **and** *Ireland* **were** loft and undone, and that there was **no other** way, but either to quit the Kingdom, or fubmit **to the** Enemy, **or** die, he refolved **upon** **the** former, and **preparing** for his journey, **afked** his Steward, **How** Much Money he **had** left? Who anfwer'd, **That he had** but 90*l.* **My** Lord not being at **all ftartled at fo fmall a** Summ, although his prefent defign **required** much more, was refolved too feek his Fortune, even with that litle ; and thereupon having taken leave of His Highnefs Prince *Rupert,* and the reft that were prefent, went to *Scarborough* (as before is mentioned) where two Ships were prepared for *Hamborough* **to fet** fail within **24** hours, **in** which he embarqued with his Company, and arrived in **four days** time to **the faid City, which was** on the 8*th* of *July,* 1644.

In one of thefe Ships was my Lord, with his two Sons, *Charles* Vifcount *Mansfield,* and Lord *Henry Cavendifh,* **now** Earl of *Ogle ;* as alfo Sir *Charles Cavendifh,* My Lord's Brother;

the then Lord Bishop of *London-derry*, Dr. *Bramhall;* the Lord *Falconbridg*, the Lord *Widdrington*, Sir *William Carnaby*, who after died at *Paris*, and his Brother Mr. *Francis Carnaby*, who went presently in the same Ship back again for *England*, and soon after was slain by the Enemy, near *Sherborne* in *York-shire*, besides many of my Lord's and their servants.   In the other Ship was the Earl of *Ethyne*, Lieutenant General of My Lord's Army, and the Lord *Cornworth*.   But before My Lord landed at *Hamborough*, his eldest Son *Charles*, Lord *Mansfield*, fell sick of the Small-Pox, and not long after his younger Son, *Henry*, now Earl of *Ogle*, fell likewise dangerously ill of the Measels; but it pleased God that they both happily recovered.

My Lord finding his Company and Charge very great, although he sent several of his Servants back again into *England*, and having no means left to maintain him, was forced to seek for Credit; where at last he got so much as would in part relieve his necessities; and whereas heretofore he had been contented, for want of a Coach, to make use of a Waggon, when his occasions drew him abroad, he was now able (with the credit he had got) to buy a Coach and nine Horfes of an *Holfatian* breed; for which Horfes he paid £160, and and was afterwards offer'd for one of them an hundred Piftols at *Paris*, but he refufed the money, and prefented feven of them to Her Majefty the Queen-Mother of *England*, and kept two for his own ufe.

After my Lord had ftay'd in *Hamborough* from *July* 1644, till *February* 164$\frac{5}{4}$, he being refolved to go into *France*, went by Sea from *Hamborough* to *Amfterdam*, and from thence to *Rotterdam*, where he fent one of his Servants with a Complement and tender of his humble Service to Her Highnefs, the then Princefs Royal, the Queen of *Bohemia*, the Princefs Dowager of *Orange*, and the Prince of *Orange*, which was received with much kindnefs and civility.

From *Rotterdam* he directed his Journey to *Antwerp*, and from thence, with one Coach, one Chariot, and two Waggons, he went to *Mechlin* and *Bruffels*, where he received a Vifit from the Governour, the Marquefs of *Caftel Rodrigo*, the Duke of *Lorrain*, and Count *Piccolomini.*

From thence he fet forth for *Valenchin* and *Cambray*, where the Governour of the Town, ufed my Lord with great refpect and civility, and defired him to give the word that night. Thence he went to *Peroon*, a Frontier Town in *France* (where the Vice-Governour, in abfence of the Governour of that place, did likewife entertain my Lord with all refpect, and defired him to give the Word that night), and fo to *Paris* without any further ftay.

My Lord being arrived at *Paris*, which was in *April*, 1645, immediately went to tender his humble duty to Her Majefty, the Queen-Mother of *England*, where it was my Fortune to fee him the firft time, I being then one of the Maids of Honour to Her Majefty; and after he had ftay'd there fome time, he was pleafed to take fome particular notice of me, and exprefs more then an ordinary affection for me; infomuch that he refolved to chufe me for his Second Wife; for he, having but two Sons, purpofed to marry me, a young Woman that might prove fruitful to him and encreafe his Pofterity by a Mafculine Off-fpring. Nay, He was fo defirous of Male-Iffue, that I have heard him fay, He cared

not (fo **God** **would** **be** pleafed **to** give **him**
many Sons), although they **came to be perfons**
of the meaneft Fortunes ; **but God** (it feems)
had ordered it otherwife, and fruftrated his
Defigns by making me barren, which **yet**
did never leffen his Love and Affection for
me.

After My Lord **was** married, **having no**
Eftate or Means left **him to** maintain **himfelf**
and his **Family, he was neceffitated** to feek
for Credit, **and live** upon **the** Courtefie of
thofe that **were** pleafed **to Truft** him ; which
although **they** did for fomewhile, and fhew'd
themfelves very civil **to** My Lord, yet they
grew weary at length, infomuch that his
Steward was forced one time **to tell** him,
That he was not able **to provide a** Dinner for
him, for his Creditors were refolved **to truft**
him no longer. **My** Lord being always a
great mafter of his Paffions, **was,** at leaft
fhew'd himfelf not in **any** manner troubled at
it, but in a pleafant **humour told me, that I**
muft of neceffity pawn my Cloaths **to** make
fo much Money as would **procure a** Dinner.
I anfwer'd, **That** my **Cloaths** would **be** but of
fmall value, and therefore defired my Waiting-

Maid[1] to pawn fome fmall toys, which I had formerly given her, which fhe willingly did. The fame day in the afternoon, My Lord fpake himfelf to his Creditors, and both by his civil Deportment, and perfwafive Arguments, obtained fo much that they did not onely truft him for more neceffaries, but lént him Mony befides to redeem thofe Toys that were pawned. Hereupon I fent my Waiting-Maid into *England* to my Brother, the Lord *Lucas*, for that fmall Portion which was left me, and my Lord alfo immediately after difpatched one of his Servants,[2] who was then Governour to his Sons, to fome of his Friends, to try what means he could procure for his fubfiftance ; but though he ufed all the induftry and endeavour he could, yet he effected but little, by reafon everybody was fo affraid of the Parliament, that they durft not relieve Him, who was counted a Traitor for his Honeft and Loyal fervice to his King and Country.

Not long after, My Lord had profers made him of fome Rich Matches in *England* for his

---

[1] Mrs. **Chaplain,** now Mrs. *Top.*   [2] Mr. *Benoift.*

two Sons, whom therefore he fent thither with one Mr. *Loving*, hoping by that means to provide both for them and himfelf; but they being arrived there, out of fome reafons beft known to them, declared their unwillingnefs to Marry as yet, continuing neverthelefs in *England*, and living as well as they could.

Some two years after my Lord's Marriage, when he had prevailed fo far with his Creditors, that they began to truft him anew, the firft thing he did was, that he removed out of thofe Lodgings in *Paris*, where he had been neceffitated to live hitherto, to a Houfe which he hired for himfelf and his Family, and furnifhed it as well as his new gotten Credit would permit; and withal, refolving for his own recreation and divertifement in his banifhed condition, to exercife the Art of Mannage, which he is a great lover and Mafter of, bought a Barbary-horfe for that purpofe, which coft him 200 Piftols, and foon after another Barbary-horfe from the Lord *Crofts*, for which he was to pay him 100l. when he returned into *England*.

About this time, there was a Council call'd at St. *Germain*, in which were prefent, befides

My Lord, **Her** Majefty the now Queen Mother of *England;* His Highnefs **the Prince,** our now **gracious** King, His Coufin **Prince** *Rupert ;* the Marquefs of *Worcefter*, the then Marquefs, now Duke of *Ormond*, the Lord *Jermyn* now **Earl** of St. *Albans*, and feveral others ; where **after** feveral debates concerning the then pre- fent **condition of** His Majefty King *Charles* the **Firft, my Lord** delivered his fentiment, **that** he could **perceive no** other probability of pro- curing Forces for His Majefty, **but an** affift- ance of the *Scots ;* **But Her Majefty** was pleafed to anfwer my Lord, **That he** was too **quick.**

Not long after, When my **Lord** had begun to fettle **himfef in** his mentioned **new** houfe, His gracious Mafter the **Prince,** having taken **a refolu**tion to **go** into *Holland* upon fome defigns, **Her** Majefty the Queen Mother **defired my Lord to** follow him, promifing to **engage** for his debts which hitherto **he** had contra&ted at *Paris*, and commanding Her **Controller**[1] and **Treafurer**[2] to be bound for **them in** Her behalf ; **which they** did, although

---

[1] Sir *Henry Wood.*   [2] Sir ———— *Fofter.*

the Creditors **would not** content themſelves, until my Lord had **joined his word** to theirs ; So great and generous **was** the bounty and favour of her Majeſty to my Lord ! conſidering ſhe had already given **him** heretofore near upon 2000l. *Sterling*, even at that time when **Her** Majeſty ſtood moſt in need of it.

My Lord, after his Highneſs the Prince was gone, being ready to execute Her Majeſties Commands in following **Him, and** preparing for his Journey, wanted the chief thing, which was Money; and **having** much endeavoured for it, at laſt had the good Fortune to obtain upon Credit three or four hundred pounds *ſterl.* With which Sum he ſet out of *Paris* in the ſame Equipage he entred, *viz.* One Coach, which he had newly cauſed to be made, (wherein were the **Lord** *Widdrington*, **my** Lord's Brother Sir *Charles Cavendiſh*, **Mr.** *Loving*, **my** Waiting-Maid, and **ſome others,** **whereof the two** later **were** then returned out of *England*) **one** little Chariot, that would onely hold **my** Lord and **my** ſelf; and three Waggons, beſides an indifferent number of Servants on Horſe-back.

That day when we left *Paris*, the Creditors

coming to take their Farwell of my Lord, expreſſed ſo great a love and kindneſs for him,
accompanied with ſo many hearty Prayers and
Wiſhes, that he could not but proſper on his
Journey.

Being come into the King of *Spain's* Dominions, my Lord found a very Noble Reception. At *Cambray* the Governour was ſo
civil, that my Lord coming to that place ſomewhat late, and when it was dark, he commanded ſome Lights and Torches to meet my
Lord, and conduct him to his Lodgings : He
offer'd my Lord the Keys of the City, and
deſir'd him to give the Word that night, and
moreover invited him to an Entertainment,
which he had made for him of purpoſe ; but
it being late, my Lord (tyred with his Journey)
excuſed himſelf as civilly as he could ; the
Governour notwithſtanding being pleaſed to
ſend all manner of Proviſions to my Lords
Lodgings, and charging our Landlord to take
no pay for any thing we had : Which extraordinary Civilities ſhewed that he was a Right
Noble *Spaniard.*

The next morning early, my Lord went on
his Journey, and was very civilly uſed in

every place of His Majefty of *Spain's* Dominions, where he arrived : At laft coming to
Antwerp, He took water to *Rotterdam* (which
Town he chofe for his refiding place, during
the time of his ftay in *Holland*) and fent
thither to a Friend of his,[1] a Gentleman of
Quality, to provide him fome Lodgings; which
he did, and procured them at the houfe of
one Mrs. *Beynham*, Widow to an Englifh
Merchant, who had always been very Loyal
to His Majefty the King of *England*, and ferviceable to His Majefties faithful Subjects in
whatfoever lay in his Power.

My Lord being come to *Rotterdam*, was informed that His Highnefs the Prince (now
our Gracious King) was gone to Sea : Wherefore he refolved to follow him, and for that
purpofe hired a Boat, and victual'd it ; but
fince nobody knew whither His Highnefs was
gone, and I being unwilling that my Lord
fhould venture upon fo uncertain a Voyage,
and (as the Proverb is) *Seek a Needle in a
Bottle of Hay*, he defifted from that defign :
The Lord *Widdrington* neverthelefs, and Sir

---

[1] Sir *William Throckmorton*, Knight.

Will. Throckmorton, being refolved to **find out**
the Prince, **but** having by **a** ftorm been driven
towards the Coaft **of** *Scotland*, and endangered
their lives, they returned without obtaining
their aim.

After fome little time, my Lord **having**
notice that **the** Prince **was** arrived **at** the
Hague, **he went** to wait on His Highnefs
(which **he alfo did** afterwards at feveral times,
fo long **as** His Highnefs continued there) ex-
pecting **fome** opportunity where **he** might be
able to fhew his readinefs **to** ferve **His King**
and Countrey, as certainly there **was** no little
hopes for it ; for firft, it **was** believed that the
Englifh fleet would come and **render** it felf
into the obedience **of** the Prince ; next, it
was reported that the Duke of *Hamilton* **was**
going out of *Scotland* with **a** great Army, into
England, to the affiftance of His Majefty,
and that His Majefty had then fome party at
Colchefter ; but **it** pleafed God that none **of**
thefe proved effectual.   For the Fleet did not
come in ; the Duke of *Hamilton's* **Army** was
deftroyed, and *Colchefter* was **taken by the**
Enemy, **where my dear** Brother Sir *Charles*
Lucas, **and his** dear Friend Sir *George* **Lile**,

were moft inhumanly murther'd and fhot to death, they being both Valiant and Heroick Perfons, good Soldiers, and moft Loyal Subjects to His Majefty; the one an excellent Commander of Horfe, the other of Foot.

My Lord having now lived in *Rotterdam* almoft fix months, at a great charge, keeping an open and noble Table for all comers, and being pleafed efpecially to entertain fuch as were excellent Soldiers, and noted Commanders of War, whofe kindnefs he took as a great Obligation, ftill hoping that fome occafion would happen to invite thofe worthy Perfons into *England* to ferve His Majefty; but feeing no probability of either returning into *England*, or doing His Majefty any fervice in that kind, he refolved to retire to fome place where he might live privately; and having chofen the City of *Antwerp* for that purpofe, went to the *Hague* to take his leave of His Highnefs the Prince, our now gracious Soveraign. My Lord had then but a fmall ftock of money left; for though the then *Marquefs* of *Hereford* (after Duke of *Somerfet*, and his Coufin-German, once removed, the now Earl of *Devonfhire* had lent him 2000 l. between them ; yet all that was fpent, and above 1000 l. more, which my Lord borrowed during the time he lived in *Rotterdam*, his Expence being the more, by reafon (as I mentioned) he lived freely and nobly.

However my Lord, notwithftanding that little provifion of Money he had, fet forth from *Rotterdam* to *Antwerp*, where for fome time he lay in a publick Inne, until one of his Friends that had a great love and refpect for my Lord, Mr. *Endymion Porter*, who was Groom of the Bed-chamber to His Majefty King *Charles* the Firft (a place not onely honourable, but very profitable) being not willing that a Perfon of fuch Quality as my Lord, fhould lie in a publick Houfe, profer'd him Lodgings at the Houfe where he was, and would not let my Lord be at quiet, until he had accepted of them.

My Lord after he had ftay'd fome while there, endeavouring to find out a Houfe for himfelf which might fit him and his fmall Family, (for at that time he had put off moft of his Train) and alfo be for his own content, lighted on one that belonged to the Widow of a famous Picture-drawer, *Van Ruben*,[1] which he took.

About this time my Lord was much necef-fitated for Money, which forced him to try feveral ways for to obtain fo much as would relieve his prefent wants. At laft Mr. *Alef-bury*, the onely Son to Sir *Th. Alefbury*, Knight and Baronet, and Brother to the now Coun-tefs of *Clarendon*, a very worthy Gentleman, and great Friend to my Lord, having fome Moneys that belonged to the now Duke of *Buckingham*, and feeing my Lord in fo great diftrefs, did him the favour to lend him 200l. (which money my Lord fince his return hath honeftly and juftly repai'd). This relief came fo feafonably, that it got my Lord Credit in the City of *Antwerp*, whereas otherwife he would have loft himfelf to his great difadvan-tage; for my Lord having hired the houfe aforementioned, and wanting Furniture for it, was credited by the Citizens for as many Goods as he was pleafed to have, as alfo for Meat and Drink, and all kind of neceffaries

---

[1] This " picture-drawer " was no other than Rubens, the eminent artift. He had a magnificent mufeum, which the duke afterwards purchafed for 1,000l.

and provifions, which certainly was a fpecial Bleffing of God, he being not onely a ftranger in that Nation, but to all appearance, a Ruined man.

After my Lord had been in *Antwerp* fometime, where he lived as retiredly as it was poffible for him to do, he gained much love and refpect of all that knew or had any bufinefs with him : At the beginning of our coming thither, we found but few Englifh (except thofe that were Merchants) but afterwards their number increafed much, efpecially of Perfons of Quality; and whereas at firft there were no more but four Coaches that went the *Tour, viz.* the Governors of the Caftle, my Lords, and two more, they amounted to the number of above a hundred, before we went from thence ; for all thofe that had fufficient means, and could go to the price, kept Coaches, and went the *Tour* for their own pleafure. And certainly I cannot in duty and confcience but give this Publick Teftimony to that place. That whereas I have obferv'd, that moft commonly fuch Towns or Cities where the Prince of that Country doth not refide himfelf, or where there is no great refort of the chief Nobility and Gentry, are but little civilifed; Certainly, the Inhabitants of the faid City of *Antwerp* are the civileft, and beft behaved People that ever I faw; fo that my Lord lived there with as much content as a man of his condition could do, and his chief paftime and divertifement confifted in the Mannage of the two afore mentioned Horfes; which he had not enjoyed long, but the *Barbary*-horfe, for which he paid 200 Piftols in *Paris*, died, and foon after the Horfe which he had from the Lord *Crofts*; and though he wanted prefent means to repair thefe his loffes, yet he endeavoured and obtained fo much Credit at laft that he was able to buy two others, and by degrees fo many as amounted in all to the number of 8. In which he took fo much delight and pleafure, that though he was then in diftrefs for Money, yet he would fooner have tried all other ways, then parted with any of them; for I have hear'd him fay, that good Horfes are fo rare, as not to be valued for Mony, and that He who would buy him out of his Pleafure (meaning his Horfes), muft pay dear for it. For inftance I fhall mention fome paſſages which happen'd when My Lord was in *Antwerp*.

Firſt ; A ſtranger coming thither, and ſeeing my Lords Horſes, had a great mind to buy one of them, which my Lord loved above the reſt, and called him his Favourite, a fine *Spaniſh* Horſe ; intreating my Lords Eſcuyer to acquaint him with his deſire, and aſk the price of the ſaid Horſe : My Lord, when he heard of it, commanded his Servant, that if the Chapman returned, he ſhould be brought before him ; which being done accordingly, my Lord aſked him, whether he was reſolved to buy his *Spaniſh* Horſe ? Yes, anſwered he, my Lord, and I'le give your Lordſhip a good price for him. I make no doubt of it, replied My Lord, or elſe you ſhall not have him : But you muſt know, ſaid he, that the price of that Horſe is 1000*l.* to day, to morrow it will be 2000*l.* next day 3000*l.* and ſo forth. By which the Chapman perceiving that my Lord was unwilling to part with the ſaid Horſe for any Money, took his leave, and ſo went his ways.

The next was, That the Duke *de Guiſe*, who was alſo a great lover of good Horſes, hearing much Commendation of a gray leaping Horfe, which my Lord then had, told the Gentleman that praifed and commended him, That if my Lord was willing to fell the faid Horfe, he would give 600 Piftols for him. The Gentleman knowing my Lords humour, anfwered again, That he was confident, my Lord would never part with him for any mony, and to that purpofe fent a Letter to my Lord from *Paris;* but my Lord was fo far from felling that Horfe, that he was difpleafed to hear that any Price fhould be offer'd for him : So great a Love hath my Lord for good Horfes! And certainly I have obferved, and do verily believe, that fome of them had alfo a particular Love to my Lord; for they feemed to rejoice whenfoever he came into the Stables, by their trampling action, and the noife they made ; nay, they would go much better in the Mannage, when my Lord was by, then when he was abfent ; and when he rid them himfelf, they feemed to take much pleafure and pride in it. But of all forts of Horfes, my Lord loved *Spanifh* Horfes and *Barbes* beft ; faying, That *Spanifh* Horfes were like Princes, and *Barbes* like Gentlemen, in their kind. And this was the chief Recreation and Paftime **my Lord** had in *Antwerp*.

I will now return to my former Difcourfe, and the Relation of fome Important Affairs and Actions which happen'd about this time: His Majefty (our now Gracious King, *Charles* the Second) fome time after he was gone out of *Holland*, and returned into *France*, took his Journey from thence to *Breda* (if I remember well) to **treat** there with **his** Subjects **of** *Scotland*, who had then made fome offers of Agreement: My Lord, according **to** his duty, went thither to wait on His Majefty, and was there in Council with His Majefty, His Highnefs **the** then Prince **of** *Orange*, His Majefties Brother-in-law, and fome other Privy-Counfellors; in which, after feveral Debates concerning that Important Affair, His Highnefs **the Prince** of *Orange*, and my Lord, agreed **in** one **Opinion,** *viz.* That they could perceive **no** other and better **way** at that prefent for His Majefty, but **to** make an Agreement with **His** Subjects of *Scotland*, upon any Condition, **and to** go into *Scotland* in **Perfon** Himfelf, **that he might but** be **fure** of **an Army,** there being **no** probability **or** appearance then **of** getting an Army any where elfe. Which Counfel, either out of the then alledged Reafons, or fome others beft known to His Majefty, was embraced ; His Majefty agreeing with the *Scots* fo far, (notwithftanding they were fo unreafonable in their Treaty, that His Majefty had hardly Patience to hear them) that he refolved to go into *Scotland* in Perfon; and though my Lord had an earneft defire to wait on His Majefty thither, yet the *Scots* would not fuffer him to come, or be in any part of that Kingdom : Wherefore out of his Loyalty and Duty, he gave His Majefty the beft advice he could, *viz.* that he conceived it moft fafe for His Majefty to adhere to the Earl of *Argyle's* Party, which he fuppofed to be the ftrongeft ; but efpecially, to reconcile *Hamilton's* and *Argyle's* Party, and compofe the differences between them ; for then His Majefty would be fure of Two Parties, whereas otherwife He would leave an Enemy behind Him, which might caufe His over-throw, and endanger His Majefties Perfon; and if His Majefty could but get the Power into his own hands, he might do hereafter what he pleafed.

His Majefty **being arrived** in *Scotland*, ordered his affairs fo wifely, **that foon** after **he got an Army to march with him into** *England*; **but whether they were all Loyal**, is **not** for **me to difpute :** However, *Argyle* was difcontented, **as it** appear'd **by two complaining Letters he fent** to my Lord, which **my Lord gave** His Majefty notice of; fo that onely **the Duke of** *Hamilton* went with His Majefty, **who fought and died** like a Valiant Man, and a **Loyal fubject.** In this fight be**tween** the *Englifh* **and** *Scots*, **His** Majefty expreffed **an** extraordinary Courage ; and though his **Army was in a manner** deftroyed, **yet the** Glory of an Heroick **Prince** remained with **our gracious Soveraign.**

In the mean time, whileft His Majefty was **yet in** *Scotland*, **and before he** marched with **His Army** into *England*, it happen'd that **the Elector of** *Brandenburg,* **and Duke of** *Newburg*, upon fome differences, having **raifed Forces againft** each **other, but** afterwards concluded **a Peace** between them, **were pleafed to** profer **thofe Forces to** my **Lord for His Majefties ufe and** fervice, which (as the Lord Chan**cellour, who** was then in *France*, fent **word to**

my Lord) was the onely Foreign profer that had been made to his Majefty. My Lord immediately gave His Majefty notice of it; but whether it was for want of convenient Tranfportation, or Mony, or that the *Scots* did not like the affiftance, that profer was not accepted.

Concerning the affairs and intrigues that pafs'd in *Scotland*, and *England*, during the time of His Majefties ftay there, I am ignorant of them; neither doth it belong to me now to write, or give an account of any thing elfe but what concerns the Hiftory of my Noble Lord and Hufbands Life, and his own Actions; who fo foon as he had Intelligence that the *Scottifh* Army, which went with His Majefty into *England*, was defeated, and that no body knew what was become of His Majefty, fell into fo violent a Paffion, that I verily believed it would have endanger'd his life; but when afterwards the happy news came of His Majefties fafe arrival in *France*, never any Subject could rejoice more then my Lord did.

About this time it chanced, that my Lords Brother Sir *Charles Cavendifh*, and my felf,

took a journey into *England*, occasioned both
by my **Lord's** extream want and **neceffity,**
and **his Brothers** Eftate ; which having been
under Sequeftration from **the time** (or foon
after) he went **out of** *England*, was then, in
cafe he did **not** return and compound for it, to
be fold out-right ; Sir *Charles* **was** unwilling
to receive his Eftate upon fuch conditions,
and would rather have loft it, then compounded **for it : But my** Lord confidering **it**
was better to recover fomething, then lofe all,
intreated the Lord Chancellour, who was then
in *Antwerp,* to perfwade his Brother **to a** compofition, which his Lordfhip **did** very effec-
tually, and proved himfelf **a Noble and** true
Friend in it. We had fo fmall **a** Provifion of
money when we **fet** forth **our** Journey **for**
England, that it was **hardly** able to carry us
to *London,* but were forced **to** ftay at *South-*
wark ; where Sir *Charles* fent into *London* **for**
one that **had** formerly **been** his Steward ; and
having declared to him his wants and neceffities, defir'd him to try his **Credit.** He feemed
ready to do his Mafter what fervice he could
in that kind ; **but pretending** withall, that his
Credit was but **fmall, Sir** *Charles* gave him his

Watch to pawn, and **with that** money paid thofe fmall **fcores we had made** in our Lodging there. From **thence we** went to fome other Lodgings that were prepared for us in *Covent-Garden* ; and having refted our felves fome **time,** I defired my Brother the Lord *Lucas,* to claim, in my behalf, **fome** fubfiftance for my felf out of my **Lords** Eftate, (for it was declared **by** the Parliament, **That the Lands** of thofe **that** were banifhed, **fhould** be fold to any that **would** buy them, **onely** their Wives and Children were allowed **to** put **in** their Claims :) **But he** received this Anfwer, That I could not expect the leaft allowance, **by** reafon my Lord and Hufband had been **the** greateft Traitor of *England* **(that is to** fay, the honefteft man, becaufe he had been moft againft them.)

Then **Sir** *Charles* intrufted fome perfons to compound **for** his Eftate ; but **it** being a good while **before** they agreed in their Compofition, and then before the Rents could be received, we having **in** the mean time nothing **to** live on, muft of neceffity **have** been ftarved, had not Sir *Charles* got fome Credit of feveral Perfons, and that not without great **difficulty;**

for all thofe that had Eftates, were afraid to come near him, much lefs to affift him, until he was fure of his own Eftate. So much is Mifery and Poverty fhun'd!

But though our Condition was hard, yet my dear Lord and Hufband, whom we left in *Antwerp*, was then in a far greater diftrefs then our felves; for at our departure he had nothing but what his Credit was able to procure him; and having run upon the fcore fo long without paying any the leaft part thereof, his Creditors began to grow impatient, and refolved to truft him no longer: Wherefore he fent me word, That if his Brother did not prefently relieve him, he was forced to ftarve. Which doleful news caufed great fadnefs and melancholy in us both, and withal made his Brother try his utmoft endeavour to procure what moneys he could for his fubfiftance, who at laft got 200 l. *fterl.* upon Credit, which he immediately made over to my Lord.

But in the mean time, before the faid money could come to his hands, my Lord had been forced to fend for all his Creditors, and declare to them his great wants and neceffities; where his Speech was fo effectual, and made fuch an

impreſſion in them, that they had all a deep
ſenſe of my Lords Misfortunes; and inſtead
of urging the payment of his Debts, promiſed
him, That he ſhould not want any thing in
whatſoever they were able to aſſiſt him;
which they alſo very nobly and civilly performed, furniſhing him with all manner of
proviſions and neceſſaries for his further ſub-
ſiſtance; ſo that my Lord was then in a
much better condition amongſt ſtrangers,
then we in our Native Countrey.

At laſt when Sir *Charles Cavendiſh* had compounded for his Eſtate, and agreed to pay
4500 l. for it, the Parliament cauſed it again
to be ſurveyed, and made him pay 500 l.
more, which was more then many others had
paid for much greater Eſtates; ſo that Sir
Charles to pay this Compoſition, and diſcharge
ſome Debts, was neceſſitated to ſell ſome Land
of his at an under-rate. My Lords two Sons
(who were alſo in *England* at that time) were
no leſs in want and neceſſity, then we, having
nothing but bare Credit to live on; and my
Lords Eſtate being then to be ſold outright,
Sir *Charles*, his Brother, endeavoured, if poſ-
ſible, to ſave the two chief Houſes, *viz. Welbeck*

and *Bolſover*, being reſolved rather to part with ſome more of his Land, which he had lately compounded for, then to let them fall into the Enemies hands ; but before ſuch time as he could compaſs the money, ſome body had bought *Bolſover*, with an intention to pull it down, and make money of the Materials ; of whom Sir *Charles* was forced to buy it again at a far greater Rate then he might have had it at firſt, notwithſtanding a great part of it was pulled down already ; and though my Lords eldeſt Son *Charles* Lord *Mansfield*, had thoſe mentioned Houſes ſome time in poſſeſſion, after the death of his Uncle ; yet for want of Means he was not able to repair them.

I having now been in *England* a year and a half, ſome Intelligence which I received of my Lords being not very well, and the ſmall hopes I had of getting ſome relief out of his Eſtate, put me upon deſign of returning to *Antwerp* to my Lord ; and Sir *Charles*, his Brother, took the ſame reſolution, but was prevented by an Ague that ſeized upon him. Not long had I been with my Lord, but we received the ſad news of his Brothers death, which was **an extream affliction** both to my Lord, and **my felf, for they loved each other** entirely : In truth, **He was a Perfon of fo great worth, fuch** extraordinary civility, fo obliging a Nature, fo full of Generofity, **Juftice and Charity,** befides all manner of Learning, efpecially in the *Mathematicks*, **that not** onely his Friends, but even **his** Enemies, **did much** lament his **lofs.**

After **my** return **out of** *England*, **to my** Lord, the Creditors **fuppofing I had brought** great ftore **of** money along with me, came all **to my Lord to** folicite **the payment** of their Debts ; **but** when my Lord had informed them of the truth of the bufinefs, and defired their patience fomewhat longer, with affurance that fo foon as he received any money, **he** would honeftly and juftly **fatisfie** them, they **were not** onely willing to forbear the payment of thofe Debts he had contracted hitherto, but to credit him for the future, and fupply him with fuch Neceffaries as he fhould defire of them. And this was the onely happinefs which my Lord had in his diftreffed condition, and the chief bleffing of the Eternal **and** Merciful God, in **whofe** Power are all **things,** who ruled the hearts and minds of men, and filled them with Charity and Compaſſion ; for certainly it was a work of Divine Providence, that they ſhewed ſo much love, reſpect and **honour to** my Lord, a ſtranger to their Nation ; **and** notwithſtanding his ruined Condition, and the ſmall appearance of recovering his own, credited him wherefoever he lived, **both** in *France*, *Holland*, *Bra-bant* and *Germany;* that although my Lord **was baniſhed his** Native Countrey, and dif-poſſeſſed **from his own Eſtate**, could neverthe-leſs live in ſo **much Splendor and** Grandure as he did.

In this Condition (and how little **ſoever the** appearance was) my Lord was never **without** hopes of ſeeing **yet** (before his death) a happy iſſue of all his misfortunes and ſufferings, **eſpe-**cially **of the** Reſtauration of His moſt Gracious King and Maſter, **to** His Throne and Kingly Rights, whereof he always had aſſured Hopes, **well** knowing, that it was impoſſible **for the Kingdom to** ſubſiſt long under ſo many changes of Government ; and whenſoever I expreſſed **how little faith I had in it, he would** gently re-prove me, ſaying, I believ'd leaſt, what I deſir'd moſt ; **and could never be happy** if I endeavour'd to exclude all **hopes, and entertain'd** nothing but doubts **and fears.**

The City **of** *Antwerp* **in which we** lived, **being** a place of great refort for Strangers and Travellers, His Majefty **(our** now gracious **King,** *Charles* the Second) paffed thorough it, when he went his Journey towards *Germany;* and after my Lord had done his **humble duty,** and waited **on** His Majefty, **He** was pleafed to Honour him with his Prefence **at his Houfe.** The fame **did** almoft all ftrangers that were Perfons of Quality; **if they** made any ftay in the Town, they would **come and** vifit my Lord, and fee the Mannage of **his** Horfes :[1] And, amongft the reft, the Duke of *Olden-burg,* and the Prince of *Eaft-Friefland,* did my Lord the Honour, and prefented him with Horfes of their own breed.

One time **it** happen'd, that His Highnefs *Dom John d' Auftria* (who was then Governour of thofe Provinces) came to *Antwerp,* **and** ftayed there fome few **days;** and then almoft all **his** Court waited on **my** Lord, fo **that** one day I reckoned about feventeen Coaches, in

---

[1] Another **Philip !**

H

which were all Perfons of Quality, who came
in the morning of purpofe to fee my Lord's
Mannage; My Lord receiving fo great an
honour thought it fit to fhew his refpect and
civility to them, and to ride fome of his Horfes
himfelf, which otherwife he never did but for
his own excercife and delight. Amongft the
reft of thofe great and noble Perfons, there
were two of our Nation, *viz.* the then Marquefs, now Duke of *Ormond*, and the Earl of
Briftol; but *Dom John* was not there in Perfon, excufing himfelf afterwards to my Lord
(when my Lord waited on him) that the mul-
tiplicity of his weighty affairs had hindred his
coming thither, which my Lord accounted as
a very high honour and favour from fo great
a Prince; and conceiving it his duty to wait
on his Highnefs, but being unknown to him,
the Earl of *Briftol*, who had acquaintance with
him, did my Lord the favour, and upon his
requeft, prefented him to his Highnefs; which
favour of the faid Earl my Lord highly refented.[1]

---

[1] This now obfolete ufe of the word *refented* founds
fingular to modern ears: we now never refent a favour, though we may refent an injury. The French

Dom John received my Lord with all kindnefs and refpect; for although there were many great and noble Perfons that waited on him in an out room, yet fo foon as his Highnefs heard of my Lord's, and the Earl of *Briftol's* being there, he was pleafed to admit them before all the reft. My Lord, after he had paffed his Complements, told His Highnefs, That he found himfelf bound in all duty to make his humble acknowledgments for the Favour he received from His Catholick Majefty for permitting and fuffering him (a banifhed man) to live in His Dominions, and under the Government of His Highnefs; whereupon *Dom John* afk'd my Lord whether he wanted any thing, and whether he liv'd peaceably without any moleftation or difturbance? My Lord anfwer'd, That he lived as much to his own content as a banifh'd man could do; and received more refpect and civility from that City then he could have expected, for which he returned his moft humble thanks to his Catholick Majefty, and His Highnefs.

---

reffentir means equally, to take well or ill; and in the feventeenth century to refent implied either an emotion of gratitude, or a feeling of revenge.

After fome fhort Difcourfe, my **Lord took his** leave of *Dom John;* Several of the *Spaniards* advifing him to go into *Spain*, and affuring him of His Catholick Majefties Kindnefs and Favour; but my Lord being engaged in the City of *Antwerp*, and befides in years, and wanting means **for** fo long and chargeable **a voyage, was** not able to embrace their motions; and furely he was fo well pleafed with the great Civilities he received from that City, that then **he** was refolved to chufe no other refiding place all the time of his banifhment but that; **he** being not onely credited there for all manner of Provifions and Neceffaries **for** his fubfiftance, but alfo free both from ordinary **and** extraordinary Taxes, and **from** paying Excife, which **was** a great favour and obliga- **tion to** my Lord.

After His Highnefs *Dom John* had left the Government of thofe Provinces the Marquefs of *Caracena* fucceeded in his place, who having a great defire to fee my Lord ride in **the Man-** nage, entreated a Gentleman of **the** City, that was acquainted with my Lord, to beg that favour of him. **My Lord** having **not been at that** Exercife fix weeks, or two months, by **reafon** of fome ficknefs that made him unfit for it, civilly begg'd his excufe ; but he was fo much importuned by the faid Gentleman that at laft he granted his Requeft, and rid one or two Horfes in prefence of the faid Marquefs of *Caracena*, and the then Marquefs, now Duke of *Ormond*, who often ufed to honour my Lord with his Company. The faid Marquefs of *Caracena* feem'd to take much pleafure and fatisfaction in it, and highly complemented my Lord; and certainly I have obferved, That Noble and Meritorious perfons take great delight in honouring each other.

But not onely ftrangers, but His Majefty Himfelf (our now Gracious Soveraign) was pleafed to fee my Lord ride, and one time did ride Himfelf, He being an Excellent Mafter of that Art, and inftructed by my Lord, who had the Honour to fet Him firft on a Horfe of Mannage, when he was His Governour ; where His Majefties Capacity was fuch, that being but Ten years of Age, he would ride leaping Horfes, and fuch as would overthrow others, and mannage them with the greateft Skill and Dexterity, to the admiration of all that beheld Him.

Nor was **this the** onely Honour my Lord received from His Majefty, **but His Majefty and all** the Royal Race ; that **is to fay, Her** Highnefs the then Princefs Royal, His Highnefs the **Duke** of *York*, with His Brother the Duke of *Glocefter*, (except the Princeffe *Henrietta*, now Duchefs of *Orleans*,) being met one time in *Antwerp*, were pleafed to honour my Lord with their Prefence, and accept of a fmall Entertainment at his Houfe, fuch **as his** prefent Condition was able **to** afford them. And fome other time His Majefty paffing through the City was pleafed **to** accept of a private Dinner at my Lord's Houfe ; after which I receiving that gracious Favour from His Majefty, **that** he was pleafed **to fee** me, he did merrily and in jeft, tell **me,** *That he perceived my Lord's* **Credit** *could procure better Meat* **then His** *own.* Again, fome other time, **upon a** merry Challenge playing a Game **at** Butts with my Lord (when my Lord had the better of Him), *What* (faid **He)** *my* **Lord,** *have you invited me to play the* **Rook** *with me?*[1]

---

[1] " To play the Rook," means to play the *fharper.* "Rook " is fynonymous with a cheat. A " rookery"

Although their **Stakes were** not at all confiderable, **but onely for Paftime.**

Thefe paffages I mention onely **to declare
my** Lord's **happinefs in his** miferies, which he
received by the honour and kindnefs not onely
of foreign Princes, but of his own **Mafter and**
Gracious Soveraign : I will not fpeak now **of**
the good efteem and repute **he** had by his **late**
Majefty King *Charles* the **Firft, and Her**
Majefty the now Queen-Mother, who always
held and **found him a very loyal** and faithful
Subjeft, **although** Fortune was pleafed to
oppofe him in the height of his endeavours ;
for his onely and chief intention was to hinder
His Majefties Enemies from executing that
cruel defign which they had upon their gracious
and merciful King ; In which **he** tried his
uttermoft power, in fo much that **I** have heard
him **fay** out **of** a paffionate Zeal **and** Loyalty,
That **he would** willingly facrifice himfelf and
all **his** Pofterity, for **the** fake **of** his Majefty
and the Royal Race. **Nor did he** ever repine

in many of our **old** towns is the **rendezvous of** difhoneft
perfons. That pleafant **bird, the** rook, **was** formerly
regarded as a thief—but he **does** far more good than
harm.

either at **his** losses or sufferings, but rejoyced rather that **he** was able **to** suffer **for His** King and Countrey.   His Army **was the** onely Army that was able to uphold His Majesties Power; which so long as it was Victorious it preserved **both His** Majesties Person and Crown; **but so** soon **as** it fell, that fell too: **and my** Lord was then in **a** manner forced to seek his own prefervation in foreign Countries, where God was pleafed **to make** ftrangers his Friends, who received and protected him when he was banifhed his native Country, and relieved him when his own Country-men fought to ftarve him, by withholding from him what was juftly his own, onely for his Honefty and Loyalty; **which** relief he received more **from the Commons** of thofe parts where he lived, **then from Princes,** he being unwilling to trouble any foreign Prince with his wants **and** miferies, well knowing, that Gifts of **Great Princes** come flowly, and not without much difficulty; neither loves **he to** petition **any** one **but** His own Soveraign.

But though **my Lord by the** civility of Strangers, **and the** affiftance **of** fome **few** Friends **of his** native Country, lived **in an in-**

different Condition, yet (as it hath been declared heretofore) he was put to great plunges and difficulties, in so much that his dear Brother Sir *Charles Cavendish* would often say, That though he could not truly complain of want, yet his meat never did him good by reason my Lord, his Brother, was always so near wanting, that he was never sure after one meal to have another: And though I was not afraid of starving or begging, yet my chief fear was, that my Lord for his debts would suffer Imprisonment, where sadness of Mind, and want of Exercise, and Air, would have wrought his destruction, which yet by the Mercy of God he happily avoided.

Some time before the Restauration of His Majesty to his Royal Throne, my Lord, partly with the remainder of his Brothers Estate, which was but little, it being wasted by selling of Land for compounding with the Parliament, paying of several debts, and buying out the two Houses aforementioned, *viz. Welbeck* and *Bolsover;* and the Credit which his Sons had got, which amounted in all to 2400l. a year, sprinkled something amongst his Creditors, and borrowed so much of Mr. *Top* and Mr.

Smith (though without aſſurance) that he could pay ſuch ſcores as were moſt preſſing, contracted from the poorer ſort of Trades-men, and ſend ready mony to Market, to avoid cozenage (for ſmall ſcores run up moſt unreaſonably, eſpecially if no ſtrict accounts be kept, and the rate be left to the Creditors pleaſure) by which means there was in a ſhort time ſo much ſaved, as it could not have been imagined.

About this **time, a** report came of a great number of Sectaries, and of ſeveral diſturbances in *England*, which heightned my Lord's former hopes into **a** firm belief **of a** ſudden Change in that Kingdom, and a happy Reſtauration of His Majeſty, which it alſo pleaſed God to ſend according to his expectation; **for His** Majeſty was invited by his Subjects, who were not able longer to endure thoſe great confuſions and encumbrances they had ſuſtained hitherto, to take poſſeſſion of **His** Hereditary Rights, and the power **of all** his Dominions : And being then at the *Hague* in *Holland*, to take ſhipping in thoſe **parts** for *England*, my Lord went thither to wait on his **Majeſty,** who uſed my Lord very Graciouſly ;

and his Highnefs the Duke of *York* was pleafed to offer him one of thofe Ships that were ordered to tranfport His Majefty; for which he returned his moft humble thanks to his Highnefs, and begg'd leave of His Highnefs that he might hire a Veffel for himfelf and his Company.

In the mean time whilft my Lord was at the *Hague*, His Majefty was pleafed to tell him, That General *Monk*, now Duke of *Albemarle*, had defired the Place of being Mafter of the Horfe: To which my Lord anfwer'd, That that gallant Perfon was worthy of any Favour that His Majefty could confer upon him: And having taken his leave of His Majefty, and His Highnefs the Duke of *York*, went towards the Ship that was to tranfport him for *England*, (I might better call it a Boat, then a Ship; for thofe that were intrufted by my Lord to hire a Ship for that purpofe, had hired an old rotten Fregat, that was loft the next Voyage after; infomuch, that when fome of the Company that had promifed to go over with my Lord, faw it, they turn'd back, and would not endanger their lives in it, except the now Lord *Wid-*

drington, who was refolved not to forfake my Lord.)

My Lord (who was fo tranfported with the joy of returning into his Native Countrey, that he regarded not the Veffel) having fet Sail from *Rotterdam,* was fo becalmed, that he was fix dayes and fix nights upon the Water, during which time he pleafed himfelf with mirth, and pafs'd his time away as well as he could ; Provifions he wanted not, having them in great ftore and plenty. At laft being come fo far that he was able to difcern the fmoak of *London,* which he had not feen in a long time, he merrily was pleafed to defire one that was near him, to jogg and awake him out of his dream, for furely, faid he, I have been fixteen years afleep, and am not throughly awake yet. My Lord lay that night at *Greenwich,* where his Supper feem'd more favoury to him, then any meat he had hitherto tafted ; and the noife of fome fcraping Fidlers, he thought the pleafanteft harmony that ever he had heard.

In the mean time my Lords Son, *Henry* Lord *Mansfield,* now Earl of *Ogle,* was gone to *Dover* with intention to wait on His Majefty, and receive My Lord his Father, with all joy and duty, thinking he had been with His Majesty ; but when he mifs'd of his defign, he was very much troubled, and more, when His Majesty was pleas'd to tell him, That my Lord had fet to Sea, before His Majesty Himfelf was gone out of *Holland*, fearing my Lord had met with fome Misfortune in his Journey, becaufe he had not heard of his Landing. Wherefore he immediately parted from *Dover*, to feek my Lord, whom at laft he found at *Greenwich* ; with what joy they embraced and faluted each other, my Pen is too weak to exprefs.

But all this while, and after my Lord was gone from *Antwerp*, I was left alone there with fome of my fervants ; for my Lord being in *Holland* with His Majesty, declared in a Letter to me his intention of going for *England*, withal commanding me to ftay in that City, as a Pawn for his debts, until he could compafs money to difcharge them ; and to excufe him to the Magiftrates of the faid City for not taking his leave of them, and paying his due thanks for their great civilities, which he defired me to do in his behalf. And certainly my Lords affection to me was fuch, that it made him very induftrious in providing thofe means ; for it being uncertain what or whether he fhould have any thing of his Eftate, made it a difficult bufinefs for him to borrow Mony; At laft he received fome of one Mr. *Afh*, now Sir *Jofeph Afh*, a Merchant of *Antwerp*, which he returned to me ; but what with the expence I had made in the mean while, and what was required for my tranfporting into *England*, befides the debts formerly contracted, the faid money fell too fhort by 400l. and although I could have upon my own word taken up much more, yet I was unwilling to leave an engagement amongft ftrangers : Wherefore I fent for one Mr. *Shaw*, now Sir *John Shaw*, a near kindfman to the faid Mr. *Afh*, intreating him to lend me 400l. which he did moft readily, and fo difcharged my debts.

My departure being now divulged in *Antwerp*, the Magiftrates of the City came to take their leaves of me, where I defired one Mr. *Duart* a very worthy Gentleman, and one of the chief of the City, though he derives his Race from the *Portuguez* (to whom and his Sifters, all very fkilful in the Art of Mufick, though for their own paftime and Recreation, both my Lord and my felf were much bound for their great civilities) to be my Interpreter. They were pleafed to exprefs that they were forry for our departure out of their City, but withal rejoyced at our happy returning into our Native Country, and wifhed me foon and well to the place where I moft defired to be : Whereupon I having excufed my Lord's hafty going away without taking his leave of them, returned them mine and my Lord's hearty Thanks for their great civilities, declaring how forry I was that it lay not in my power to make an acknowledgment anfwerable to them. But after their departure from me, they were pleafed to fend their Under-Officers (as the cuftom there is) with a Prefent of Wine, which I received with all refpe&t and thankfulnefs.

I being thus prepar'd for my Voyage, went with my Servants to *Fluffing*, and finding no *Englifh* Man of War there, being loth to truft my felf with a lefs Veffel, was at laft informed that a *Dutch* man of War lay there ready to Convoy fome Merchants ; I forthwith fent for the Captain thereof, whofe name was *Bankert*, and afked him whether it was poffible to obtain

the favour of having the ufe of his Ship to
tranfport me into *England?*   To which he
anfwered, That he queftion'd not but I might;
for the Merchants which he was to convey,
were not ready yet, defiring me to fend one of
my fervants to the State, to requeft that favour
of them; with whom he would go himfelf,
and affift him the beft he could; which he
alfo did.   My fuit being granted, my felf and
my chief fervants embarqued in the faid Ship;
the reft, together with the Goods, being conveyed in another good ftrong Veffel, hired for
that purpofe.

After I was fafely arrived at *London*, I
found my Lord in Lodgings; I cannot call
them unhandfome; but yet they were not fit
for a Perfon of his Rank and Quality, nor of
the capacity to contain all his Family: Neither
did I find my Lord's Condition fuch as I expected: Wherefore out of fome paffion I
defir'd him to leave the Town, and retire into
the Countrey; but my Lord gently reproved
me for my rafhnefs and impatience, and foon
after removed into *Dorfet*-houfe; which,
though it was better then the former, yet not
altogether to my fatisfaction, we having but

a part of the said House in possession. By this
removal I judged my **Lord would not hastily**
depart from *London ;* **but not long after, he**
was pleased to tell me, That he had dispatched
his business, and **was now** resolved to remove
into the Country, having already given order
for Waggons to transport **our goods,** which
was no unpleasant news to me, who **had a**
great desire for **a** Countrey-life.

My Lord before he began his Journey, went
to his Gracious Soveraign, **and begg'd** leave
that he might retire into the Countrey, to reduce and settle, if possible, his confused, en-
tangled, and almost ruined Estate, *Sir,* said he
to His Majesty, *I am not ignorant, that many
believe I am discontented ; and 'tis probable they'l
say, I retire through discontent : But I take God
to witness, That I am in no kind or ways dif-
pleas'd;* **for** *I am so joyed at your Majesties
happy Restauration,* **that** *I cannot be sad* **or**
troubled for **any Concern to** *my own particular ;
but whatsoever Your Majesty is pleased to command me, were* **it** *to sacrifice* **my** *Life, I shall
most obediently perform it ; for* **I** *have no other
Will, but Your Majesties Pleasure.*

Thus he kissed His Majesty's hand, **and**

went the next day into *Nottingham-fhire*, to his Mannor-houfe call'd *Welbeck;* but when he came there, and began to examine his Eftate, and how it had been ordered in the time of his Banifhment, he knew not whether he had left any thing of it for himfelf, or not, till by his prudence and wifdom he inform'd himfelf the beft he could, examining thofe that had moft knowledg therein.   Some Lands, he found, could be recover'd no further then for his life, and fome not at all : Some had been in the Rebels hands, which he could not recover, but by His Highnefs the Duke of *York*'s favour, to whom His Majefty had given all the Eftates of thofe that were condemned and executed for murdering his Royal Father of bleffed memory, which by the Law were forfeited to His Majefty ; whereof His Highnefs gracioufly reftor'd my Lord fo much of the Land that formerly had been his, as amounted to 730l. a year.   And though my Lord's Children had their Claims granted, and bought out the life of my Lord, their Father, which came near upon the third part, yet my Lord received nothing for himfelf out of his own Eftate, for the fpace of eighteen years, viz. During the time from the firft entring into Warr, which was *June* 11. 1642, till his return out of Banifhment, *May* 28. 1660; for though his Son *Henry*, now Earl of *Ogle*, and his eldeft Daughter, the now Lady *Cheiny*, did all what lay in their power to relieve my Lord their Father, and fent him fome fupplies of moneys at feveral times when he was in banifhment ; yet that was of their own, rather then out of my Lord's Eftate; for the Lady *Cheiny* fold fome few Jewels which my Lord, her Father, had left her, and fome Chamber-Plate which fhe had from her Grandmother, and fent over the money to my Lord, befides 1000l. of her Portion : And the now Earl of *Ogle* did at feveral times fupply my Lord, his Father, with fuch moneys as he had partly obtained upon Credit, and partly made by his Marriage.

After my Lord had begun to view thofe Ruines that were neareft, and tried the Law to keep or recover what formerly was his, (which certainly fhew'd no favour to him, befides that the Act of Oblivion proved a great hinderance and obftruction to thofe his defigns, as it did no lefs to all the Royal Party)

and had fetled fo much of his Eftate as poffibly
he could, he caft up the **Summ** of his Debts,
and fet out feveral parts of Land for the payment of them, or of fome of them (for fome
of his Lands could not be eafily **fold, being**
entailed) and fome he fold in *Derbyfhire* to
buy the Caftle of *Nottingham*, which although
it is quite ruined and demolifht, yet, it being
a feat which had **pleafed** his Father very much,
he would not leave **it** fince it was offer'd to
be fold.

His two Houfes *Welbeck* and *Bolfover* he
found much out of repair, and this later half
pull'd down, no furniture or **any neceffary**
Goods were left in them, but **fome few**
Hangings and Pictures, which had been faved
by the care and induftry of his Eldeft Daughter
the Lady *Cheiny*, and were bought over again
after the death of his eldeft Son *Charles*, Lord
Mansfield; for they being given to him, and
he leaving fome debts to be paid after his
death, My Lord fent to his other Son *Henry*,
now Earl of *Ogle*, to endeavour for fo much
Credit, **that** the faid Hangings and Pictures
(which **my** Lord efteemed very much, the
Pictures being drawn by *Van Dyke*) might be

faved; which he **alfo** did, and My Lord hath paid the debt fince his return.

Of eight Parks, which my Lord had before the Wars, there was but one left that was not quite deftroyed, *viz. Welbeck-*Park **of** about four miles compafs; for my Lord's Brother Sir *Charles Cavendifh*, who bought out the life of my Lord in that Lordfhip, faved moft part of it from being cut down; and in *Blore-*Park there were fome **few** Deer left: **The** reft **of** the Parks were totally defaced and deftroyed, both Wood, Pales and Deer; amongft which was alfo *Clipfton-*Park of feven miles compafs, wherein my Lord had taken much delight formerly, it being rich of Wood, and con- taining the greateft and talleft Timber-trees of all the Woods he had; in **fo** much, **that** onely the Pale-row **was** valued at 2000l. **It was** water'd by a pleafant **River that** runs through it, **full of fifh** and Otters; was **well** ftock'd with Deer, full of Hares, **and had great** ftore of Partriges, Poots,[1] Pheafants, *&c.*

---

[1] *Poots.* **I had a** difficulty **as** to the meaning of this word; but through two **able** ornithologifts I learn that *powt* fignifies **either** the Black-cock or the Red-groufe, **but more probably** the former, which is **a** great fre-

befides all forts of Water-fowl; fo that this Park afforded all manner **of** fports, for Hunting, Hawking, Courfing, Fifhing, &c. for which my Lord efteemed it very much: And although **his** Patience and Wifdom is fuch, that I never perceived him fad **or** dif-contented for his own Loffes and Misfortunes, yet when **he** beheld the ruines of that Park, I obferved him troubled, though he did little exprefs it, onely faying, he had been in hopes **it** would not **have** been fo much defaced as he found it, there being not one Timber-tree **in** it left for fhelter. However he patiently **bore** what could not be helped, and gave pre-fent order for the cutting down of fome Wood that was left him in **a** place near adjoining, **to** repale it, and got from feveral Friends Deer **to** ftock it.

Thus though his Law-fuits and other un-avoidable expences were very chargeable to him, yet he order'd his affairs fo prudently,

---

quenter of woods. Primarily **it** fignifies **a chicken** of any kind, efpecially a young game bird. **The word** is doubtlefs of common etymology with *pullet, poultry,* &c. In fome provincial dialects the **word *polt*** is applied to a young pigeon.

that by degrees he ftock'd and manur'd thofe Lands he keeps for his own ufe, and in part repaired his Mannor-houfes, *Welbeck*, and *Bol-fover*, to which latter he made fome additional building; and though he has not yet built the Seat at *Nottingham*, yet he hath ftock'd and paled a little Park belonging to it.

Nor is it poffible for him to repair all the ruines of the Eftate that is left him, in fo fhort a time, they being fo great, and his loffes fo confiderable, that I cannot without grief and trouble remember them; for before the Wars my Lord had as great an Eftate as any fubject in the Kingdom, defcended upon him moft by Women, *viz.* by his Grandmother of his Father's fide, his own Mother, and his firft Wife.

What Eftate his Grandfather left to his Father Sir *Charles Cavendifh*, I know not; nor can I exactly tell what he had from his Grandmother, but fhe was very rich; for her third Hufband Sir *Will.* Saint *Loo*, gave her a good Eftate in the Weft, which afterwards defcended upon my Lord, my Lord's Mother being the younger daughter of the Lord *Ogle*, and fole Heir, after the death of her eldeft

Sifter *Jane*, Countefs of *Shrewsbury*, whom King *Charles* the Firft reftored to her Fathers Dignity, *viz.* Baronefs of *Ogle :* This Title defcended upon my Lord and his Heirs General, together with 3000l. a year in *Northumberland ;* and befides the Eftate left to my Lord, fhe gave him 20000l. in Money, and kept him and his Family at her own charge for feveral years.

My Lord's firft Wife, who was Daughter and Heir to *William Baffet* of *Blore*, Efq ; Widow to **Henry Howard**, younger Son to *Thomas* Earl of *Suffolk*, brought my Lord 2400l. a Year Inheritance, between fix and feven thoufand Pounds in Money, and a jointure for her life of 800l. a Year. Befides my Lord increafed his own Eftate before the Wars, to the value of 100000l. and had increafed it more, had not the unhappy Wars prevented him ; for though he had fome difadvantages in his Eftate, even before the Wars, yet they are not confiderable to thofe he fuffered afterwards for the fervice of his King and Country : For example, His Father Sir *Charles Cavendifh* had lent his Brother in Law *Gilbert* Earl of *Shrewfbury* 16000l. for

which, although afterward before his death he
fetled 2000l. a year upon him ; yet he having
injoyed the faid Money for many years without paying any ufe for it, it might have been
improved to my Lord's better advantage, had
it been in his Fathers own hands, he being a
Perfon of great prudence in managing his
Eftate ; and though the faid Earl of *Shrewf-*
bury made my Lord his Executor, yet my Lord
was fo far from making any advantage by that
Truft, even in what the Law allowed him,
that he loft 17000l. by it ; and afterwards delivered up his Truft to *William* Earl of *Pem-*
brook, and *Thomas* Earl of *Arundel*, who both
married two Daughters of the faid Earl of
Shrewfbury ; And fince his return into *Eng-*
land, upon the defire of *Henry Howard*, Second
Son to the late Earl of *Arundel*, and Heir
apparent, (by reafon of his Eldeft Brother's
Diftemper) he refigned his Truft and Intereft
to him, which certainly is a very difficult bufinefs, and yet queftionable whether it may
lawfully be done, or not ?   But fuch was my
Lord's Love to the Family of the *Shrewfburies*,
that he would rather wrong himfelf, then it.

To mention fome lawful advantages which

my Lord might have made by the faid Truft,
it may be noted in the firft place, That the
Earl of *Shrewfbury*'s Eftate was **Let** in long
Leafes, which, by the **Law**, fell to the Executor.   Next, that after fome Debts and
Legacies **were** paid out of thofe Lands, which
were fet out for that purpofe, they were fetled
fo, that they fell to my Lord.   Thirdly, Seven
hundred pounds a year was left as a Gift to
my Lord's Brother, Sir *Charles Cavendifh*, in
cafe the Countefs of *Kent*, Second Daughter
to the faid Earl of *Shrewfbury*, had no Children. But my Lord never made any advantage
for himfelf, of all thefe ; neither was **he** in-
quifitive whether the faid Countefs of *Kent*
cut off the Entail of that Land, although fhe
never had a Child ; for my Lord's Nature is
fo generous, that he hates to be Mercenary,
and never minds his own Profit or Intereft in
any Truft or Employment, more then the
good and benefit of him that intrufts or em-
ploys him.

But, as I faid heretofore, thefe are but petty
Loffes in comparifon of thofe he fuftained by
the late Civil Warrs, whereof I fhall partly
give you an account : I fay partly ; for though

it may be computed what the lofs of the Annual Rents of his **Lands** amounts to, of which he never received the leaft worth **for** himfelf and his own profit, during the time both of his being employed in the Service of Warr, and his Sufferings in Banifhment; **as** alfo the lofs of thofe Lands that are alienated from him, both in **prefent** poffeffion, **and in** reverfion; and of his Parks and **Woods that** were cut **down;** yet it is impoffible to render an exact account of **his Perfonal Eftate.**

As for **his** Rents during **the time he** acted in the Warrs, though he fuffer'd others to gather theirs **for their** own ufe, yet his own either went for the ufe of the Army, or fell into the hands of the Enemy, or were fup-prefs'**d** and with-held from **him** by the Cozenage **of** his Tenants and Officers, **my** Lord being then not able to look after them himfelf.

About the time when **His late** Majefty un-dertook the expedition into *Scotland* for the fuppreffing of fome infurrection that happened there; My Lord, **as** afore is mentioned, amongft **the** reft, lent **His** Majefty 10000l. *fterling;* But having newly married a Daughter to the then Lord *Brackly*, now Earl of *Bridg-water*, whofe portion was 12000l. the moiety whereof was paid in Gold on the day of her marriage, and the reft foon after (although fhe was too young to be bedded.) This, together with fome other expences, caufed him to take up the faid 10000l. at Intereft, the Ufe whereof he paid many years after.

Alfo when after his fixteen years Banifh-ment, he returned into *England*, before he knew what Eftate was left him, and was able to receive any Rents of his own, he was neceffitated to take 5000l. upon Ufe for the maintenance of himfelf and his Family; whereof the now Earl of *Devonfhire*, his Coufin German, once removed, lent him 1000l. for which and the former 1000l. men-tioned heretofore, he never defired nor re-ceived any Ufe from my Lord, which I men-tion, to declare the favour and bounty of that Noble Lord.

But though it is impoffible to render an exact account of all the loffes which My Lord has fuftained by the faid Wars, yet as far as they are accountable, I fhall endeavour to reprefent them in thefe following Particulars :

In the firft place, I fhall give you a juft particular of My Lords Eftate in **Lands,** as it was before the Wars, partly according to the value of his own Surveighers, and partly according to the rate it is let, at this prefent.

Next, I fhall accompt the Woods cut **down** by the Rebellious **Party,** in feveral places of My Lords Eftate.

Thirdly, I fhall **compute the** Value of **thofe** Lands **which My Lord** hath **loft,** both in prefent poffeffion, and **in reverfion;** that is to fay, thofe which **he has loft** altogether, both for himfelf, **and his** Pofterity ; **and** thofe he has recovered onely during the time of his life, and which his **onely** Son and Heir, the now Earl of *Ogle,* muft lofe after **his** Fathers deceafe.

Fourthly, I fhall make mention, how much **of Land my** Lord **hath** been forced to fell for the payment of fome **of** his Debts, contracted during the time of **the** late Civil Wars, **and** when his Eftate was fequeftred ; I fay fome, **for** there **are a** great **many to** pay yet.

To which I fhall, Fifthly, add the Compofition of his Brothers **Eftate ;** and the lofs of it for Eight years.

A Particular of My Lords Eſtate in plain Rents, as it was partly ſurveighed in the Year 1641, and partly is let at this preſent.

Nottingham-ſhire.

	l.	s.	d.
THE Mannor of *Welbeck* .	600	0	0
The Mannor of *Norton, Carbarton,* and the *Granges* .	454	19	1
Warkſopp	51	6	8
The Mannor-houſe of *Soakholm*	308	10	3
The Manor of *Clipſton* & *Edwin-ſtow*	334	9	8
Drayton	8	16	6
Dunham	99	17	8
Sutton	185	0	5
The Mannor of **Kirby**, &c. . .	1075	7	2
The Mannor of *Cotham* . . .	833	18	8
The Mannor of *Sitthorp* . . .	704	1	0
Carcholſton	450	3	0
Hauksworth, &c.	139	4	
Flawborough	512	11	8
Mearing and *Holm*-Meadow .	471	2	0
	6229	7	11

Lincoln-shire.

	l.	s.	d.
Wellinger and *Ingham* Meales .	100	0	0

Derby-shire.

	l.	s.	d.
The Barrony of *Bolsover* and *Woodthorp*	846	8	11
The Mannor of *Chesterfield* . .	378	0	0
The Mannor of *Barlow* . . .	796	17	6
Tissington	159	11	0
Dronfield	486	15	10
The Mannor of *Brampton* . .	142	4	8
Little-*Longston*	87	2	0
The Mannor of *Stoak* . . .	212	3	0
Birth-Hall, and *Peak*-Forrest .	131	8	0
The Mannor of *Gringlow* . .	156	8	0
The Mannor of *Hucklow* . .	162	10	8
The Mannor of *Blackwall* . .	306	0	4
Buxton and *Tids-Hall* . . .	153	2	0
Mansfield-Park	100	0	0
Mappleton and *Thorp*	207	5	0
The Mannor of *Windly*-Hill .	238	18	0
The Mannor of *Litchurch* and *Markworth*	713	15	1
Church and *Meynel Langly* Mannor	850	1	0
	6128	11	10

Stafford-shire.

	l.	s.	d.
The Mannor of *Bloar* with *Caulton*	573	13	4
The Mannor of *Grindon, Cauldon*, with *Waterfull* . . .	822	3	0
The Mannor of *Cheadle* with *Kinſly*	259	18	0
The Mannor of *Barleſton*, &c. .	694	3	0
	2349	17	4

Gloceſter-ſhire.

	l.	s.	d.
The Manor of *Tormorton* with *Litleton*	1193	16	0
The Mannor of *Acton Turvil* .	388	3	2
	1581	19	2

Summerſet-ſhire.

	l.	s.	d.
The Mannor of *Chewſtoak* . .	816	15	6
Knighton Sutton	300	14	4
Stroud and *Kingſham*-Park . .	186	4	0
	1303	13	10

York-shire.

The Manors of *Slingsby, Ho-*
verngham and *Friton, Nor-*
thinges and *Pomfret* . . . 1700 0 0

Northumberland.

The Barrony of *Bothal, Ogle*
and *Hepple*, &c. 3000 0 0

Totall 22393 10 1

That this Particular of My Lords Eſtate
was no leſs then is mentioned, may partly
appear by the rate, as it was ſurveighed, and
ſold by the Rebellious Parliament; for they
raiſed, towards the later end of their power,
which was in the year 1652, out of my Lord's
Eſtate, the ſumme of 115593l. 10s. 11d. at
five years and a half Purchaſe, which was at
above the rate of 18000l. a year, beſides
Woods; and his Brother Sir *Charles Caven-*
diſh's Eſtate, which Eſtate was 2000l. a year,
which falls not much ſhort of the mentioned
account; and certainly, had they not ſold ſuch
Lands at eaſie rates, few would have bought
them, by reaſon the Purchaſers were uncer-

tain how long they fhould enjoy their purchafe: Befides, Under-Officers do not ufually **refufe** Bribes; and it is well known that the Surveighers did under-rate Eftates according as **they were feed by the** Purchafers.

Again, many of the **Eftates of** banifhed **Perfons were** given to Soldiers for the payment of their Arrears, who again fold **them to others which** would buy them at eafier rates. **But chiefly, it** appears by the **rate** as my **Lords E**ftate **is** let at prefent, there being feveral of the mentioned Lands that are let at a higher rate now then they were furveighed; nor are they all valued in the mentioned particular according to the furveigh, but many of them which were **not** furveighed, are accounted according to the rate they are **let at at this** prefent.

The **Lofs of** my Lords Eftate, in plain Rents, as alfo upon ordinary Ufe, and Ufe upon Ufe, is as followeth:

The Annual Rent of My Lords Lands, *viz.* 22393l. 10s. 1d. being loft for the fpace of 18 years, which was the time of **his** acting in the Wars, and **of his** Banifhment, without any benefit to him, reckoned without any Intereft, amounts **to 40308l. But being** accounted with the ordinary Ufe at Six in the Hundred, and Ufe upon Ufe for the mentioned fpace of 18 Years, it amounts to 733579l.

But fome perhaps will fay, That if **My Lord** had enjoyed his Eftate, he would have fpent it, at leaft fo much as to maintain himfelf according to his degree and quality.

I anfwer; That it is very improbable **My Lord** fhould have fpent all his Eftate, **if he** had enjoyed it he being a man of great Wifdom **and** Prudence, knowing well **how** to fpend, and how to manage ; for though he lived nobly before the time of the Wars, yet not beyond the Compafs of his Eftate ; nay, fo far he would have been from fpending his Eftate, that no doubt but he would have increaft it to a vaft value, as he did before the Wars ; where notwithftanding his Hofpitality and noble Houfe-keeping, his charges **of** Building **came** to about 31000l ; the portion **of his** fecond Daughter, which was 12000l ; **the** noble entertainments he gave King *Charles* the Firft, one whereof came to almoft 15000l. another to above 4000l, and a third to 1700l. as hereafter fhall be mentioned ; and his great expences during the time of his being Governour to **his** Majefty that now **is, he** yet encreafed **his** Eftate to the value of 100000l. which is 5000 *per annum*, when it was by fo much lefs.

But if any one will reckon the charges of his Houfe-keeping during the time of his Exile, and when **he** had not the enjoyment of his Eftate, he may fubftract the fum accounted **for the** payment of his debts, contracted **in the time of** his Banifhment, which went to the maintenance of himfelf and his Family; or in lieu thereof, confidering that I do not account all My Lords loffes, **but** onely thofe that are certainly known, he may compare it **with** the lofs of his perfonal Eftate, whereof I fhall make fome mention anon, and he'll find that I do not heighten my Lords Loffes, but **rather** diminifh them; for furely the loffes of his perfonal Eftate, and thofe I account **not, will** counterballance the charges of **his** Houfe-keeping, if not exceed them.

Again, others **will** fay, That there **was** much Land fold in the time of My Lords Banifhment by his Sons, and Feoffees in Truft.

I anfwer, Firft, That whatfoever was fold, **was** firft bought of the Rebellious Power: Next, although they fold fome Lands, yet **My Lord knew** nothing of it, neither did he receive a penny worth for himfelf, neither of what they purchafed, nor fold, all the time of his Banifhment till his return.

And thus much of the lofs of My Lords Eftate in Rents: Concerning the lofs of his Parks and Woods, as much as is generally known, (for I do not reckon particular Trees cut down in feveral of his Woods yet ftanding) 'tis as follows:

1. *Clipfton*-Park and Woods cut down to the value of 20000 l.

2. *Kirkby*-Woods, for which my Lord was formerly proferr'd 10000 l.

3. Woods cut down in *Derbyfhire* 8000 l.

4. *Red-lodg*-Wood, *Rome*-wood and others near *Welbeck* 4000 l.

5. Woods cut down in *Stafford*-fhire 1000 l.

6. Woods cut down in *York*-fhire 1000 l.

7. Woods cut down in *Northumberland* 1500 l.

The *Total* 45000 l.

The Lands which My Lord hath loft in prefent pofeffion are 2015 l. *per annum*, which at 20 years purchafe come to 40300 l. and thofe which he hath loft in Reverfion, are 3214 l. *per annum*, which at 16 years purchafe amount to the value of 51424 l.

The Lands which my Lord fince his return has fold for the payment of fome of his debts, occafioned by the Wars (for I do not reckon thofe he fold to buy others) come to the value of 56000 l. to which out of his yearly revenue he has added 10000 l. more, which is in all 66000 l.

Laftly, The Compofition of his Brothers Eftate was 5000 l. and the lofs of it for eight years comes to 16000 l.

All which, if fumm'd up together, amounts to 941303 l.

Thefe are the accountable loffes, which My Dear Lord and Hufband has fuffered by the late Civil Wars, and his Loyalty to his King and Country. Concerning the lofs of his perfonal Eftate, fince (as I often mentioned) it cannot be exactly known; I fhall not endeavour to fet down the Particulars thereof, onely in General give you a Note of what partly they are:

1. The pulling down of feveral of his dwelling or Mannor-houfes.

2. The disfurnifhing of them, of which the Furniture at *Bolfover* and *Welbeck* was very noble and rich: Out of his *London*-houfe at *Clarken-well*, there were taken, amongft other

Goods, fuits **of Linnen,** *viz.* Table-Cloths, Sideboard-cloths, Napkins, *&c.* whereof one fuit coft 160 l. **they being** bought **for** an Entertainment which My Lord made for Their Majefties, King *Charles* the Firft, **and** the Queen, at *Bolfover*-Caftle ; And of 150 Suits **of** Hangings of all forts **in** all **his** Houfes, **there** were not above 10 or 12 faved.

Of Silver-plate, My Lord had **fo much as** came **to the value of** 3800 l. befides feveral Curiofities of Cabinets, Cups, and other **things,** which after My Lord was gone out of *England,* were taken out **of** his Mannor-houfe, *Welbeck,* by a Garifon of the Kings Party that lay therein, whereof he recovered onely 1100 l. which Money was **fent** him beyond the Seas, the reft was loft.

As for Pewter, Brafs, Bedding, Linnen, **and** other Houfhold-ftuff, there was nothing elfe left but fome **few** old Feather-beds, and thofe **all** fpoiled, and **fit** for no ufe.

3. My Lord's Stock **of** Corn, Cattel, *&c.* was very great before **the Warrs, by** reafon **of** the largenefs **and** capacity of thofe grounds, and the great number of Granges he kept for his own **ufe;** as for example, *Barlow, Carkholfton, Gleadthorp, Welbeck,* **and** feveral more, which were all well manured and ftockt. But all this ftock was loft, befides **his Race** of Horfes in his Grounds, Grange-Horfes, Hackny-Horfes, Mannage-Horfes, Coach-Horfes, and others he kept for his ufe.

To thefe Loffes **I** may well and juftly join **the** charges which my Lord hath been put **to** **fince his** return into *England*, by reafon they were caufed by the ruines of the faid **Warrs**; whereof **I reckon,**

1. **His Law-fuits,** which have been very chargeable to him, more than advantagious.

2. The Stocking, Manuring, Paling, Stubbing, Hedging, &c. of his Grounds and **Parks;** where it is to be noted, That no advantage or benefit can be made of Grounds, **under the** fpace of **three** years, and of Cattel not under five or fix.

3. **The** repairing and furnifhing of fome of his Dwelling-Houfes.

4. **The** fetting up a Race or Breed of Horfes, as he **had** before the Warrs; for which purpofe he hath bought **the** beft Mares **he** could get for money.

In fhort, **I** can reckon 12000 l. laid out barely for **the** repair of fome Ruines, which

my Lord could not be without, there being
many of them to repair yet ; neither is this all
that is laid out, but much more which I cannot well remember ; nor is there more but
one Grange ſtock'd, amongſt ſeveral that were
kept for furniſhing his Houſe with Proviſions :
As for other Charges and Loſſes, which My
Lord hath ſuſtained ſince his return, I will
not reckon them, becauſe my deſign is onely
to account ſuch loſſes as were cauſed by the
Wars.

By which, as they have been mentioned,
it may eaſily be concluded, That although
My Lord's Eſtate was very great before the
Wars, yet now it is ſhrunk into a very narrow
compaſs, that it puts his Prudence and Wiſdom
to the Proof, to make it ſerve his neceſſities,
he having no other aſſiſtance to bear him up ;
and yet notwithſtanding all this, he hath ſince
his return paid both for Himſelf and his Son,
all manner of Taxes, Lones, Levies, Aſſeſſ-
ments, &c. equally with the reſt of His
Majeſties Subjects, according to that Eſtate
that is left him, which he has been forced to
take upon Intereſt.

The *

Life of the Moſt Illuſtrious Prince, William Duke of Newcaſtle.

THE THIRD BOOK.

HUS having given you a faithful Account of all My **Lords Actions**, both before, in, **and** after the **Civil** Warrs, and **of his** Loſſes; I ſhall now conclude with ſome particular **heads** concerning the deſcription of his own Perſon, his Natural Humour, Diſpoſition, Qualities, Vertues; his Pedigree, Habit, Diet, Exerciſes, *&c.* together with ſome **other Re-**marks **and** Particulars which **I thought** requiſite to be inſerted, both **to illuſtrate** the former **Books, and to** render the Hiſtory of his **Life more** perfect and compleat.

1. *Of his Power.*

AFTER His Majesty King *Charles* the First, had entrusted **my** Lord with the Power of raising Forces for **His** Majesties Service, he effected that which never any Subject did, nor was (in all probability) able to do; for though many Great and Noble Persons did also raise Forces for His Majesty, yet they were Brigades, rather then well-formed Armies, **in** comparison **to** my Lord's. The reason was, That my Lord, by his Mother, the Daughter of *Cuthbert* Lord *Ogle*, being allyed to most of the most ancient Families in *Northumberland*, and other the Northern parts, could pretend a greater Interest in them, then a stranger; for they through **a** natural affection **to my** Lord as their own Kinsman, would sooner follow **him,** and under his Conduct sacrifice their Lives for His Majesty's Service, then **any** body else, well knowing, That by deserting **my Lord, they** deserted **themselves; and by this** means my Lord raised first a Troup of Horse consisting **of a** hundred and twenty, and a Regiment of Foot; and then an Army of Eight thousand

Horfe, Foot and Dragoons, in thofe parts; and afterwards upon this ground, at feveral times, and in feveral places, fo many feveral Troups, Regiments and Armies, that in all from the firft to the laft, they amounted to above 100000 men, and thofe moft upon his own Intereft, and without any other confiderable help or affiftance; which was much for a particular Subject, and in fuch a conjuncture of time; for fince Armies are fooneft raifed by Covetoufnefs, Fear and Faction; that is to fay, upon a conftant and fettled Pay, upon the Ground of Terrour, and upon the Ground of Rebellion; but very feldom or never upon uncertainty of Pay; and when it is as hazardous to be of fuch a Party, as to be in the heat of a Battel; alfo when there is no other defign but honeft duty; it may eafily be conceived that my Lord could have no little love and affection when He raifed his Army upon fuch grounds as could promife them but little advantage at that time.

Amongft the reft of his Army, My Lord had chofen for his own Regiment of Foot, 3000 of fuch Valiant, ftout and faithful men, (whereof many were bred in the Moorish-grounds of the Northern parts) that they were ready to die at my Lord's feet, and never gave over, whenſoever they were engaged in action, until they had either conquer'd the Enemy, or loſt their lives. They were called White-coats, for this following reaſon: My Lord being reſolved to give them new Liveries, and there being not red Cloth enough to be had, took up ſo much of white as would ſerve to cloath them, deſiring withal, their patience until he had got it dyed; but they impatient of ſtay, requeſted my Lord, that he would be pleaſed to let them have it un-dyed as it was, promiſing they themſelves would die it in the Enemies Blood: Which requeſt my Lord granted them, and from that time they were called White-Coats.

To give you ſome inſtances of their Valour and Courage, I muſt beg leave to repeat ſome paſſages mentioned in the firſt Book. The Enemy having cloſely beſieged the City of *York*, and made a paſſage into the Mannor-yard, by ſpringing a Mine under the Wall thereof, was got into the Mannor-houſe with a great number of their Forces; which My

Lord perceiving, he immediately went and drew 80 of the faid White-coats thither, who with the greateft Courage went clofe up to the Enemy, and having charged them, fell Pell-mell with the But-ends of their Mufquets upon them, and with the affiftance of the reft that renewed their Courage by their example, kill'd and took 1500, and by that means faved the Town.

How valiantly they behaved themfelves in the laft fatal Battel upon *Heffom-moor* near *York*, has been alfo declared heretofore; in fo much, that although moft of the Army were fled, yet they would not ftir, until by the Enemies Power they were overcome, and moft of them flain in rank and file.

Their love and affection to my Lord was fuch, that it lafted even when he was deprived of all his power, and could do them little good; to which purpofe I fhall mention this following paffage:

My Lord being in *Antwerp*, received a Vifit from a Gentleman, who came out of *England*, and rendred My Lord thanks for his fafe Efcape at Sea; My Lord being in amaze, not knowing what the Gentleman meant, he was pleafed to acquaint Him, that in his coming over Sea out of *England*, he was fet upon by Pickaroons,[1] who having examined him, and the reft of his Company, at laft fome afked him, whether he knew the Marquefs of *Newcaftle?* To whom he anfwered, That he knew him very well, and was going over into the fame City where my Lord lived. Where-upon they did not onely take nothing from him, but ufed him with all Civility, and de-fired him to remember their humble duty to their Lord General, for they were fome of his White-Coats that had efcaped death ; and if my Lord had any fervice for them, they were ready to affift him upon what Defigns foever, and to obey him in whatfoever he fhould be pleafed to Command them.

This I mention for the Eternal Fame and Memory of thofe Valiant and Faithful Men. But to return to the *Power* my Lord had in the late Warrs : As he was the Head of his own Army, and had raifed it moft upon his own Intereft for the Service of His Majefty ; fo he was never Ordered by His Majefty's

---

[1] **Rogues**, from the Spanifh *Picaro.*

Privy Council, (except that fome forces of His were kept by His late Majefty, (which he fent to Him) together with fome Arms and Ammunition heretofore mentioned) until His Highnefs Prince *Rupert* came from His Majefty, to join with him at the Siege of *York*. He had moreover the Power of Coyning, Printing, Knighting, *&c.* which never any Subject had before, when His Soveraign Himfelf was in the Kingdom; as alfo the Command of fo many Counties, as is mentioned in the Firft Book, and the Power of placing and difplacing what Governours and Commanders he pleafed, and of conftituting what Garifons he thought fit; of the chief whereof I fhall give you this following lift.

A Particular of the Principal Garifons, and the Governors of them, conftituted by my Lord.

In Northumberland.

NEWCASTLE upon *Tyne*, Sir *John Marley* Knight.

Tynmouth Caftle and *Sheilds*, Sir *Thomas Riddal*, Knight.

In the Bishoprick of Durham.

Hartlepool, Lieutenant Colonel *Henry Lambton.*

Raby-Castle, Sir *William Savile,* Knight and Baronet.

In Yorkshire.

The City of *York,* Sir *Thomas Glenham* Knight and Baronet; and afterwards when he took the Field, the Lord *Jo. Bellasyse.*

Pomfret-Castle, Colonel *Mynn,* and after him Sir *Jo. Redman.*

•*Sheffield-Castle,* Major *Beamont.*

Wortly-Hall, Sir *Francis Wortley.*

Tickhill-Castle, Major *Mountney.*

Doncaster, Sir *Francis Fane,* Knight of the Bath, afterwards Governour of *Lincoln.*

Sandal-Castle, Captain *Bonivant.*

Skipton-Castle, Sir *John Mallary,* Baronet.

Bolton-Castle, Mr. *Scroope.*

Hemsley-Castle, Sir *Jordan Crosland.*

Scarborough-Castle and Town, Sir *Hugh Chomley.*

Stamford-Bridg, Colonel *Galbreth.*

Hallifax, Sir *Francis Mackworth.*

L

Tadcaster, Sir *Gamaliel Dudley*.

Eyrmouth, Major *Kaughton*.

In Cumberland.

The City of *Carlisle*, Sir *Philip Musgrave*, Knight and Baronet.

Cockermouth, Colonel *Kirby*.

In Nottinghamshire.

Newark upon *Trent*, Sir *John Henderson*, Knight; **and** afterwards, Sir *Richard Byron*, Knight, now **Lord** *Byron*.

Wyrton-House, Colonel *Rowland Hacker*.

Welbeck, Colonel *Van Peire*; **and after,** Colonel *Beeton*.

Shelford-House, Col. *Philip Stanhop*.

In Lincolnshire.

The City of *Lincoln*, first Sir *Francis Fane*, Knight of the Bath; secondly, Sir *Peregrine Bartu*.

Gainsborough, Colonel St. *George*.

Bullingbrook - Castle, Lieutenant Colonel *Chester*.

Beluoir-Castle, Sir *Gervas Lucas*.

In Derbyſhire.

Bolſover-Caſtle, **Colonel** *Muſchamp.*
Wingfield **Mannor, Colonel** *Roger Molyneux.*
Staly-Houſe, the now Lord *Fretchwile.*

A LIST *of the General* OFFICERS *of the ARMY.*

1. THE **Lord** General, **the now Duke of** *Newcaſtle*, **the Noble** Subject of this Book.

2. The Lieutenant General **of the Army ;** firſt the Earl **of** *Newport*, afterwards the Lord *Eythin.*

3. The General **of the** Ordnance, *Charles* Viſcount *Mansfield.*

4. **The** General **of the** Horſe, *George* Lord *Goring.*

5. The Colonel General of the **Army, Sir** *Thomas Glenham.*

6. The Major General of the Army, Sir *Francis Mackworth.*

7. The Lieutenant General of the Horſe, Firſt Mr. *Charles Cavendiſh*, after him Sir *Charles* **Lucas.**

8. Commiſſary General **of** Horſe, Firſt Colonel *Windham*, after **him** Sir *William Throckmorton*, and after him **Mr.** *George Porter*.

9. Lieutenant General of the Ordnance, Sir *William Davenant*.

10. Treaſurer **of** the Army, Sir *William Carnaby*.

11. **Advocate**-General **of** the Army, **Dr.** *Liddal*.

12. Quarter-Maſter General of the Army, **Mr.** *Ralph Errington*.

13. Providore-General **of** the **Army,** Mr. *Gervas Nevil*, **and** after Mr. *Smith*.

14. Scout-Maſter-General of the **Army, Mr.** *Hudſon*.

15. **Waggon-Maſter-General of the** Army, *Baptiſt Johnſon*.

William **Lord** *Widdrington* was Preſident **of the Council of** War, **and Commander in** chief **of** the three Counties of *Lincoln*, *Rutland* **and** *Nottingham*, **and** the forces there.

When my Lord marched with his Army to *Newcaſtle* againſt the *Scots*, then the Lord *John Bellaſſis* was conſtituted Governour of

York, and Commander in Chief, or Lieutenant General of *York-fhire*.

As for the reft of the Officers and Commanders of every particular Regiment and Company, they being too numerous, cannot well be remembred, and therefore I fhall give you no particular accompt of them.

2. *Of His Misfortunes and obftruftions.*

ALTHOUGH Nature had favour'd My Lord, and endued him with the beft Qualities and Perfections fhe could infpire into his foul; yet Fortune hath ever been fuch an inveterate Enemy to him, that fhe invented all the fpight and malice againft him that lay in her power; and notwithftanding his prudent Counfels and Defigns, caft fuch obftructions in his way, that he feldom proved fuccefsful, but where he acted in Perfon. And fince I am not ignorant that this unjuft and partial Age is apt to fupprefs the worth of meritorious perfons, and that many will endeavour to obfcure my Lords noble Actions and Fame, by cafting unjuft afperfions upon him, and laying (either out of ignorance or malice) Fortunes **envy to his charge, I** have purpofed to **reprefent thefe obftructions** which confpired to render his good intentions **and** endeavours ineffectual, and at laft did **work his ruine** and deftruction, in thefe following particulars.

1. At the time when the Kingdom became fo **infatuated, as to oppofe and** pull down **their** Gracious King and Soveraign, **the** Treafury **was** exhaufted, **and no** fufficient means to raife and maintain Armies to reduce **His** Majefties Rebellious Subjects; **fo that My** Lord had little **to** begin withal but what his own Eftate would allow, and his Intereft procure him.

2. **When** his late **Majefty, in** the beginning **of the** unhappy **W**ars, fent My Lord to *Hull,* **the** ftrongeft place **in the** Kingdom, where **the** Magazine of Arms and Ammunition **was kept, and he** by his prudence had gained **it to his** Majefties fervice; My Lord was **left to the mercy** of the Parliament, **where he had furely** fuffered for **it,** (though he acted not without His Majefties Commiffion) **if** fome **of** the contrary **party** had not **quitted** him, in hopes **to** gain him on their fide.

3. After His Majefty had fent My Lord to *Newcaftle* upon *Tyne,* to take upon him the Government of that place, and he had raifed there, of Friends and Tenants, a troup of Horfe and Regiment of Foot, which he ordered to conveigh fome Arms and Ammunition to His Majefty, fent by the Queen out of *Holland;* His Majefty was pleafed to keep the fame Convoy with him to encreafe his own Forces, which although it was but of a fmall number, yet at that prefent time it would have been very ferviceable to my Lord, he having then but begun to raife Forces.

4. When Her Majefty the now Queen-Mother, after her arrival out of *Holland* to *York,* had a purpofe to conveigh fome Armes to His Majefty, My Lord order'd a Party of 1500 to conduct the fame, which His Majefty was pleafed to keep with him for his own fervice.

5. After Her Majefty had taken a refolution to go from *York* to *Oxford,* where the King then was ; my Lord for Her fafer conduct quitted 7000 men of his Army, with a convenient Train of Artillery, which likewife never returned to my Lord.

6. When the Earl of *Montroſs* was going into *Scotland*, he went to my Lord at *Durham*, **and** deſired of him a ſupply of ſome Forces for His Majeſties ſervice; where **my** Lord gave him 200 Horſe and Dragoons, even at ſuch a time when he ſtood moſt in need of a ſupply himſelf, and thought every day to encounter the *Scottiſh* Army.

7. When my Lord out **of the** Northern parts went into *Lincoln-* and *Derby-ſhires* with his Army, to order and reduce them to their Allegiance and Duty to His Majeſty, and from thence reſolved to march into the Aſſociate Counties, (where in all probability he would have made an happy end of the Warr) he was ſo importuned by thoſe he left behind him, and particularly the Commander in Chief, **to** return into *York-ſhire*, alledging the Enemy grew ſtrong, and would ruine them all, if **he** came **not** ſpeedily to ſuccour and aſſiſt them; that in honour and duty he could do no otherwiſe but grant their Requeſts; when as yet being returned into thoſe parts, **he** found them ſecure and ſafe enough from the Enemies Attempts.

8. **My Lord (as** heretofore mentioned) had

as great private Enemies about **His** Majefty, as he had **publick** Enemies in the Field, **who** ufed all **the** endeavour they could to pull him down.

9. There was fuch Jugling, Treachery, and Falfhood in his own Army, and amongft fome of his own Officers, that it was impof-fible for my Lord to be profperous and fuccefs-ful in his Defigns and Undertakings.

10. My Lord's Army being the chief and greateft Army which His Majefty **had,** and in which confifted His prime Strength and Power; the Parliament refolved **at** laft, to join all their Forces with the Army of the *Scots,* (which when it came out of *Scotland,* **was** above Twenty thoufand Men) to oppofe, and if poffible, to ruine it; well knowing, that if they did **pull** down my Lord, they fhould be Mafters **of** all the Three King-doms; fo that there were Three Armies againft One. But although my Lord fuffered much by the Negligence (and fometimes Treachery) of his Officers, and was unfor-tunately called back **into** *York-fhire,* from his March he defigned for the Affociate Counties, and was forced to part with a great number

of his Forces and Ammunition, as aforementioned; yet he would hardly have been overcome, and his Army ruined by the Enemy,
had he but had fome timely fupply and affiftance at the Siege of *York*, or that his Counfel
had been taken in not fighting the Enemy
then, or that the Battel had been differ'd fome
two or three dayes longer, until thofe Forces
were arrived which he expected, namely three
thoufand men out of *Northumberland*, and Two
thoufand drawn out of feveral Garifons. But
the chief Misfortune was, That the Enemy
fell upon the Kings Forces before they were
all put into a *Battallia*, and took them at their
great difadvantage; which caufed fuch a
Panick fear amongft them, that moft of the
Horfe of the right Wing of His Majefty's
Forces, betook themfelves to their heels; infomuch, that although the left Wing (commanded by the Lord *Goring*, and my Brother
Sir *Charles Lucas*) did their beft endeavour,
and beat back the Enemy three times, and
My Lord's own Regiment of Foot charged
them fo couragioufly, that they never broke,
but died moft of them in their Ranks and
Files; yet the Power of the Enemy being

too ftrong, put them at **laft to** a total rout and confufion. Which unlucky difafter put an end to all future hopes of His Majefties **Party;** fo that **my** Lord feeing he had **nothing** left in **his** Power to do His Majefty any further fervice in that kind (for had he ftayed, **he would** have been forced to furrender all thofe **Towns** and Garifons in thofe **parts,** that were yet in His Majefties Devotion, as afterwards **it alfo** happen'd) **refolved to quit the Kingdom, as** formerly is mentioned.

And **thefe** are chiefly **the** obftru&tions to the good fuccefs of my **Lord's** Defigns in the late Civil Wars; which being rightly confidered, will fave him blamelefs from what otherwife would be laid to his charge ; for, **as** according to the old faying, *'Tis eafie for men to fwim; when they* **are** *held up* **by** *the chin :* **So** on **the other** fide, **it is** very dangerous **and** difficult **for** them to endeavour it, **when they are** pulled down by the Heels, **and beaten upon their** Heads.

3. *Of His Loyalty and Sufferings.*

I DARE boldly and juftly fay, That there never **was,** nor is a **more** Loyal and Faithful

Subject then **My** Lord: Not to mention the Truft he difcharged in all thofe imployments, which either King *James*, or King *Charles* the Firft, or His now Gracious Mafter King *Charles* the Second, were pleafed to beftow upon him, which he performed with fuch **care** and fidelity, that he never difobeyed their Commands in the leaft; I will onely note,

1. That he was the Firft that appear'd in Armes for His Majefty, and engaged Himfelf and all his **Friends he** could for His Majefties Service; and though he had but two Sons which were young, and one onely Brother, yet they all were with him in the Wars: **His** two Sons had Commands, but His Brother, though he had no Command, by reafon of the weaknefs of his body, yet he was never from My Lord when he was in action, even to the laft; **for he** was the laft with my Lord in the Field in that fatal Battel upon *Heffom-moor*, near *York*; and though my Brother, Sir *Charles Lucas*, defired my Lord to fend his fons away, when the faid Battel was fought, **yet** he **would** not, faying, **His** fons fhould fhew **their** Loyalty and Duty to His Majefty, in venturing their lives, as well as Himfelf.

2. My **Lord** was the **chief** and **onely Perſon,** that kept **up the** Power **of** His **late** Majeſty ; for when his Army was **loſt,** all the Kings **Party** was ruined in all three of his Majeſties Kingdoms ; becauſe in his Army lay the chief ſtrength of all the Royal Forces ; it being the greateſt and beſt formed Army which His Majeſty had, and the onely ſupport both of his Majeſties Perſon and Power, and of the hopes of all **his** Loyal Subjects in **all his Do-** minions.

3. My **Lord** was 16 Years in Baniſhment, and hath **loſt** and ſuffered moſt **of** any ſubject, that ſuffer'd either by War, or otherways, ex- cept thoſe that loſt their lives, and even that **he** valued not, but expoſed it to ſo eminent dangers that nothing but Heavens Decree had ordained to ſave it.

4. **He** never minded his own **intereſt more then his** Loyaltie and Duty, and upon **that** account never deſired nor received any thing from the Crown to enrich himſelf, but ſpent great ſums in His Majeſties Service ; ſo that after his long baniſhment and return into *England,* I obſerved his ruined Eſtate was like **an** Earthquake, and his Debts like Thunder-

bolts, by which he was in danger of being utterly undone, had not Patience and Prudence, together with Heavens Bleſſings, ſaved him from that threatening Ruine.

5. He never repined at his Loſſes and Sufferings, becauſe he loſt and ſuffered for his **King** and Countrey; nay, ſo far was he from that, that I have heard him ſay, If the ſame Warrs ſhould happen again, and he was ſure to loſe both his life, and all he had left him, yet **he** would moſt **willingly** ſacrifice it for His Majeſties Service.

6. He never connived **or conſpired** with the Enemy, neither directly nor indirectly; for though ſome Perſon of Quality being ſent in the late Wars to him into the North, from His late Majeſty, **who** was then at *Oxford*, with ſome Meſſage, did withal in private acquaint him, that ſome of the Nobility that were with the King, deſired him to ſide with them againſt His Majeſty, alledging that if His Majeſty ſhould become an abſolute Conqueror, both himſelf and the reſt of the Nobility would loſe all their Rights and Priviledges; yet he was ſo far from conſenting to it, that he returned him this anſwer, namely,

That he entred into actions of War, for no other end, but for the service of **His King** and **Mafter**, and to keep up His Majefties Rights and Prerogatives, for which he was refolved to venture both his **Life**, Pofterity and **Eftate**; for certainly, faid **he**, the No-bility cannot fall if **the** King be Victorious, nor can they keep up their **Dignities**, if the King be overcome.

This Meffage **was delivered by word or** mouth, but none **of their names mentioned**; fo that it is not certainly known **whether it** was a **real truth** or not; more **probable** it was, that they intended **to** found my **Lord, or to** make, if poffible, more divifion; **for** certainly not all that pretended to be **for the** King, **were** His **Friends**; and I my felf remember very well, when **I was** with Her Majefty, **the** now Queen-Mother, in *Oxford,* (although I was **too** young to perceive their intrigues, yet I was **old** enough **to** obferve) that there were great Factions **both** amongft **the Cour-**tiers and Soldiers. **But** my Lords Loyalty was fuch, **that** he kept always faithful and true to His Majefty, **and** could by no means be brought to fide with the Rebellious Party, or to juggle and mind his own Intereſt **more** then his Majeſties Service ; and this was the cauſe that he had as great private Enemies at Court, as he had publick Enemies **in** the Field, who ſought as much his ruine and de-ſtruction privately, and would caſt aſperſions upon his Loyalty and Duty, as theſe did publickly oppoſe him.

In ſhort, that it may appear the better what loyal **and** faithful ſervices my Lord has done both for His late Majeſty King *Charles* the Firſt, and His now Gracious Maſter King *Charles* the Second, I have thought fit to ſubjoin both Their Majeſties Commendations which they were pleaſed **to give** him, when for his Great **and** Loyal Services they con-fer'd upon him the Titles and Dignities of *Marqueſs*, and *Duke of Newcaſtle.*

A Copy **of** the Preamble of My Lord's Patent for *Marqueſs*, Engliſhed.

Rex *&c.* Salutem.

WHEREAS *it appears* **to Us**, *That* Wil-liam *Earl of* Newcaſtle *upon* Tyne, *befides his moſt Eminent Birth and ſplendid Alli-ances, hath equalled all thoſe Titles with which* he is adorned by *Defert*, and hath **alfo** *wonne* them by *Virtue*, *Induftry*, *Prudence*, and **a fted-faft** *Faith* : **Whileft with dangers and expences** *gathering together Soldiers*, **Armes, and** *all other War-like Habiliments ;* **and applying them as well in Our** *Affairs*, *as moft plentifully fending* **them to Us,** *(having fore-thought of Our Dignity and fecurity) he was* **ready with Us in, all** *Actions in* York-fhire, *and* **governed the Town of New-**caftle, *and Caftle* **in** *the mouth* **of** Tyne, *at the time of* **that** *fatal Revolt* **of the People who** *were got together;* **and with a** *Bond* **of his** *Friends did opportunely feize* **that** *Port, and fettled it* **a Garifon;** *bringing Armes to Us (then Our onely relief :)* *In which Service fo ftrongly going on, (which was of grand moment* **to** *our affairs)* **We** *do gratefully remember him ftill* **to have** *ftood* **to :** *Afterwards, having Muftered* **together a good** *Army,* **(Our felf being** *gone* **elfe-where)** *the* **Rebels** *now enjoying almoft* **all** York-fhire, *and the chiefeft* **Fortrefs** *of all* **the** *Country* **now** *appearing to have fcarce refuge or fafety for him againft* **the fwelling** *Rebels,* *(the whole Country then defiring and praying for his coming,* **that** *he might timely relieve them in their defperate condition)* *And leading his faid*

Army in the midſt of Winter, gave the Rebels Battel in his paſſage, vanquiſh'd **them,** *and put them to flight, and took from them ſeveral Gariſons, and places of Refuge, and reſtored* **Health** *to the Subjeɛts, and by his many Viɛtories, Peace and Security to the Countryes : Witneſs thoſe places, made Noble by the death and flight of the Rebels :* in *Lincoln-ſhire,* Gainsborough and Lincoln ; *in Derby-ſhire,* Cheſterfield ; *but in York-ſhire,* Peirce-bridge, Seacroft, Tankerly, Tadcaſter, Sheffield, Rotheram, **Yarum,** Beverly, Cawood, Selby, Halifax, Leeds, *and above all,* Bradford ; *where when the* York-ſhire-*and* Lancaſhire-*Rebels were united, and Battel joined with them ; when Our* **Army as** *well by the great numbers of the Rebels, as much more the badneſs of Our ground, was ſo preſt upon, that the Soldiers now ſeemed to think of flying ; He, their General, with a full Carier, commanding two Troops to follow him, broke into the very rage of the Battel, and with ſo much violence fell upon the right Wing of thoſe Rebels, That thoſe who were but now certain of Viɛtory, turn'd their backs, and fled from the Conqueror, who by* **his** *Wiſdom, Virtue and his own Hand, brought death and flight to the Rebels, Viɛtory* *and Glory* **to** *Himself,* **Plunder to** *the Soldiery, and* 22 *great Guns, and* **many** *Enſigns* **to Us.** *Nor was there before this, wanting* **to ſo much** *Virtue,* **equal** *Felicity, for* **Our moſt** *beloved Conſort, after a diſmal Tempeſt coming from* **Holland,** *being drove aſhore at* Burlington, *and undergoing a more grievous danger, by the excurſions of the Rebels, then the toſſing and tumbling of the Sea;* He *having heard of it, ſpeedily goes to* Her **with** *his Army, and dutifully receiveth* Her, *in ſafety brings* **her,** *and with* **all ſecurity** *conducts* **her to Us at** Oxford. *Whereas therefore the aforeſaid Earl hath raiſed* **ſo** *many Monuments of His Virtue and Fidelity towards* **Us, Our** *Queen, Children, and Our Kingdom; when alſo he doth at this time eſtabliſh with ſafety, and with His* **Power** *defend the Northern* **parts** *of Our Kingdom againſt the Rebels;* **when laſtly,** *nothing* **more** *concerns Mankind* **and** *Princes, and nothing* **can** *be more juſt, then* **that** *he* **may** *receive for his Deeds, a Reward ſuitable* **to** *his name, which requires that he who defends the Borders, ſhould be created by Us,* Governour or Marqueſs of the Borderers. *Know therefore,* &c.

A Copy of the Preamble of My Lord's
Patent for *DUKE*, Englished.

Rex *&c.* Salutem.

WHEREAS *Our most beloved and faithful Cousin and Counsellor*, William *Earl and Marquess of* Newcastle upon Tyne, &c. *worthy by his famous Name, Blood and Office, of large Honours, has been eminent in so many, and so great Services performed to Us and Our Father (of ever blessed memory) that his Merits are still producing new effects, We have decreed likewise to add more Honour to his former. And though these his such eminent Actions, which he hath faithfully and valiantly performed to Us, Our Father, and Our Kingdom, speak loud enough in themselves ; yet since the valiant Services of a good Subject are always pleasant to remember, We have thought fit to have them in part related for a good Example and Encouragement to Virtue.*

The great proofs of his Wisdom and Piety are sufficiently known to Us from Our younger years, and We shall always retain a sense of those good Principles he instilled into Us ; the Care of Our Youth which he happily undertook for Our good, he as faithfully **and well discharged.** *Our years growing up* **amidst** *bad* **Times,** *and* **the** *harsh* **Necessities of Warr,** *a new* **Charge** *and* **Care** *of* **Loyaltie, the** *Kingdom and Religion call'd him* **off** *to make use of his further* **Diligence and Valour.** *Rebellion spread abroad, he levied* **Loyal** *Forces in great numbers, opposed* **the Enemy,** *won so many and so great Victories in the Field, took in so many* **Towns, Castles and Garisons, as well in Our Northern parts, as** *elsewhere;* **and behaved** *himself with so great* **Courage and Valour in the** *defending also what he had* **got,** *especially* **at** *the Siege* **of** York, *which he maintain'd against three Potent Armies of* Scots *and* English, *closely beleaguering, and with emulation assaulting it for three Months (till Relief was brought)* **to the wonder and envy** *of the Enemy; that,* **if** *Loyal and Humane Force* **could have** *prevailed, he had soon* **restored Fidelity, Peace** *and* **his KING to the** *Nation,* **which was** *then* **hurrying** *to* **Ruine by an** *unhappy* **Fate;** **So** *that Rebellion getting* **the** *upper hand, and no place being* **left** *for him* **to** *act further valiantly in, for his* **King** *and* **Countrey,** *he still retain'd the same Loyalty and Valour in suffering, being* **an** *inseparable Follower* **of Our** *Exile; during*

which *sad* **Cataſtrophe,** *his whole Eſtate was
ſequeſtred and* **ſold from** *him, and his Perſon
alwayes one* **of** *the firſt of thoſe few who were
excepted both for Life and Eſtate (which* **was**
offer'd **to all** *others.)   Beſides, his Virtues are
accompanied with* **a** *Noble Blood, being of a
Family* **by each** *Stock equally adorn'd and en-
dow'd with great Honours and Riches.   For
which Reaſons We have reſolv'd to grace the ſaid
Marqueſs with* **a new Mark** *of our Favour, he
being every way deſerving of it, as one who lov'd
vertue equal to his Noble Birth, and poſſeſs'd
Patrimonies ſuitable to both,* **as** *long as loyalty
had any place to ſhew it ſelf in our Realm ; which
poſſeſſions he ſo well employ'd, and* **at laſt for** *Us
and* **Our** *Fathers ſervice loſt, till he was with*
Us *reſtor'd.   Know therefore, &c.*

4. *Of his Prudence and Wiſdom.*

MY Lord's Prudence and Wiſdom hath
been ſufficiently apparent both in his
Publick and Private Actions **and** Imployments ; for he hath ſuch **a** Natural Inſpec-
tion, and Judicious Obſervation of things,
that he ſees beforehand what will come to

paſs, and orders his affairs accordingly. To
which purpoſe I cannot but mention, that
Laud, the then Archbiſhop of *Canterbury*, between whom and my Lord, interceded a great
and intire Friendſhip, which he confirmed by
a Legacy of a Diamond, to the value of 200 l.
left to my Lord when he died, which was
much for him to bequeath ; for though he
was a great Stateſman, and in favour with his
late Majeſty, yet he was not covetous to hoard
up wealth, but beſtowed it rather upon the
Publick, repairing the Cathedral of St. *Pauls*
in *London*, which, had God granted him life,
he would certainly have beautified, and rendred as famous and glorious as any in Chriſ-
tendom : This ſaid Arch-Biſhop was pleaſed
to tell His late Majeſty, that my Lord was
one of the Wiſeſt and Prudenteſt Perſons that
ever he was acquainted with.

For further proof, I cannot paſs by that
my Lord told His late Majeſty King *Charles*
the Firſt, and Her Majeſty the now Queen-
Mother, ſome time before the Wars, That
he obſerved by the humours of the People,
the approaching of a Civil War, and that His
Majeſties Perſon would be in danger of being

depofed, if timely care was not taken to prevent it.

Alfo when my Lord was at *Antwerp*, the
Marquefs of *Montrofs*, before he went into
Scotland, gave my Lord a Vifit, and acquainted
him with his intended Journey, afking my
Lord whether he was not alfo going for *England?* My Lord anfwer'd, He was ready to
do His Majefty what fervice he could, and
would fhun no opportunity, where he perceived he could effect fomething to His Majefties advantage ; Nay, faid he, if His Majefty
fhould be pleafed to Command my fingle Perfon to go againft the whole Army of the
Enemy, although I was fure to lofe my life,
yet out of a Loyal Duty to His Majefty, and
in Obedience to his Commands, I fhould
never refufe it. But to venture (faid he) the
life of my Friends, and to betray them in a
defperate action, without any probability of
doing the leaft good to His Majefty, would be
a very unjuft and unconfcionable act ; for my
Friends might perhaps venture with me upon
an implicite Faith, that I was fo honeft as not
to engage them without a firm and folid foundation ; but I wanting that, as having no Ships,

Armes, Ammunition, Provifion, **Forts, and**
places of **Rendezvous, and what is the** chief
thing, Money; **To what** purpofe would it be
to draw them into fo hazardous an Action,
but to **feek** their ruine **and** deftruction, without the leaft benefit to His Majefty? **Then**
the Marquefs of *Montrofs* afked my Lord's
Advice, and what **he fhould do in fuch a cafe?**
My Lord anfwer'd, **That he** knowing **beft his**
own Countrey, **Power** and Strength, and what
probability **he** had **of Forces, and other Ne-**
ceffaries **for** Warr, **when he came** into *Scot-*
land, could give himfelf the beft advice; but
withall told him, That if he had no **Provifion**
nor Ammunition, Armes and places of Rendezvous for his men to meet and join, he
would likely be forced to hide his head, **and**
fuffer for **his** rafh undertaking: Which unlucky Fate did alfo accordingly befall **that**
worthy Perfon.

Thefe paffages I mention **to no** other end,
but to declare my Lord's Judgment and Prudence in worldly Affairs; whereof there are
fo many, that **if I fhould fet them all** down, it
would fwell this Hiftory to a big Volume.
They may in fome fort be gather'd from his

actions mentioned heretofore, especially the ordering of his affairs in the time **of Warr**, **with** such Conduct, Prudence and Wisdom, that notwithstanding at the beginning of his Undertaking that great Trust and honourable Employment which **His** late Majesty was pleased to confer upon him, he saw so little appearance of performing his Designs with good success, His Majesty's Revenues being then much weakned, and the Magazines and publick Purse, in the Enemies Power, besides several other obstructions and hindrances; yet as he undertook it chearfully, and out of pure Loyalty and Obedience to His Majesty; so he ordered it so wisely, that so long as he acted by his own Counsels, and was personally present at the execution of his Designs, he **was** always prosperous in his Success. And although he had so great an Army, as afore-**mentioned, yet by** his wife and prudent Conduct, there appear'd no visible sign of devastation in any of the Countreys where he marched; for first, he setled a constant Rule for the Regular levy of money for the convenient Maintenance of the Soldiery. Next, **he** constituted such Officers of his Army, that most of them were known to be Gentlemen of large and fair Eſtates, which drew a good part of their private Revenues, to ſerve and ſupport them in their publick Employments; wherein my Lord did lead them the way by his own good Example.

To which may be added his wiſdom in ordering the Government of the Church, for the advancement of the Orthodox Religion, and ſuppreſſion of Factions; as alſo in Coyning, Printing, Knighting, and the like, which he uſed with great diſcretion and prudence, onely for the Intereſt of His Majeſty, and the benefit of the Kingdom, as formerly has been mentioned.

The Prudent mannage of his private and domeſtick affairs, appears ſufficiently: 1. In his Marriage. 2. In the ordering and increaſing his Eſtate before the Wars, which notwithſtanding his Noble Houſekeeping and Hoſpitality, and his Generous Bounty and Charity, he increaſed to the value of 100000 l. 3. In the ordering his Affairs in the time of Baniſhment, where although he received not the leaſt of his own eſtate, during all the time of his exile, until his return; yet maintained himſelf handſomely and nobly, according to his Quality, as much **as** his Condition **at that** time would permit. 4. In reducing **his** torn **and** ruined Eſtate after his return, which beyond all probability, himſelf hath ſetled and order'd ſo, that his Poſterity will have reaſon gratefully **to** remember it.

In ſhort; Although **my** Lord naturally **loves** not buſineſs, eſpecially thoſe of State, (though he underſtands them as well **as** any body) **yet what** buſineſs **or** affairs he cannot avoid, none will do them better then himſelf. **His** private affairs he orders without any noiſe or trouble, not over-haſtily, **but** wiſely : Neither is he paſſionate in acting **of buſineſs,** but **hears** patiently, and orders ſoberly, and **pierces** into the heart or bottom of a buſineſs at **the** firſt encounter ; **but** before all things, he conſiders well before he undertakes a buſineſs, whether **he** be able to go through it or no, for he never ventures upon either publick or private buſineſs, beyond his ſtrength.

And **here I** cannot forbear to mention, that **my Noble** Lord, when he was **in** baniſhment, **preſumed** out of his Duty and Love to **his** Gracious Maſter our now Soveraign **King**

Charles the **Second, to write** and fend **him** a little **Book, or** rather **a** Letter, wherein **he** delivered his Opinion concerning the Government of his Dominions, whenfoever God fhould be pleafed to reftore him **to his** Throne, together with fome other **Notes and** Obfervations of Foreign States and Kingdoms; but it being **a** private offer **to His** facred Majefty, I **dare not** prefume **to** publifh it.

5. *Of his Bleſſings.*

ALTHOUGH my Lord hath **been** one of the moft Unfortunate Perfons of his Rank and Quality, which this later age did produce ; yet Heaven hath been fo propitious to him, that it beftowed fome bleffings upon him even **in** the midft of his Misfortunes, **and** fupported him againft Fortunes Malice, **which** otherwife, **as it** feems, had defigned his **total** ruine and deftruction : Of thefe Bleffings I **may** name **in** the firft **place,**

1. The Royal Favours of His Gracious Soveraign's, and the good efteem they had of his Fidelity and Loyalty *;* which as **it** was the chief of his endeavours, fo he efteemed it

above all the reſt. To repeat them particularly would be too tedious, and **they** are ſufficiently apparent out of the precedent Hiſtory; onely this I may add, that King *Charles* the Firſt, out of a ſingular Favour to **my** Lord, was pleaſed upon his moſt humble requeſt, to create ſeveral Noble-men; the Names of them, left I commit an offence, I ſhall not mention, by reaſon moſt men uſually pretend ſuch claimes upon **the** Ground of their own **Merit**.

2. That God was pleaſed to bleſs him with **W**ealth and Power, to enable him the better **for** the ſervice of his King and Country.

3. That he made him happy in his Marriage; (for his firſt Wife was a very kind, loving and Virtuous Lady) and bleſs'd him with Dutiful and Obedient Children, free from Vices, Noble and Generous both in ther Natures and Actions; who did all that lay in their power to ſupport and relieve **my** Lord their Father in his Baniſhment, as before is mentioned.

4. The Kindneſs and Civility which my Lord received from Strangers, and the Inhabitants **of thoſe** places, where he lived

during the time of his Banifhment; for had it not been for them, he would have perifhed in his extream wants; but it pleafed God fo to provide for him, that although he wanted an Eftate, yet he wanted not **Credit**; and although he was banifhed and forfaken by his own Friends and Countrymen, yet he was **civilly** received and relieved by ftrangers, until God blefs'd him.

Laftly, With a happy return to his **Native** Country, his dear Children, **and his own** Eftate; **which** although he found much ruined and broke, yet by his Prudence and Wifdom, hath order'd **as** well as he could; and I hope, and pray God to add this blefling to all the reft, That he may live long to encreafe it for the benefit of his Pofterity.

6. *Of his Honours and Dignities.*

THE Honours, Titles and Dignities which were conferr'd upon my Lord, by King *James*, King *Charles* the Firft, and King *Charles* the Second, **partly** as an encouragement for future Service, and a reward for paft, are following.

1. He was made Knight of the *Bath*, when

he was but 15 or 16 years of Age, at the Creation of *Henry*, Prince of *Wales*, King *James's* Eldeſt Son.[1]

2. King *James* Created him Viſcount *Mansfield*, and Baron of *Bolſover*.

3. King *Charles* the Firſt conſtituted him Lord Lieutenant of *Nottinghamſhire*, and

4. **Lord Warden of** the Forreſt of *Sher-wood*; **as** alſo,

5. Lord Lieutenant **of** *Derby-ſhire*.

6. **He** choſe **him Governour to** His Son *Charles*, our now gracious King ; and

7. Made him one of **his Honourable Privy** Council.

8. He conſtituted **him** Governour **of** the Town and County of *Newcaſtle*, and **General** of **all** His Majeſties Forces raiſed, and **to be** raiſed in the **Northern** parts **of** *England* ; as alſo of the ſeveral Counties **of** *Nottingham*, *Lincoln*, *Rutland*, *Derby*, *Stafford*, *Leiceſter*, *Warwick*, *Northampton*, *Huntington*, *Cam-bridg*, *Norfolk*, *Suſſex*, *Eſſex* and *Hereford*, together with all the Appurtenances belong-

---

[1] This is probably the **only** inſtance **of** a knighthood conferred upon ſo young a boy.

ing to fo great a Power, as is formerly declared.

9. He conferr'd upon him the Honour and
Title of Earl of *Newcaftle,* and Baron of
Bothal and *Hepple.*

10. He created him Marquefs of *Newcaftle.*

11. His Majefty King *CHARLES* the
Second, was pleafed, when my Lord was in
banifhment, to make him Knight of the moft
Noble Order of the Garter ; And

12. After his Return into *England,* Chief
Juftice in *Eyre Trent-North.*

13. He created him Duke of *Newcaftle,*
and Earl of *Ogle.*

7. *Of the Entertainments He made for King*
CHARLES *the Firft.*

THOUGH my Lord hath alwayes been
free and noble in his Entertainments
and Feaftings, yet he was pleafed to fhew his
great Affection and Duty to his Gracious
King, *Charles* the Firft, and Her Majefty the
Queen, in fome particular Entertainments
which he made of purpofe for them before
the late Warrs.

When his Majefty was going into *Scotland* to be Crowned, he took His way through *Nottinghamfhire*; and lying at *Workfop-*Mannor, hardly two miles diftant from *Wel-beck*, where my Lord then was, my Lord invited His Majefty thither to a Dinner, which he was **gracioufly** pleafed to accept of: This Entertainment **coft** my Lord between Four and Five thoufand pounds; which His Majefty liked fo well, that **a year** after His Return out of *Scotland*, **He** was pleafed **to** fend my Lord word, That **Her Majefty the Queen** was refolved to make **a Progrefs** into the Northern **parts,** defiring **him to prepare** the like Entertainment for **Her, as he had formerly done** for Him: Which **My Lord did, and endeavour'd** for **it with all poffible** Care and Induftry, fparing nothing that might add fplendor to that Feaft, which both Their Majefties were pleafed to honour with their Prefence: *Ben Johnfon* he employed in fitting fuch Scenes and Speeches as he could beft devife; and fent for all the Gentry of the Country to come and wait on their Majefties; **and in** fhort, did all that ever he could imagine, **to** render it Great, and worthy **Their Royal** Acceptance.

This Entertainment he made at *Bolfover-Caftle* in *Derbyfhire*, fome five miles diftant from *Welbeck*, and refigned *Welbeck* for Their Majefties Lodging; it coft him in all between Fourteen and Fifteen thoufand pounds.

Befides thefe two, there was another fmall Entertainment which my Lord prepared for His late Majefty, in his own Park at *Welbeck*, when His Majefty came down, with his two Nephews, the now Prince Elector Palatine, and His Brother Prince *Rupert*, into the Forreft of *Sherwood*; which coft him Fifteen hundred pounds.

And this I mention not out of a vain-glory, but to declare the great love and Duty, my Lord had for His Gracious King and Queen, and to correct the miftakes committed by fome Hiftorians, who not being rightly informed of thofe Entertainments, make the World believe Falfhood for Truth. But as I faid, they were made before the Warrs, when my Lord had the poffeffion of a great Eftate; and wanted nothing to exprefs his Love and Duty to his Soveraign in that manner; whereas now he fhould be much to feek to do the like, his Eftate being fo much ruined

by the late **Civil** Wars, **that** neither himfelf
nor his Pofterity will **be** able fo foon to
recover **it**.

8. *His Education.*

HIS Education was according to his
Birth; for **as** he was born a Gentleman, fo he was bred like **a** Gentleman. To
School-Learning he **never** fhew'd **a great**
inclination; **for** though he was fent **to** the
Univerfity, and was a Student of St. *John's*
Colledg in *Cambridg,* and **had** his Tutors to
inftruct him; yet they could not perfwade
him to read or ftudy much, he taking **more**
delight **in** fports, then in learning; fo that
his Father being **a** wife man, and feeing that
his **Son** had a good natural Wit, and was of a
very good Difpofition, fuffer'd him to follow
his **own** Genius; whereas his other Son
Charles, in whom he found a greater love and
inclination to Learning, he encouraged **as**
much that way, as poffibly he **could**.

One time it hapned that a young Gentleman,
one of my Lord's Relations, **had** bought fome
Land, at the fame **time** when my Lord had

bought a Singing-Boy for 50 l. a Horſe for 50 l. and a Dog for 2 l.[1] which humour his **Father** Sir *Charles* liked ſo well, that **he** was pleaſed to ſay, That if he ſhould find his **Son to be** ſo covetous, that he would **buy Land** before **he** was 20 years of Age, **he** would disinherit him. But above **all the reſt,** my Lord **had a** great inclination to **the Art of** Horſemanſhip and Weapons, in **which** later, **his Father Sir** *Charles,* **being a** moſt **ingenuous and un-** parallell'd Maſter **of that Age, was his** onely Tutor, **and** kept him alſo ſeveral **Maſters in** the Art of Horſemanſhip, and ſent **him to the** *Mewſe* to *Mons. Antoine,* who was then **ac-** counted the beſt Maſter in **that Art.** But **my** Lord's delight in thoſe Heroick Exerciſes was ſuch, that he ſoon became Maſter thereof Himſelf, which encreaſed much his Father's hopes of his future perfections, who being himſelf **a** perſon **of a** Noble and Heroick

---

[1] What a curious collocation;—a Horſe for £50, a Dog for £2, and a "Singing-Boy" for £50! As the days of feudaliſm, ſo far **as** poſſeſſing one's fellow-creature was concerned, **had** paſſed, we muſt conclude that "My Lord" had engaged the boy for his amuſement at the coſt of £50, and not purchaſed him as a chattel.

nature, was extreamly well pleafed to obferve his Son take delight in fuch Arts and Exercifes as were proper and fit for a perfon of Quality.

9. *His Natural Wit and Underftanding.*

ALTHOUGH my Lord has not fo much of Scholarfhip and Learning as his Brother Sir *Charles Cavendifh* had, yet he hath an excellent Natural Wit and Judgment, and dives into the bottom of every thing; as it is evidently apparent in the forementioned Art of Horfemanfhip and Weapons, which by his own ingenuity he has reformed and brought to fuch perfection, as never any one has done heretofore: And though he is no Mathematician by Art, yet he hath a very good Mathematical brain, to demonftrate Truth by natural reafon, and is both a good Natural and Moral Philofopher, not by reading Philofophical Books, but by his own Natural Underftanding and Obfervation, by which he hath found out many Truths.

To pafs by feveral other inftances, I'le but mention, that when my Lord was at *Paris*, in

his Exile, it happen'd one time, that he difcourfing with fome of his Friends, amongft
whom was alfo that Learned Philofopher
Hobbes, they began amongft the reft, to argue
upon this fubject, namely, *Whether it were
poffible to make Man by Art fly as Birds do;* and
when fome of the Company had delivered
their Opinion, *viz.* That they thought it
probable to be done by the help of Artificial
Wings : My Lord declared, that he deemed
it altogether impoffible, and demonftrated it
by this following Reafon : Man's Armes, faid
he, are not fet on his fhoulders in the fame
manner as Bird's wings are; for that part of
the Arm which joins to the Shoulder, is in
Man placed inward, as towards the breaft,
but in Birds outward, as toward the back;
which difference and contrary pofition or
fhape, hinders that man cannot have the fame
flying-action with his Armes, as Birds have
with their Wings; Which Argument Mr.
Hobbes liked fo well, that he was pleafed to
make ufe of it in one of his Books called
Leviathan, if I remember well.

Some other time they falling into a Difcourfe concerning Witches, Mr. *Hobbes* faid,

That though **he could not** rationally believe there were Witches, yet he could **not** be fully satisfied to believe there were none, by **reafon** they would themfelves confefs **it,** if ftrictly examined.

To which my Lord anfwer'd, That though for his part he cared not whether there were Witches or no; yet his Opinion was, That the Confeffion of Witches, and their fuffering **for it,** proceeded from an Erroneous Belief, *viz.* That they had **made a** Contract with the Devil to ferve him for fuch Rewards as were **in** his Power to give them; and that **it** was their Religion to worfhip and adore him; in which Religion they had fuch a firm and conftant belief, that if any thing came to pafs according to their defire, they believed **the** Devil had heard their prayers, and granted their requefts, for which they gave him thanks; **but if** things fell out contrary to their prayers and defires, then they were troubled at it, fearing they had offended him, or not ferved him as they ought, and afked him forgivenefs **for** their offences. Alfo (faid **my Lord**) they **imagine that their** Dreams are real exterior actions; for example, if **they dream they flye** in the Air, **or** out of the Chimney top, **or that** they are **turned into** several shapes, **they be-** lieve **no** otherwife, **but that** it is really fo: **And** this wicked Opinion makes **them induf-** trious to perform fuch Ceremonies **to** the Devil, **that** they adore and worfhip him as their God, and chufe to live and dye for him.

Thus **my** Lord declared himfelf concerning Witches, which Mr. *Hobbes* **was alfo** pleafed to infert **in his fore-mentioned Book:** But yet my **Lord** doth **not** count this Opinion **of his** fo univerfal, as **if** there were **none** but imaginary Witches; **for** he doth **not** fpeak but of fuch a fort of Witches as make it their Religion to worfhip the Devil in the manner aforefaid. Nor doth he think **it** a Crime to entertain what Opinion feems moft probable **to** him, in things indifferent; for in **fuch cafes men** may difcourfe **and** argue as they pleafe, **to** exercife their Wit, and may change **and** alter their Opinions upon **more** probable Grounds **and** Reafons; whereas **in** Funda- mental **matters** both **of** Church **and** State, he is fo ftrict **an** Adherent to them, that he will never maintain or defend fuch Opinions which are in the leaft prejudicial to either.[1]

One proof more I'le add **to confirm his** Natural Underftanding and Judgment, which was upon fome Difcourfe I held with him one time, concerning that famous Chymift *Van Helmont,* who in his Writings is very invective againft the School-men, and amongft the **reft,** accufes them for taking the Radical moifture for the fat of Animal Bodies. Whereupon my Lord anfwer'd, That furely the School-men were too wife to commit fuch an Error; for, faid he, the Radical moifture is not the fat or tallow of **an** Animal, but an Oily and Balfamous Subftance; **for the fat** and tallow, as alfo the watery parts, are cold; whereas the Oily and Balfamous parts, have **at all** times **a** lively heat; which makes that thofe Creatures which have much of that Oyle or Balfom, **are** long-liv'd, and appear young; and not onely Animals, but alfo Vegetables, which have much of that Oyle or Balfom, as Ivy, Bayes, Laurel, Holly, and the like, live

---

[1] **It is** not neceffary **here to comment upon** witchcraft; but it **is** pretty clear that the Duke was in advance **of popular** opinions and notions on that fubject.

long, and appear **freſh** and green, not onely
in Winter, **but** when **they** are old.   Then I
aſk'd my **Lord's** Opinion concerning the
Radical **heat**: To which he anſwer'd, That
the Radical heat lived in the Radical moiſture;
and when the one decayed, the other decayed
alſo; and then was produced either an unnatural heat, which cauſed an unnatural **dry-**
neſs; or an unnatural moiſture, which cauſed
Dropſies, and **theſe, an** unnatural coldneſs.

Laſtly; **His** Natural Wit appears by his
delight in **Poetry;** for **I may** juſtly call him
the beſt *Lyrick* and *Dramatick* **Poet of** this
Age: **His** Comedies do ſufficiently ſhew his
great Obſervation and Judgment, for they are
compoſed of theſe three Ingredients, *viz. Wit,
Humour* and *Satyre;* and his chief Deſign in
them, is **to divulge and laugh at the** follies of
Mankind; to perſecute Vice, and **to** encou-
rage Virtue.

10. *Of his Natural Humour and Diſpoſition.*

MY Lord may juſtly **be** compared to *Titus*
the *Deliciæ* of Mankind, by reaſon of
his ſweet, gentle and **obliging** Nature; for

though his Wifdom and Experience found it impoffible to pleafe all men, becaufe of their different humours and difpofitions; yet his Nature is fuch, that he will be forry when he feeth that men are difpleafed with him out of their own ill Natures, without any caufe; for he loves all that are his Friends, and hates none that are his Enemies: He is a Loyal Subject, a kind Hufband, a Loving Father, a Generous Mafter, and a Conftant Friend.

His natural Love to his Parents has been fo great, that I have heard him fay, he would moft willingly, and without the left repining, have begg'd for his daily relief, fo God would but have let his Parents live.

He is true and juft both in his words and actions, and has no mean or petty Defigns, but they are all juft and honeft.

He condemns not upon Report, but upon Proof; nor judges by Words, but Actions; he forgets not paft Service, for prefent Advantage; but gives a prefent Reward to a prefent Defert.

He hath a great Power over his Paffions, and hath had the greateft tryals thereof; for certainly He muft of neceffity have a great fhare of Patience, that can forgive fo many falfe, treacherous, malicious and ungrateful Perfons as **he** hath done; but he is fo wife, that **his** Paffion never out-runs his Patience, **nor** his Extravagancies his Prudence; and although his Private Enemies have been numerous, yet I verily believe, there is **never** a fubject more generally beloved then He is.

He hates Pride and loves Humility; is civil to Strangers, **kind to his** Acquaintance, and refpectful **to all perfons, according** to their Quality; **He** never regards **Place, except it be** for Ceremony : To the meaneft perfon he'll **put** off his Hat, and fuffer every **body** to fpeak **to** him.

He never refufes any Petition, but accepts them; and being informed **of** the bufinefs, **will give a** juft, and as much **as** lies in him, **a** favourable anfwer **to** the Petitioning Party.

He eafily Pardons, **and** bountifully Rewards; **and always** praifes particular mens Virtues, but covers **their** Faults with filence.

He is **full** of Charity and Compaffion to perfons that **are** in mifery, and full of Clemency **and** Mercy; **in** fo much, that when he was General of a great Army, **he** would never fit in

Council himſelf upon Cauſes of Life and **Death,** but **granted** Pardon to many Delinquents that were condemned by his **Council of War**; ſo that ſome **were** forced **to Petition** him **not to** do it, by reaſon it **was an ill** preſident for others. To which my Lord merrily anſwer'd, That if they **did** hang **all, they** would leave him none to fight.

His **Courage** he always ſhew'd in Action, more then in **Words, for he** would Fight, **but** not **Rant.**

He is not Vain-glorious to heighten or brag of his Heroick Actions; Witneſs that great Victory upon *Atherton-moor*, after **which he** would not ſuffer his **Trumpets to** ſound, but came quietly **and ſilently into the** City of *York,* for **which** he **would certainly** have been **blamed** by thoſe **that make a** great noiſe upon ſmall **cauſes; and love to be** applauded, **though their** actions little deſerve it.

His **noble** Bounty and Generoſity is ſo mani-feſt **to all the** World, that I ſhould light a Candle to the Sun, if **I** ſhould ſtrive **to** illuſtrate it; for **he** has **no** ſelf-deſigns or ſelf-intereſt, but will rather **wrong and** injure himſelf then others. To give you but one proof of this noble **Vertue, it** is known, that where he hath **a legal right to** Felons Goods, as he hath in a great part of his Eſtate, yet he never took **or** exacted more then **ſome** inconſiderable ſhare for acknowledgment of his **Right;** ſaying, That he was reſolved never to grow **rich** by other **mens** misfortunes.

In ſhort, **I** know **him** not addicted **to any** manner **of Vice, except that** he has **been** a **great** lover **and admirer of** the Female **Sex;** which whether it be ſo great **a crime** as **to** condemn **him** for it; I'le leave **to** the judgment **of young** Gallants and beautiful Ladies.

11. *Of His outward Shape and Behaviour.*

HIS Shape is neat, and exactly proportioned; his Stature of a middle ſize, and **his** Complexion ſanguine.[1]

---

[1] **There is an** excellent portrait of **the Duke** in "**Lodge's** Portraits." **It was** painted by Vandyke. It repreſents him as a man under forty years of age, with clear, bright, eyes, flowing **hair,** a mouſtache and a *barbe de bouc.* He wears **the** elaborate lace collar of **the** period. The expreſſion of the countenance is extremely pleaſing, amiable, and agreeable. No wonder that the Ducheſs could dote **on ſuch** a huſband !

His Behaviour is such, that it might be a Pattern for all Gentlemen; for it is Courtly, Civil, easie and free, without Formality or Constraint; and yet hath something in it of grandure, that causes an awful respect towards him.

12. *Of His Discourse.*

HIS Discourse is as free and unconcerned, as his Behaviour, Pleasant, Witty, and Instructive; He is quick in Reparties or sudden answers, and hates dubious disputes, and premeditated Speeches. He loves also to intermingle his Discourse with some short pleasant stories, and witty sayings, and always names the Author from whom he hath them; for he hates to make another man's Wit his own.

13. *Of His Habit.*

HE accouters his Person according to the Fashion, if it be one that is not troublesome and uneasie for men of Heroick Exercises and Actions. He is neat and cleanly; which makes him to be somewhat long in

dreffing, though **not fo long as many** effeminate perfons are.   **He fhifts** ordinarily **once a**
day, and every time when he ufes Exercife, or
his temper is more hot then ordinary.

14. *Of his DIET.*

IN his Diet he is fo fparing and temperate,
that he never **eats nor** drinks **beyond his**
fet proportion, fo as to fatisfie onely his natural
appetite : **He makes but one Meal a** day, **at**
which **he drinks two good Glaffes of Small-**
Beer, **one** about the **beginning, the** other at
the end thereof, and a little Glafs of Sack in
the middle **of his Dinner ; which** Glafs **of**
Sack he alfo ufes **in** the morning for his
Breakfaft, with **a** Morfel **of** Bread.   His
Supper confifts of **an Egg, and a draught of**
Small-beer.   And by this **Temperance he**
finds himfelf very healthful, and may yet live
many **years, he being** now **of** the Age **of**
Seventy three, which I **pray God** from **my**
foul, to grant him.

15. *His Recreation and Exercife.*

HIS prime Paftime **and** Recreation hath
always been the Exercife of Mannage

and Weapons; which Heroick Arts he ufed to practife every day; but I obferving that when he had over-heated himfelf, he would be apt to take cold, prevail'd fo far, that at laft he left the frequent ufe of the Mannage, ufing neverthelefs ftill the Exercife of Weapons; and though he doth not ride himfelf fo frequently as he hath done; yet he takes delight in feeing his Horfes of Mannage rid by his Efcuyers, whom he inftructs in that Art for his own pleafure. But in the Art of Weapons (in which he has a method beyond all that ever were famous in it, found out by his own Ingenuity and Practice) he never taught any body, but the now Duke of *Buckingham*, whofe Guardian He hath been, and his own two fons.

The reft of his time he fpends in Mufick, Poetry, Architecture and the like.

16. *Of His Pedigree.*

HAVING made promife in the beginning of the firft Book, that I would join a more large Defcription of the Pedigree of my Noble Lord and Hufband, to the end of the

Hiftory of his life : I fhall now difcharge my felf ; and though I could derive it from a longer time, and reckon up a great many of his Anceftors, even from the time of *William* the Conqueror, He being defcended from the moft ancient family of the *Gernouns,* as *Cambden* relates in his *Britannia,* in the De-fcription of *Derbyfhire* ; yet it being a work fitter for Heralds, I fhall proceed no further then his Grandfather, and fhew you onely thofe noble Families which my Lord is allied to by his Birth.

My Lord's Grandfather, by his Father, (as is formerly mentioned) was Sir *William Cavendifh,* Privy-Counfellor and Treafurer of the Chamber to King *Henry* the Eighth, *Edward* the Sixth, and Queen *Mary* ; who married two Wives ; by the firft he had onely two Daughters ; but by the fecond, *Elizabeth,* who was my Lords Grandmother, he had three Sons and four Daughters, whereof one Daughter died young. She was Daughter to *John Hardwick* of **Hardwick,** in the County of *Derby,* Efq. ; and had four Hufbands : The firft was — *Barlow,* Efq. ; who died before they were bedded together, they being both very **young**. The fecond was Sir *William Cavendifh*, my Lord's Grandfather, who being fomewhat in years, married her chiefly for her beauty; fhe had fo much power in his affection, that fhe perfwaded him to fell his Eftate which he had in the Southern parts of *England* (for he was very rich) and buy an **Eftate** in the Northern parts, *viz.* in *Derby-fhire*, **and** thereabout, where her own friends and kindred liv'd, which he did; and having there fetled himfelf, upon her further perfwafion, built **a** Mannor-houfe **in** the fame County, call'd *Chattefworth*, **which, as I** have heard, coft firft and laft above 80,000 l. *fterling*. But before this Houfe **was finifh'd,** he died, and left fix Children, viz. three Sons and three Daughters, **which** before they **came to** be marriageable, **fhe** married **a** third Hufband, **Sir William** St *Loo* Captain of the Guard **to** Queen *Elizabeth*, and Grand Butler **of** *England;* **who** dying without Iffue, fhe married **a fourth** Hufband, *George*, **Earl of** *Shrewfbury*, **by whom fhe** left no iffue.

The Children **which fhe had by her** fecond Hufband, Sir *William Cavendifh*, **being** grown marriageable; **the** eldeft Son *Henry*, married

Grace the youngeft **Daughter of his Father in** Law, the faid *George* **Earl** of *Shrewfbury,* which he had by his former **Wife** *Gertrude,* Daughter of *Thomas Manners,* Earl **of** ***Rut-**land,* but died without Iffue.

The fecond Son *William,* after Earl **of** *Devonfhire,* had two **Wives;** the firft was **an** Heirefs, by whom he **had** Children, **but all** died fave one **Son,** whofe name **was alfo** *Wiliam,* **Earl of** *Devonfhire:* His fecond Wife was **W**iddow to **Sir** *Edward Wortly,* **who had** feveral Children **by her** firft **Hufband, and** but one Son **by the faid** *Will. Cavendifh,* **after** Earl of *Devonfhire,* who dyed **young.**

His Son by his firft Wife, (*William* Earl of *Devonfhire*) married *Chriftian,* Daughter of *Edward* Lord *Bruce,* **a** *Scots*-man, by whom he had **two** Sons, and one Daughter; the Eldeft **Son** *William,* now Earl of *Devonfhire,* married *Elizabeth,* **the** fecond Daughter of *William* **Earl** of *Salifbury,* by whom **he has** three children, *viz.* Two Sons and one Daughter, whereof **the** Eldeft Son *William* is married to **the** fecond Daughter of *James* now Duke of *Ormond;* the fecond Son *Charles* is yet a youth : The Daughter *Anne* married the

Lord *Rich*, **the** onely Son and Child to *Charles* now Earl of *Warwick*; but he dyed **without** Iſſue.

The ſecond Son of *William* Earl of *Devon-ſhire*, and Brother to the now Earl of *Devon-ſhire*, was unfortunately ſlain in the late **Civil** Warrs, **as is** before mentioned.

The Daughter of the ſaid *William* Earl of *Devonſhire*, **Siſter to** the now Earl of *Devon-ſhire*, married *Robert* Lord *Rich*, Eldeſt Son **to** *Robert* Earl **of** *Warwick*, by whom ſhe had **but** one Son, who married, **but** dyed without Iſſue.

The third and youngeſt Son **of** Sir *William Cavendiſh, Charles Cavendiſh,* (my Lord's **Father) had two** Wives; the firſt was Daughter and Coheir **to** Sir *Thomas Kidſon*, who dyed a year **after her** Marriage, without iſſue : The ſecond was the younger Daughter of **Cuthbert** Lord *Ogle*, and after her Elder **and onely** Siſter *Jane*, Wife to *Edward* Earl of *Shrewſbury*, who dyed without Iſſue, be-came Heir to her Father's Eſtate and Title ; **by** whom he had **three Sons;** whereof the eldeſt dyed in **his** Infancy; the ſecond was *William*, **my** dear Lord and Huſband; the third, *Charles*, who dyed a Batchelour about the age of **Sixty** three.

My Lord **hath** had two Wives; **the** firſt **was** *Elizabeth*, Daughter and Heir to *William Baſſet* of *Bloore*, in the County **of** *Stafford*, Eſq.; and Widow to *Henry Howard*, younger Son to *Thomas* Earl of *Suffolk;* by whom **he had** ten Children, *viz.* **Six** Sons, and **four** Daughters;[1] whereof **five, *viz*.** four **Sons,** and one Daughter, dyed young; the **reſt,** *viz.* Two Sons and three Daughters, came **to be** married.

His Elder Son, *Charles*, Viſcount of *Manſ-field*, married the Eldeſt Daughter and Heir of Mr. *Richard Rogers*, by whom he had but **one** Daughter, who dyed ſoon after her birth; **and** he dyed alſo without any other Iſſue.

His ſecond Son *Henry*, now Earl of *Ogle*, **married** *Francis* the eldeſt Daughter of Mr. *William Pierrepont*, by whom he hath **had three** Sons, and **four** Daughters; two Sons

---

[1] In the copy of **the** " Life " before me this ſeems **to** be a misſtatement, **and** from ſome obliterations and correſtions **(made,** I think, by the Ducheſs herſelf), the number of **children** appears **to** have been ſix ſons and four daughters.

were born before their natural time; the third, *Henry* Lord *Mansfield* is alive: The four Daughters are, the Lady *Elizabeth*, Lady *Frances*, Lady *Margaret*, and Lady *Catherine*.

My Lords three Daughters were thus married; The eldeſt, Lady *Jane*, married *Charles Cheiney*, Eſq.; deſcended of a very noble and ancient family; by whom ſhe hath one Son and two Daughters. The ſecond, Lady *Elizabeth*, married *John* now Earl of *Bridgwater*, then Lord *Brackly*, and eldeſt Son to *John* then Earl of *Bridgwater;* who died in Childbed, and left five Sons, and one Daughter, whereof the eldeſt Son *John* Lord *Brackly*, married the Lady *Elizabeth*, onely Daughter and Child to *James* then Earl of *Middleſex.*

My Lords third Daughter, the Lady *Frances*, married *Oliver* Earl of *Bullingbrook*, and hath had no Child yet.

After the death of my Lords firſt Wife, who died the 17*th* of *April*, in the Year 1643, he married me, *Margaret*, Daughter to *Thomas Lucas* of St. *Johns* near *Colcheſter*, in *Eſſex*, Eſquire; but hath no Iſſue by me.

And this is the Posterity of the three Sons of Sir *William Cavendish,* my Lords Grandfather by his Fathers side; The three Daughters were disposed of as followeth :

The eldest, *Frances Cavendish,* married Sir **Henry Pierrepont** of *Holm Pierrepont,* in the County of *Nottingham,* by whom she had two Sons, whereof the first died young; The second, *Robert,* after Earl of *Kingston* upon *Hull,* married **Gertrude,** the eldest Daughter, and Co-heir to *Henry* **Talbot,** fourth Son to *George* Earl of *Shrewsbury,* by whom he had five Sons and three Daughters, whereof the eldest Son, *Henry,* now Marquess of *Dorchester,* hath had two Wives ; the first **Cecilia,** Eldest Daughter to the Lord Viscount *Bayning,* by whom he had several Children, of which there are living onely two Daughters; the eldest *Anne,* who married *John Rosse,* onely Son to *John* now Earl of *Rutland;* the second, *Grace,* who is unmarried. **His** second Wife **was** *Catharine,* second Daughter to *James* Earl of *Derby,* by whom he has no Issue living.

The second Son of the Earl of *Kingston,* *William,* married the sole Daughter and Heir of Sir *Thomas Harries,* by whom he had Issue five Sons, and five Daugters, whereof **two** Sons and two Daughters **died** unmarried: The other six are,

Robert the Eldeſt, who married *Elizabeth*, Daughter and Co-heir to Sir *John Evelyne*, by whom he has three Sons, and one Daughter. The ſecond Son *George*, and the third *Gervas*, are yet unmarried.

The eldeſt Daughter of *William Pierrepont*, *Frances*, is married to my Lords now onely Son and Heir, **Henry** Earl of *Ogle*, as before is mentioned.

The ſecond, *Grace*, is married to *Gilbert* now Earl of *Clare*, by whom he hath Iſſue, Two ſons, and three daughters.

The third, *Gertrude*, is unmarried.

The third ſon of the Earl of *Kingſton*, *Francis Pierrepont*, married *Elizabeth* the eldeſt daughter of Mr. *Bray*, by whom he had Iſſue, one ſon, and one daughter; the ſon, *Robert*, married *Anne* the daughter of *Henry Murray*. The daughter, *Frances*, married *William Pagatt*, eldeſt ſon to *William* Lord *Pagatt*. (Paget.)

The fourth ſon of the Earl of *Kingſton*, *Gervaſe*, is unmarried.

The fifth fon, *George Pierrepont,* married the daughter of Mr. *Jonas,* by whom he had two fons unmarried, *Henry* and *Samuel.*

The three daughters of the faid Earl of *Kingſton,* are, *Frances* the eldeſt, who was married to *Philip Rowleſton;* the fecond, *Mary,* dyed young; the third, *Elizabeth,* is unmarried.

The fecond daughter of Sir *William Cavendiſh, Elizabeth,* married the Earl of *Lennox,* Unkle to King *James;* by whom ſhe had onely one daughter, the Lady *Arabella,* who againſt King *Jame's* Commands (ſhe being after Him and His Children, the next Heir to the Crown) married *William,* the fecond fon to the Earl of *Hereford;* for which ſhe was put into the Tower, where not long after ſhe dyed.

The youngeſt daughter *Mary Cavendiſh,* married *Gilbert Talbot,* fecond fon to *George* Earl of *Shrewſbury;* who after the deceafe of his Father, and his elder Brother *Francis,* who dyed without Iſſue, became Earl of *Shrewſbury;* by whom ſhe had Iſſue, four fons, and three daughters; the fons all dyed in their Infancy, but the daughters were married.

The eldeſt, *Mary Talbot*, **married** *William Herbert*, Earl of *Pembroke*, **by whom** (ſome eighteen years after her Marriage) **ſhe** had **one ſon, who** dyed young.

The ſecond daughter, *Elizabeth*, married Sir *Henry Gray*, after *Earl* of *Kent*, (the fourth Earl of *England*) by whom ſhe had no Iſſue.

The third **and** youngeſt daughter *Aletheia*, married **Thomas** *Howard*, Earl of *Arundel*, the firſt **Earl, and** Earl-Marſhal of *England* ; **by** whom ſhe left two ſons, *James*, **who** died beyond the ſeas without Iſſue ; and *Henry*, **who** married *Elizabeth*, daughter **of** *Eſme Stuart*, Duke of *Lennox* ; by whom he had Iſſue, ſeveral ſons, and one daughter ; whereof the eldeſt ſon, **Thomas**, (ſince the Reſtauration **of** King *Charles* the **Second**) was reſtored to the **Dignity of** his Anceſtors, *viz*. Duke **of** *Norfolk*, **next to** the Royal Family, the firſt Duke of *England*.

And **this is** briefly the Pedigree **of my** dear **Lord** and Huſband, from his Grandfather by his Fathers ſide ; concerning his Kindred and alliances by his Mother, who was *Katherine*,

Daughter to *Cuthbert* Lord *Ogle*, they are so many, that it is impossible for me to enumerate them all, My Lord being by his Mother related to the chief of the most ancient Families of *Northumberland*, and other the Northern parts; onely this I may mention, that My Lord is a Peer of the Realm, from the first year of King *Edward* the Fourth his Reign.

The
Life of the Moſt Illuſtrious
Prince, William Duke of
Newcaſtle.

THE FOURTH BOOK:

CONTAINING SEVERAL ESSAYS AND DISCOURSES

GATHER'D FROM THE MOUTH OF MY

NOBLE LORD AND HVSBAND.

With ſome few Notes of mine own.

I have heard My Lord ſay,

I.

HAT thoſe which command the Wealth of a Kingdom, command the hearts and hands of the People.

II.

That He is a great Monarch, who hath a Soveraign Command over Church, Laws and

Armes; and He **a wife** Monarch, that imploys his fubjects **for their own** profit, (for their profit **is** his) encourages Tradefmen, and affifts and defends Merchants.

III.

That it is a part of Prudence in a Commonwealth or Kingdom to encourage **drayners**; **for drowned Lands** are onely fit **to** maintain **and encreafe fome** wild **Ducks,** whereas **being drained, they are able** to afford nourifhment **and food to Cattel, befides** the producing **of** feveral **forts of** Fruit and **Corn.**

IV.

That without **a well** order'd force, a Prince doth but reign **upon** the courtefie **of others.**

V.

That great Princes fhould **not** fuffer **their** chief Cities to be ftronger then themfelves.

VI.

That great Princes **are half-armed, when** their fubjects are unarmed, **unlefs it be in time** of Foreign Wars.

VII.

That the Prince is **richeft,** who **is** Mafter of the Purfe; **and he ftrongeft** that is Mafter of the Armes; and he wifeft that can tell how to fave the one, and ufe the other.

VIII.

The Great Princes fhould be the onely Pay-Mafters of their Soldiers, and pay them out of their own Treafuries; for all men follow the Purfe; and fo they'l have both the Civil and Martial Power in their hands.

IX.

That Great Monarchs fhould rather ftudy men, then Books; for all affairs or bufinefs are amongft Men.

X.

That a Prince fhould advance Foreign Trade or Traffik to the utmoft of his Power, becaufe no State or Kingdom can be Rich without it; and where Subjects are poor, the Soveraign can have but little.

XI.

That Trade and Traffick brings Honey to the Hive; that is to fay, Riches to the Commonwealth; whereas other Profeffions are fo far from that, that they rather rob the Commonwealth, inftead of enriching it.

XII.

That it is not fo much unfeafonable Weather that makes the Countrey complain of Scarcity, but want of Commerce; for whenfoever Commodities are cheap, it is a fign that Commerce is decayed; becaufe the cheapnefs of them, fhews a fcarcity of money; for example, put the cafe five men came to Market to buy a Horfe, and each of them had no more but ten pounds, the Seller can receive no more then what the Buyer has, but muft content himfelf with thofe ten pounds, if he be neceffitated to fell his Horfe : But if each one of the Buyers had an hundred pounds to lay out for a Horfe, the Seller might receive as much. Thus Commodities are cheap or dear, according to the plenty or fcarcity of money; and though we had Mynes of Gold and Silver at home, and no Traffick into Foreign parts, yet we fhould want neceffaries from other Nations, which proves that no Nation can live or fubfift well, without Foreign Trade and Commerce ; for God and Nature have order'd it fo, That no particular Nation is provided with all things.

XIII.

That Merchants by carrying out more Commodities then they bring in; that is to say, by felling more then they buy, do enrich a State or Kingdom with money, that hath none in its own bowels; but what Kingdom or State foever hath Mynes of Gold and Silver, there Merchants buy more then they fell, to furnifh and accommodate it with neceffary provifions.

XIV.

That debafing, and fetting a higher value upon money, is but a prefent fhift of poor and needy Princes; and doth more hurt for the future, then good for the prefent.

XV.

That Foraign Commerce caufes frequent Voyages; and frequent Voyages make fkilful and experienced Seamen, and Skilful Sea men are a Brazen Wall to an Ifland.

XVI.

That he is the Powerfulleft Monarch that hath the beft fhipping; and that a Prince fhould hinder his Neighbours as much as he can, from being ftrong at Sea.

XVII.

That wife States-men ought to underſtand the Laws, Cuſtomes and Trade of the Commonwealth, and have good intelligence both of Foraign Tranſactions and Deſigns, and of Domeſtick Factions; alſo they ought to have a Treaſury, and well-furniſhed Magazine.

XVIII.

That it is a great matter in a State or Kingdom, to take care of the Education of Youth, to breed them ſo, that they may know firſt how to obey, and then how to command and order affairs wiſely.

XIX.

That it is great Wiſdom in a State, to breed and train up good States-men : As, firſt, To let them be ſome time at the Univerſities : Next, To put them to the Innes of Court, that they may have ſome knowledg of the Laws of the Land; then to ſend them to travel with ſome Ambaſſador, in the quality of Secretary; and let them be Agents or Reſidents in Foraign Countreys. Fourthly, To make them Clerks of the Signet, or Council :

And laftly, To make them Secretaries of State, or give them fome **other** Employment in State-Affairs.

XX.

That there fhould **be more** Praying, and lefs Preaching ; for much Preaching breeds Faction ; but much Praying caufes Devotion.

XXI.

That young people fhould **be** frequently Catechifed, and that **Wife Men** rather then Learned, fhould be chofen **heads of** Schools and Colledges.

XXII.

That the **more** divifions there **are** in **Church and State, the** more trouble **and** con-fufion is apt to enfue : Wherefore too many Controverfies and Difputes in the one, and **too many** Law-Cafes and Pleadings **in** the other ought **to be** avoided and fuppreffed.

XXIII.

That Difputes and Factions amongft Statef-men, are fore-runners of future diforders, if not total ruines.

XXIV.

That **all** Books of Controverfies fhould be **writ in** Latin, that none but the Learned may read them, and that there fhould be no Difputations but in Schools, left it breed Factions amongft the Vulgar; for Difputations **and** Controverfies are a kind of Civil War, main**tained by** the Pen, and often draw out the fword foon after : Alfo **that all** Prayer-Books **fhould be writ** in the **native Language;** that Excommunications fhould not be too frequent for every little and petty trefpafs ; that every Clergy-man fhould be kind and loving to his Parifhioners, not proud and quarrelfome.

XXV.

That Ceremony is nothing in it felf, and **yet** doth every thing ; for without Ceremony **there** would be **no** diftinction neither in **Church nor** State.

XXVI.

That Orders and Profeffions ought not to entrench upon each other, left in time they make a confufion amongft themfelves.

XXVII.

That in a Well-ordered State or Government, care fhould be taken left any degree or profeffion whatfoever fwell too big, or grow too numerous, it being not onely a hinderance to thofe of the fame profeffion, but a burden to the Commonwealth, which cannot be well if it exceeds in extreams.

XXVIII.

That the Taxes fhould not be above the riches of the Commonwealth, for that muft upon neceffity breed Factions and Civil Wars, by reafon a general poverty united, is far more dangerous then a private Purfe; for though their Wealth be fmall, yet their Unity and Combination makes them ftrong; fo that being armed with neceffity, they become outragious with defpair.

XXIX.

That Heavy Taxes upon Farmes, ruine the Nobility and Gentry; for if the Tenant be poor, the Landlord cannot be rich, he having nothing but his Rents to live on.

XXX.

That **it is not fo much Laws and Religion,**
nor Rhetorick, that keeps a State or Kingdom
in **order, but** Armes; which if they **be not**
imploy'd to an evil ufe, keep up the right **and**
priviledges both of Crown, Church and State.

XXXI.

That no equivocations fhould be ufed either
in Church **or Law; for the one** caufes feveral
Opinions **to** the difturbance **of** mens Con-
fciences; the other long and tedious Suits, **to**
the difturbance of mens private Affairs; and
both do oftentimes ruine and impoverifh the
State.

XXXII.

That **in** Cafes of Robberies and Murthers,
it is better to be fevere, then merciful; for
the hanging of a few, will fave the lives and
Purfes **of** many.

XXXIII.

That many Laws **do** rather entrap, then
help the fubject.

XXXIV.

That no Martial Law fhould **be** executed,
but in an Army.

XXXV.

That the Sheriffs in this Kingdom of *Eng-land* have been fo expenfive in Liveries and Entertainments in the time of their Sheri-falty, as it hath ruined many Families that had but indifferent Eftates.

XXXVI.

That the cutting down of Timber in the time of Rebellion, has been an ineftimable lofs to this Kingdom, by reafon of Shipping; for though Timber might be had out of Foreign Countries that would ferve for the building of Ships, yet there is none of fuch a temper as our *Englifh* Oak; it being not onely ftrong and large, but not apt to fplint, which renders the Ships of other Nations much inferior to ours; and that therefore it would be very beneficial for the Kingdom, to fet out fome Lands for the bearing of fuch Oaks, by fowing of Acorns, and then tranf-planting them; which would be like a Store-houfe for fhipping, and bring an incomparable benefit to the Kingdom, fince in Shipping confifts our greateft ftrength, they being the onely Walls that defend an Ifland.[1]

XXXVII.

That the Nobility and Gentry in this Kingdom, have done themfelves a great injury, by giving away (out of a petty pride) to the Commonalty, the power of being Juries and Juftices of Peace; for certainly they cannot but underftand, that that muft of neceffity be an act of great Confequence and Power, which concerns mens Lives, Lands and Eftates.

XXXVIII.

That it is no act of Prudence to make poor and mean perfons Governours or Commanders, either by Land or Sea; by reafon their poverty

---

[1] This is the firft allufion I have met with to the " Wooden Walls of Old England." Of all the oak grown in this country, the Suffex oak was accounted the tougheft and beft. For ftatements refpecting the almoft wanton deftruction of the forefts and woods of that county, fee my " Contributions to Literature," pp. 115-119. I wifh the Duke's fuggeftion of fowing acorns would be acted upon by our great landed proprietors; for if they did not perfonally derive benefit, their fucceffors would furely do fo.

caufes them to take Bribes, and fo betray their Truft; at beft, they are apt to extort, which is a great grievance to the people; befides, it breeds envy in the Nobility and Gentry, who by that means rife into Factions, and caufe difturbances in a State or Commonwealth: Wherefore the beft way is to chufe Rich and Honourable Perfons, (or at leaft, Gentlemen) for fuch Employments, who efteem Fame and Honourable Actions, above their Lives; and if they want fkill, they muft get fuch under-Officers as have more then themfelves, to inftruct them.

XXXIX.

That great Princes fhould confider, before they make War againft Foreign Nations, whether they be able to maintain it; for if they be not able, then it is better to fubmit to an honourable Peace, then to make Warr to their great difadvantage; but if they be able to maintain Warr, then they'l force (in time) their Enemies to fubmit and yeild to what Tearms and Conditions they pleafe.

XL.

That, when a State or Government is enfnarled and troubled, it is more **eafie** to raife the common people **to a** Factious Mutiny, then to draw them **to a Loyal** Duty.

XLI.

That in a Kingdom where Subjects **are** **apt to rebel,** no Offices or Commands fhould be fold ; **for** thofe **that buy, will** not onely ufe extortion, and practice unjuft wayes **to make** out their purchafe, **but be** ableft to rebel, by reafon **they** are **more** for private **gain,** then the publick good; **for it is probable** their Principles **are** like their Purchafes.

But, that **all** Magiftrates, Officers, Commanders, Heads and Rulers, **in** what Profeffion foever, both in Church and State, fhould be chofen according **to** their Abilities, Wifdom, Courage, Piety, Juftice, Honefty and Loyalty ; **and** then they'l mind the public Good, **more** then their particular Intereft.

XLII.

That thofe which have Politick Defigns, are for the moft part difhoneft, by reafon their Defigns tend **more** to Intereft, then Juftice.

XLIII.

That Great Princes fhould onely have Great, Noble and Rich Perfons to attend them, whofe Purfes and Power may alwayes be ready to **affift** them.

XLIV.

That a Poor Nobility is apt to be Factious; and **a** Numerous Nobility **is** a burden to a Commonwealth.

XLV.

That in **a** Monarchical **Government,** to be for the King, is to be for the Commonwealth; for when Head and Body are divided, **the** Life of Happinefs dies, and the Soul of Peace is departed.

XLVI.

That, **as** it **is** a great Error in a State to have all Affairs put into *Gazettes,* (for it over-heats the peoples brains, and makes them neglect their private Affairs, by over-bufying themfelves with State-bufinefs ;) **fo it** is great Wifdom for a Council of State **to** have good Intelligences (although they be bought with great Coft and Charges) as well of Domeftick,

as Foreign Affairs and Tranfactions, and to
keep them in private for the benefit of the
Commonwealth.

XLVII.

That there is no better Policy **for a Prince**
to pleafe his People, then to have many **Holy-
dayes** for their eafe, **and order** feveral Sports
and Paftimes for **their** Recreation, **and to** be
himfelf fometime Spectator thereof; by which
means **he'l** not onely gain **love** and refpect from
the people, but bufie their **minds in** harmlefs
actions, fweeten their Natures, **and** hinder
them from Factious Defigns.

XLVIII.

That **it** is more difficult and dangerous for
a Prince or Commander to **raife** an Army **in**
fuch **a time when the** Countrey is embroiled
in **a** Civil Warr, then **to** lead out an Army to
fight a Battel; for when an Army is raifed,
he hath ftrength; **but in** raifing **it, he** hath
none.

XLIX.

That good Commanders, and experienced
Soldiers, are like fkilfull Fencers, who defend

with Prudence, and aſſault with Courage, and **kill their** Enemies by Art, not truſting their Lives to Chance **or** Fortune; for as a little man with ſkill, may eaſily kill an ignorant **Giant;** ſo a ſmall **Army** that hath experienced Commanders, may eaſily overcome a great **Army** that **hath** none.

L.

That Gallant men having no employment for Heroick Actions, become lazy, as hating any other buſineſs; whereas Cowards and baſe perſons **are** onely active and ſtirring in times of Peace, working ill deſigns **to** breed Factions, **and** cauſe diſturbances **in a** Common-wealth.

LI.

That there **have been** many Queſtions and Diſputes concerning the Governments of Princes; **as,** Whether they ought to govern by Love, **or** Fear? But the beſt way **of** Government **is,** and has alwayes been **by** juſt **Rewards and** Puniſhments; for that State **which cannot** tell how and **when to** puniſh and reward, does not know how to govern, by reaſon all the **World** is governed that way.

LII.

That if **the ancient** *Britains* had **had** skill, according **to** their Courage, they **might** have conquer'd all the World, **as the** *Romans* did.

LIII.

That it would be **very** beneficial for great Princes to be sometimes present **in** Courts of Judicature, **to** examine the Causes **of** their poor Subjects, and find out the Extortions and Corruptions of Magiftrates and Officers; **by** which glorious Act they would gain much Love and Fame from the People.

LIV.

That **it** would be very advantagious for Subjects, and not in the least prejudicial to the Soveraign, to have **a** general Regifter in every County, for the Entry of all manner of **Deeds**, and Conveyance of Land between **party and** party, and Offices of Record ; **for** by this means, whofoever buyes, would fee clearly what Intereft and Title there is in any Land **he** intends **to** purchafe, whereby he fhall be affur'd that the Sale made to him is good and firm, and prevent many Law-fuits touching the Title of his Purchafe.

LV.

That there fhould be **a** Limitation for Law-Suits ; **and** that the **longeft** Suit fhould not **laft** above **two Tearms, at** length **not above a Year ;** which would certainly **be a** great **benefit to** the Subjects in general, though **not** to **Lawyers ;** and though fome Polititians object, That the more the people is bufie about their private Affairs, the lefs time have they to make difturbance in the publick ; yet this is **but a weak Argument, fince** Law-fuits are as apt to breed Factions, **as any thing elfe ;** for they bring people into poverty, that **they** know **not** how to live, which **muft** of neceffity breed difcontent, and put them upon ill defigns.

LVI.

That Power, for the moft part, does more then Wifdom ; for Fools with Power, feem wife ; whereas wife men, without Power, feem Fools ; **and** this is the reafon that the **World takes Power for Wifdom ;** and the **want** of **Power for Foolifhnefs.**

LVII.

That a valiant man will not refuse an honourable Duel; nor a wife man fight upon a Fools Quarrel.

LVIII.

That men are apt to find fault with each other's actions; believing they prove themselves wife in finding fault with their Neighbours.

LIX.

That a wife man will draw feveral occafions to the point of his defign, as a Burning-Glafs doth the feveral beams of the Sun.

LX.

That although actions may be prudently defigned, and valiantly performed; yet none can warrant the iffue; for Fortune is more powerful then Prudence, and had *Cæfar* not been fortunate, his Valour and Prudence would never have gained him fo much applaufe.

LXI.

That ill Fortune, makes wife and honeft men feem Fools and Knaves; but good

Fortune makes Fools and Knaves seem wise and honeſt men.

LXII.

That ill Fortune doth oftner ſucceed good, then good Fortune ſucceeds ill; for thoſe that have ill Fortune, do not ſo eaſily recover it, as thoſe that have good Fortune are apt to loſe it.

LXIII.

That he had obſerved, That ſeldom any perſon did laugh, but it was at the follies or misfortunes of other men; by which we may judg of their good natures.

LXIV.

I have heard my Lord ſay, That when he was in Baniſhment, He had nothing left him, but a clear Conſcience, by which he had and did ſtill conquer all the Armies of misfortunes that ever ſeized upon him.

LXV.

Alſo I have heard him ſay, That he was never beholding to Lady Fortune; for he had ſuffered on both ſides, although he never was but on one ſide.

LXVI.

I have **heard him** fay, That his Father one time, upon fome difcourfe of expences, fhould tell him, *It was but juft that every* **man** *fhould have his time.*

LXVII.

I have heard **my Lord** fay, That bold foliciting **and** intruding men, **fhall gain more** by their **importunate** Petitions, then **modeft** honeft men fhall get by filence (as being **loath to** offend, **or be** too troublefome) both in the manner and matter **of** their requefts : **The** reafon is, faid he, That Great Princes will rather grant fometimes an unreafonable **fuit,** then be tired with frequent Petitions, **and** hindered from their ordinary Pleafures ; And when I afked my Lord, whether the Grants **of** fuch importunate **fuits** were fitly and properly placed ? He anfwered, Not fo well **as** thofe that are placed **upon** due confideration, **and** upon trial and proof.

LXVIII.

I have heard my Lord fay, That it is a great Error, and weak Policy in a State, to advance their Enemies, and endeavour to make them friends by bribing them with Honours and Offices, saying, They are shrewd men, and may do the State much hurt: And on the other side, to neglect their Friends, and those that have done them great service, saying, they are Honest men, and mean the State no harm: For this kind of Policy comes from the Heathen, who pray'd to the Devil, and not to God, by reason they supposed God was Good, and would hurt no Creature; but the Devil they flatter'd and worshipp'd out of fear, lest he should hurt them: But by this foolish Policy, said he, they most commonly encrease their Enemies, and lose their Friends; for first, it teaches men to observe, that the onely way to Preferment, is to be against the State or Government: Next, Since all that are Factious, cannot be rewarded or preferr'd, by reason a State hath more Subjects, then Rewards or Preferments, there must of necessity be numerous Enemies; for when their hopes of Reward fail them, they grow more Factious and Inveterate then ever they were at first: Wherefore the best Policy in a State or Government, said my

Lord, is **to reward** Friends, and **punifh** Enemies, **and prefer** the Honeft before the Factious ; and then all will be real Friends, and profer their honeft fervice, either out of pure Love and Loyalty, **or** in hopes **of** Advancement, feeing **there** is none but **by** ferving the State.

LXIX.

I have **heard him fay feveral times, That** his love **to** his gracious **Mafter** King *Charles* the Second, **was above the love he bore to his** Wife, **Children, and all** his **Pofterity,** nay to his own life : **And when,** fince His Return into *England*, **I** anfwer'd **him, That I ob-** ferved His Gracious Mafter **did not** love him **fo well as** he lov'd Him ; he replied, That he **cared not** whether **His** Majefty lov'd **him again or not;** for he was refolved **to love** him.

LXX.

I afking **my** Lord **one time, What kind** of Fate it was, that reftored our Gracious King, *Charles* the Second, to His Throne ? He anfwer'd, It was a bleffed kind of Fate. I replied, That I had **obferved** a perfect contrariety between the **Fortunes of His Royal Father**, of bleſſed memory, and Him ; for as there was a diviſion amongſt the generality of the people, in the Reign of King *Charles* the Firſt, tending to His Deſtruction ; ſo there was a general Combination and Agreement between them in King *Charles* the Second His Reſtauration ; and as there was a general malice amongſt the people againſt the Father to Depoſe Him ; ſo there was a general Love for the Son to Enthrone Him.   My Lord anſwer'd, I had obſerved ſomething, but not all ; for, ſaid he, there was a Neceſſity for the people to deſire and Reſtore King *Charles* the Second ; but there was no Neceſſity to Murder King *Charles* the Firſt.   For the Kingdom being through ſo many Alterations and Changes of Government, divided into ſeveral Factions and Parties, was at laſt hurried into ſuch a Confuſion, that it was impoſſible in that manner to ſubſiſt, or hold out any longer ; Which Confuſion having opened the Peoples Eyes, the generality being tyred with the evil effects and conſequences of their unſetled Governments under unjuſt Uſurpers, and frightned with the apprehenfion of future dangers, began **to call to mind** the happy Times, when in an uninterrupted Peace they enjoyed their own, under the **happy Reign** of their Lawful Soveraigns ; and **hereupon** with an unanimous **confent** Re-**call'd and** Reftor'd **our** now gracious **King** ; which, although **it** was oppofed by fome Factious Parties, **yet** the generality **of the** people outweigh'd **the** reft ; **neither was the** Royal **Party** wanting in their **endeavours.**

LXXI.

Afking my Lord one time, Whether **it** was eafie or difficult to govern **a State or** Kingdom ? He anfwer'd me, That moft States were govern'd by fecret Policy, and fo with difficulty ; for thofe that govern, are (at leaft, fhould be) wifer then the State or Commonwealth they govern. I replied, That in **my** opinion, **a** State was eafily govern'd, if their Government was like unto God's ; that is **to** fay, If Governours did Reward and Punifh according to the defert. My Lord anfwer'd, I faid well ; but he added, the Follies of the People are many times too hard for the Prudence of the Governour ; like as the fins of men work more evil effects in them, then the Grace of God works good ; for if this were not, there would **be** more good then bad, which, alas, Experience proves otherwife.

LXXII.

Some Gentlemen making a complaint **to** my Lord, That fome **he** employed in His Majefty's Affairs, **were too** hafty and over-bufie.   My Lord told them, That he would rather chufe **fuch perfons for His** Majefties fervice **as were** over-active, **then fuch** that would be fuller of Queftions then Actions. The fame he would do for **his own particular** affairs.

LXXIII.

Some condemning My Lord for having *Roman-Catholicks* and *Scots* in His Army ; He anfwered them, that he did not examine their Opinions in Religion, but look'd more upon their Honefty and Duty ; for certainly there were honeft men and loyal Subjects amongft *Roman Catholicks*, as well as Proteftants ; and amongft *Scots* as well as *Englijh*.   Neverthelefs, **my** Lord, as he was for the King, fo he was alfo for the Orthodox Church of *England*, as fufficiently appears by the care he took in ordering the Church-Government, mentioned in the Hiftory. To which purpofe, when my Lord was walking one time with fome of His Officers in the Church at *Durham*, and wonder'd at the greatnefs and ftrength of the Pillars that fupported that ftruaure; My Brother, Sir *Charles* **Lucas**, who was then with him, told my Lord, that he muft confefs, thofe Pillars were very great, and of a vaft ftrength; But faid he, Your Lordfhip is a far greater Pillar of the Church then all thefe: Which certainly was alfo a real truth, and would have more evidently appear'd, had Fortune favour'd **my Lord more** then fhe did.

LXXIV.

My **Lord** being in Banifhment, I told him, that **he was** happy in **his** misfortunes, for he **was** not fubjea to any State or Prince. To which he jeftingly anfwer'd, That as he was fubjea **to no Prince**, fo he was a Prince of no Subjeas.

LXXV.

In fome Difcourfe which I had with my

Lord concerning Princes and their Sujects ; I declared that I had obferved Great Princes were not like the Sun, which fends forth out of it felf Rays of Light, and Beams of Heat ; effects that did both glorifie the Sun, and nourifh and comfort fublunary Creatures; but **their glory and** fplendor proceeded rather from the **Ceremony** which they received from their fubjects. To which my Lord anfwer'd, **That** Subjects were fo far from giving fplendor **to** their Princes, that all **the** Honours and Titles, in which confifts the chief fplendor of a fubject, were principally derived from them ; **for,** faid he, were there no **Princes,** there would be none to confer Honours and Titles **upon** them.

LXXVI.

My Lord entertaining one time fome Gentlemen with a merry Difcourfe, told them, **that** he would not keep them Company except they had **done** and fufferd as much for their King and Country as he had. They anfwer'd, That they had not a power anfwerable to my **Lords.** My Lord replied, They fhould do their endeavour according to their Abilities :

No, said they, if we did, we should be like your Self, lose all, and get but little for our pains.

LXXVII.

I being much grieved that my Lord for his loyalty and honest Service, had so many Enemies, used sometimes to speak somewhat sharply of them ; but he gently reproving me, said, *I should do like experienced Sea-men, and as they either turn their Sails with the wind, or take them down; so should I either comply with Time, or abate my Passion.*

LXXVIII.

A Soldiers Wife, whose Husband had been slain in my Lord's Army, came one time to beg some relief of my Lord ; who told her, That he was not able to relieve all that had been loyal to His Majesty ; for said he, My losses are so many, that if I should give away the remainder of my Estate, my Wife and Children would have nothing to live on : She answer'd, That His Majesty's Enemies were preferr'd to great Honours, and had much Wealth : Then it is a sign (replied my Lord) that your Husband and I were Honest Men.

LXXIX.

A Friend of my Lord's, complaining that he had done the State much Service, but received little Reward for it; my Lord anſwer'd him, That States did not uſually reward paſt Services; but if he could do ſome preſent Service, he might perhaps get ſomething; but (ſaid he) thoſe men are wiſeſt that will be paid before-hand.

LXXX.

I obſerving that in the late Civil Warrs, many were deſirous to be employed in States Affairs, and at the noiſe of **Warr**, endeavoured to be Commanders, though but of ſmall Parties, aſked my Lord the reaſon thereof, and what advantage they could make by their Employments? My Lord ſmilingly anſwer'd, That for the generality, he knew not what they could get, but danger, loſs and labour for their pains. Then I aſk'd him, Whether Generals of Great Armies were ever enriched by their Heroick Exploits, and great Victories? My Lord anſwer'd, That ordinary Commanders gained more, and were better rewarded then great Generals. To which I added, That **I had obferv'd** the fame in **Hif-**tories, namely, **That Men** of great **Merit** and Power, had not onely no Rewards, but were either **found** fault withall, **or** laid afide when **they had no** more bufinefs or employment for them; and that I could not conceive any reafon for it, but that States were afraid **of** their Power: My Lord anfwer'd, The reafon was, That **it** was far more eafie to reward Under-Officers, then Great Commanders.

LXXXI.

My Lord having fince the Return from his Banifhment, fet up a Race of Horfes, inftead of thofe he loft **by** the Warrs, ufes often to ride through his Park **to** fee his Breed. One time **it** chanced when **he** went thorough it, that **he** efpied fome labouring-men fawing **of** Woods that were blown down by the Wind, **for fome** particular **ufes;** at which my Lord turning to **his Attendants,** faid, That **he had been** at that Work a **great part of his life.** They not knowing what **my** Lord meant, but thinking he jefted; **I** fpeak very ferioufly, (added he) and not in **jeft;** for you fee that this Tree which is blown **down** by the Wind, although it was found and ftrong, yet it could not withftand its force ; **and now it is down, it muft be cut in pieces, and** made ferviceable for feveral **ufes ;** whereof fome will **ferve for** Building, fome for **Paling, fome for Firing,** *&c.* In the like manner, faid he, have I been cut down **by** the Lady Fortune ; and being **not** able to refift fo Powerful a Princefs, I **have** been forced **to** make the beft ufe **of** my Misfortunes, as the Chips of my Eftate.

LXXXII.

My Lord difcourfing **one time with fome** of his Friends, of judging **of** other **mens** Natures, Difpofitions and Actions ; **and** fome obferving that men could not poffibly **know** or judg of **them, the** events of mens actions falling out oftentimes contrary to their intentions ; fo that **where** they hit once, they fail'd twenty times in their Judgments. My Lord anfwer'd, That his Judgment in that **point** feldom did mifs, although **he** thought it weaker then theirs : **The** reafon is, faid he, Becaufe I judg moft men to be like my felf ; that is to fay, Fools ; when as you do judg them all according to your felf, that is, Wife men ;

and since there are more **Fools in the World** then Wise men, **I may** sooner guess right then you : for though my judgment **roves** at random, yet it can never miss of Errors; which **yours** will never do, except **you can dive into** other mens Follies by the length of **your own** line, and found their bottom **by the** weight of your own Plummet, **for the depth of Folly is** beyond **the** line of **Wisdom.**

Besides, said he, **You believe that other** men would **do** as you **would have them, or as** you would **do** to them ; wherein **you are** mistaken, for most men do the contrary. **In** short, Folly is bottomless, and hath no end ; **but** Wisdom hath bounds to all her designs, otherwise she would never compass them.

LXXXIII.

My Lord discoursing some **time** with **a** Learned Doctor of Divinity concerning Faith, said, That in **his** opinion, the wisest **way for a man,** was to **have as** little Faith **as** he could for **this** World, **and as** much as he **could** for **the** next World.

LXXXIV.

In some Discourse with **my Lord, I** told him

that **I did** fpeak fharpeft to thofe I loved beft.
'To which he jeftingly anfwered, That if fo,
then he would not have me love him beft.

LXXXV.

After my Lords return from a long Banifhment, when he had been in the Countrey
fome time, and endeavoured to pick up fome
Gleanings **of** his ruined Eftate; it chanced
that the **Widow** of *Charles* Lord *Mansfield*,
My **Lords Eldeft** Son, afterwards Duchefs of
Richmond, to whom **the faid Lord of** *Manf-*
field had made a joynture **of** 2000l. a Year,
died not long after her fecond marriage; **for**
whofe death, though My Lord was heartily
forry, and would willingly have loft **the** faid
Money, had **it** been able to fave her **life**; Yet
difcourfing one time merrily with his Friends,
was pleafed to fay, That though his Earthly
King and **Mafter** feem'd to have forgot him,
yet the King **of** Heaven **had** remembred him,
for he had given him 2000l. **a Y**ear.

Some Few Notes of the Authoreſſe.

I.

IT was far more difficult in the late Civil Wars, for my Lord to raiſe an Army for His Majeſties Service, then it was for the Parliament to raiſe an Army againſt His Majeſty: Not onely becauſe the Parliament were many, and my Lord but one ſingle Perſon; but by reaſon a Kingly or Monarchical Government was then generally diſliked, and moſt part of the Kingdom proved Rebellious, and aſſiſted the Parliament either with their Purſes or Perſons, or both; when as the Army which my Lord raiſed for the defence and maintenance of the King, and his Rights, was raifed moft upon his own and his Friends Intereft : For **it is** frequently feen and known by woful Experience, that rebellious **and** fa&ctious Parties do **more fud-denly and numeroufly flock** together **to** a&ct **a** mifchievous defign, then loyal and honeft men **to affift or** maintain **a** juft Caufe ; and certainly 'tis much to be lamented, that **evil** men **fhould be** more induftrious and profper-**ous then** good, and that the Wicked fhould have a **more defperate Courage,** then the Virtuous, an a&ctive Valour.

II.

I have obferved, That many **by** flattering Poets, have been compared **to** *Cæfar*, without defert ; but **this I** dare freely and without flattery fay of my **Lord,** That though he had not *Cæfars* Fortune, yet he wanted not *Cæfars* Courage, nor his Prudence, nor his good Nature, **nor** his Wit ; Nay, in fome particu-lars he did more then *Cæfar* ever did ; for though *Cæfar* had a great Army, yet he was firft fet ont by the State or Senators **of** *Rome,* who were Mafters almoft of **all** the World ; **when** as **my** Lord raifed his Army (as before is mentioned) moſt upon his own Intereſt (he having many Friends and Kindred in the Northern parts) at ſuch a time when his Gracious King and Soveraign was then not Maſter of his own Kingdoms, He being over-power'd by his rebellious Subjeꞓts.

III.

I have obſerved, That my Noble Lord has always had an averſion to that kind of Policy, that now is commonly praꞓtiſed in the world, which in plain tearms is Diſſembling, Flattery and Cheating, under the cover of Honeſty, Love and Kindneſs : But I have heard him ſay, that the beſt Policy is to aꞓt juſtly, honeſtly and wiſely, and to ſpeak truly ; and that the old Proverb is true ; *To be wiſe is to be honeſt* : For, ſaid he, That man of what Condition, Quality or Profeſſion ſoever, that is once found out to deceive either in words. or aꞓtions, ſhall never be truſted again by wiſe and honeſt men. But, ſaid he, A wiſe man is not bound to take notice of all Diſſem-blers, and their cheating Aꞓtions, if they do not concern him ; nay, even of thoſe he would not always take notice, but chuſe his time ; for the chief part of a wife man is to time bufinefs well, and to do it without Partiality and Paffion.   But, faid he, The folly of the world is fo great, that one honeft and wife man may be overpowred by many Knaves and Fools; and if fo, then the onely benefit of a wife man confifts in the fatif-faction he finds by his honeft and wife actions, and that he has done what in Con-fcience, Honour and Duty he ought to do ; and all fucceffors of fuch worthy Perfons ought to be more fatisfied in the worth and merit of their Predeceffours, then in their Title and Riches.

IV.

I have heard that fome noble Gentleman, (who was fervant to His Highnefs then Prince of *Wales*, our now Gracious Sove-raign, when my Lord was Governour) fhould relate, that whenfoever my Lord by his prudent infpection and forefight did foretell what would come to pafs hereafter ; it feemed fo improbable to him, that both him-felf and fome others believed my Lord fpoke extravagantly : But fome few years after, his predictions proved **true, and** the event **did** confirm what **his Prudence had** obferved.

v.

I **have** heard, That in our late Civil Warres there were many petty Skirmifhes, and **Forti-fications of** weak and inconfiderable **Houfes,** where fome fmall Parties would be fhooting **and** pottering at each other; **an action more** proper for Bandites **or** Thieves, **then** ftout and valiant Soldiers; **for** I **have** heard **my** Lord fay, **That** fuch fmall Parties divide the Body of an Army, and by that means weaken **it** ; whereas the bufinefs might be much eafier decided in one or two Battels, with **lefs** ruine both to the Country and Army : For **I** have heard my Lord fay, That as it **is** dangerous to divide a Limb from the Body ; fo **it** is alfo dangerous **to** divide Armies **or** Navies **in** time **of** Warr **;** and there are often more menloft in fuch petty Skirmifhes, **then** in fet-Battels, by reafon thofe **happen** almoft every day, nay every hour in feveral places.

VI.

Many in our late Civil-Warres, had more Title then Power; for though they were

Generals, or chief Commanders, yet their Forces were more like a Brigade, then a well-formed Army ; and their actions were accordingly, not set-battels, but petty Skirmishes between small Parties ; for there were no great Battels fought, but by my Lord's Army, his being the greatest and best-formed Army which His Majesty had.

VII.

Although I have observed, That it is a usual Custom of the World, to glorifie the present Power and good Fortune, and vilifie ill Fortune and low conditions ; yet I never heard that my Noble Lord was ever neglected by the generality ; but was on the contrary, alwayes esteemed and praised by all ; for he is truly an Honest and Honourable man, and one that may be relied upon both for Trust and Truth.

VIII.

I have observed, That many instead of great Actions, make onely a great Noise, and like shallow Fords, or empty Bladders, found most when there is least in them ; which expresses a flattering Partiality, rather then Honesty and Truth ; for Truth and Honefty lye at the bottom ; and have more Action then Shew.

IX.

I have obferved, That **good** Fortune adds Fame to mean Actions, when **as** ill Fortune darkens the fplendor of the moft meritorious ; **for** mean Perfons plyed with good Fortune, **are** more famous then **Noble Perfons** that **are** fhadowed **or** darkned **with ill Fortune** ; fo that Fortune, **for** the moft **part, is** Fame's Champion.

X.

I obferve, That as **it** would **be a** grief **to** covetous and miferable perfons, to be rewarded **with** Honour, rather then with Wealth, be-caufe they love Wealth, before Honour and **Fame** ; fo on the other fide, Noble, Heroick and Meritorious **Perfons,** prefer Honour and Fame before Wealth ; well knowing, That **as Infamy is** the greateft Punifhment of **un-**worthinefs, fo Fame **and** Honour is the **beft** Reward of worth and merit.

XII.

I obferve, that fpleen and malice, efpecially in this age, is grown **to that** height, that none

will **endure the** praife of any **body** befides
themfelves ; nay, they'l **rather praife** the
wicked then the good ; the Coward rather
then the Valiant ; the Miferable **then** the
Generous ; the Traytor, then the Loyal :
which makes Wife men meddle as little with
the Affairs of the world as ever they **can.**

XIII.

I have obferved, **as** well as former Ages
have done, **That** Meritorious perfons, for
their noble actions, moft commonly get Envy
and Reproach, inftead of Praife and Reward ;
unlefs their Fortunes be above **Envy,** as
Cæfar's and *Alexander's* were ; **But had** thefe
two Worthies been **as** Unfortunate **as** they
were Fortunate, they would have been as
much vilified, as **they are** glorified.

XIV.

I have obferved, that it **is** more eafie to
talk, then **to** act ; to forget, then to remember ;
to punifh, then to reward ; **and** more common
to prefer Flattery before **Truth, Intereft** be-
fore Juftice, and prefent fervice before paft.

XV.

I have obferved, that many old **Proverbs** are very **true,** and **amongft** the reft, this : It is better **to** be at the latter end of a **Feaft,** then **at the** beginning **of** a Fray; for moft commonly, thofe that **are** in the beginning of a **Fray, get** but little **of** the Feaft ; **and thofe** that have undergone the greateft dangers, **have** leaft **of the** fpoils.

XVI.

I have obferved, That Favours of Great Princes **make** men often thought Meritorious; whereas without them, they would be efteemed but as ordinary Perfons.

XVII.

I obferve, That **in** other Kingdoms **or** Countries, **to** be **the** chief Governour **of** a Province, **is** not onely a place of Honour, but much Profit; for they have a great Revenue to themfelves ; whereas in *England,* **the** Lieutenancy of a County **is barely a** Title of Honour, without **Profit ;** except it be the Lieutenancy **or** Government of the Kingdom of *Ireland;* efpecially **fince** the late Earl of

Stafford enjoyed that dignity, who fetled that Kingdom very wifely both for Militia and Trade.

XVIII.

I have obferved, That thofe that meddle leaft in Wars, whether Civil or Foreign, are not onely moft fafe and free from danger, but moft fecure from Loffes ; and though Heroick Perfons efteem Fame before Life, yet many there are, that think the wifeft way is to be a Spectator, rather then an Actor, unlefs they be neceffitated to it ; for it is better, fay they, to fit on the Stool of Quiet, then in the Chair of Troublefome Bufinefs.

FINIS.

Natures Pictures

DRAWN BY

FANCIES PENCIL

TO THE LIFE.

WRITTEN BY THE

THRICE NOBLE, ILLUSTRIOUS, AND EXCELLENT PRINCESS,

The LADY MARCHIONESS of NEWCASTLE.

In this Volume there are several feigned Stories of Natural Descriptions, as Comical, Tragical, and Tragi-comical, Poetical, Romancical, Philosophical and Historical, both in Prose and Verse, some all Verse, some all Prose, some mixt, partly Prose, and partly Verse. Also, there are some Morals, and some Dialogues; but they are as the advantage, Loaves of Bread as a Baker's Dozen; and a true Story at the latter End, wherein there is no feignings.

LONDON:

PRINTED BY J. MARTIN AND J. ALLESTRYE, AT THE BELL,

IN SAINT PAUL'S CHURCH YARD.

1656.

A TRUE RELATION

OF THE

Birth, Breeding, and Life,

OF

MARGARET CAVENDISH,

DUCHESS OF NEWCASTLE.

WRITTEN BY HERSELF.

WITH A

Critical Preface, &c.

BY

SIR EGERTON BRYDGES, M.P.

" What taste, and elegance, and genius does,
Still favours something greater than its place,
However low, or high."—*Shakesp.*

" **Though** Fortune, visible an enemy,
Should chase a virtuous pair, no jot **of power**
Hath she to change their loves."—*Ibid.*

KENT :

Printed at the private Press of Lee Priory;

BY JOHNSON AND WARWICK.

1814.

Sir Egerton Brydges' Preface.

UTO-BIOGRAPHY is fo attractive, that in whatever manner it is executed, it feldom fails both to entertain and inftruct. The Memoirs of *Margaret, Duchefs of Newcaftle*, written by herfelf, appear to me very eminently to poffefs this double merit. Whether they confirm or refute the character of the literary and moral qualities of her Grace given by Lord Orford, I muft leave the reader to judge. The fimplicity by which they are marked will, in minds conftituted like that of the noble critic, feem to approximate to folly: others, lefs inclined to farcafm, and lefs infected with an artificial tafte, will probably think far otherwife.

That the Duchefs was **deficient in a** cultivated judgment ; that **her knowledge** was
more multifarious than **exact ; and** that her
powers of fancy **and fentiment were** more
active than her powers of reafoning, **I** will
admit : but that her productions, mingled **as**
they are with great abfurdities, are wanting
either in talent, or in virtue, or even in genius,
I cannot concede.

There is an ardent **ambition,** which may
perhaps **itfelf be** confidered to prove fuperiority
of intellect. " I fear my ambition," fays the
Duchefs, " inclines to vain-glory ; **for I** am
very ambitious ; yet 'tis **neither for beauty,**
wit, titles, wealth, **or power, but** as **they** are
fteps to raife **me to** Fancy's Tower, **which is**
to live by remembrance in after-ages !" In
another **place fhe** exhibits traits of herfelf, fuch
as generally accompany genius. " I was
addicted," her Grace obferves, " from **my**
childhood to contemplation, rather then converfation ; **to** folitarinefs, rather then **fociety ;**
to melancholy rather then **mirth ; to** write
with the pen then **to work with the** needle,
paffing **my** time with harmlefs fancies, their
company being pleafing, their converfation

innocent, in which I take such pleasure, as I neglect my health ; for it is as great a grief to neglect their society, as a joy to be in their company." Again, she says : " my disposition is more inclining to melancholy then merry ; but not crabbed or peevish melancholy, but soft, melting, solitary, and contemplating melancholy ; and I am apt to weep rather than laugh."

Perhaps, however, it will be impossible to acquit the Duchess of vanity, as well as ambition, if it be vanity to indulge a too general and indiscriminate love of distinction ; and to expatiate with too much minuteness about oneself. Some of these minutiæ now afford amusement, arising from other pretensions than those with which they were written.

Her Grace was the companion of the Duke's misfortunes, the solace of his exile, the sharer of his poverty. In these gloomy days she had less opportunity of being acquainted with the splendour of courts, and the characters and manners of men eminent on the theatre of practical life, than with the scenes and actions of her own lonely imagination. We do not, therefore, find this Memoir full of anecdote, or hiftory, or political delineation. It is all domeftic ; and this domeftic painting is its charm.

If the Duchefs herfelf were out of the queftion, it is not uninterefting to have fuch a circumftantial account of the reft of the noble family of LUCAS. Whether their mode of life be confidered as common to others of their rank, or peculiar to themfelves, the picture is pleafing and inftructive. The mother's character excites refpect and affection. The burfting of the ftorms of civil war upon thofe days of peace, and virtue, and plenty, which fmiled fo treacheroufly on the youth of the Duchefs, is truly affecting. "In fuch misfortunes," fays her Grace, "my mother was of an heroick fpirit, in fuffering patiently where there is no remedy ; or to be induftrious where fhe thought fhe could help. She was of a grave behaviour, and had fuch a majeftick grandeur, as it were continually hung about her, that it would ftrike a kind of awe to the beholders, and command refpect from the rudeft." "She lived to fee the ruin of her children, in which was her ruin, and then died !"—"Not onely the family I am linked to is ruined, but the family from which I fprung, by thefe unhappy wars."

At pp. 11· and 12, the Duchefs has given with exquifite *naivetè* the account of her own going into the world, as maid of honour to the Queen, when the Court was at Oxford, and her fubfequent attachment and marriage to the Duke, then Marquis of Newcaftle. Not long after their marriage, the lofs of the battle of Marfton-moor drove them into exile. They moved from Paris to Holland, whence neceffity forced the Duchefs to come to England to folicit relief out of the Duke's immenfe eftates, which the prevailing Powers had feized.

Her Grace remained a year and half in England, during which fhe wrote her "*Poems*," and her "*Philofophical Fancies*;" to which fhe made large additions after fhe returned abroad. After her return alfo fhe wrote the volume from which this "*Life*" is extracted; and another book. Her "*World's Olio*" was, for the moft part, written before fhe went to England.

In this exile, and under the difappointment of her ineffectual efforts for relief, fhe fays,

" Heaven hitherto hath kept us, and though Fortune **hath** been crofs, **yet** we do fubmit, and are both content with what is, and cannot **be** mended ; and are fo prepared, that the worſt of fortunes ſhall not afflict our minds, fo as to make us unhappy, howfoever it doth pinch our **lives** with poverty; for, if tranquillity lives in an honeſt mind, the mind lives in peace, although the body fuffer."

What can be more amiable and virtuous, than a **refort** to the confolations **of** literature in fuch a ſtate? After **the** enjoyment of high and flattering rank, and fplendid fortune, noble **is** the fpirit that will **not be** broken **by** the gripe of Poverty, **the expulfion** from home, **and** kindred, and friends, and the defertion of **the world!** Under **the** blighting gloom of fuch oppreffion to create wealth and a kingdom " within the mind," ſhews an intellectual energy, which ought not to be defrauded of its praife.

After **the** Reſtoration, peace and **affluence** once **more ſhone** upon them amid **the long-** loſt domains **of** the Duke's **vaſt** hereditary property. Welbeck opened **her** gates to her Lord; **and the** caſtles of the North **received** with joy their heroic chieftain, whofe maternal anceftors, the baronial houfe of OGLE, had ruled over them for centuries in Northumberland. But Age had now made the Duke defirous only of repofe; and **her Grace,** the **faithful** companion of his fallen fortunes, was **little** difpofed to quit **the** luxurious **quiet of** rural grandeur, which was as foothing to her **difpofition, as** it was concordant with her duty. To fuch a **pair** the noify **and intoxicated joy of a** profligate court would probably have been **a** thoufand times more painful than all the wants of their late chilling, but calm, poverty. They came not, therefore, to palaces **and** levees; but amufed themfelves in the country **with** literature and the arts. **This** folitary **ftate,** this innocent magnificence, feems to have afforded contempt and jefts to the fophifticated mob of diffolute wits, who crowded round **King** Charles **II.** Thefe momentary **buzzers in the** artificial funfhine **of the regal** prefence, probably thought that **they, who** having the power to mix with fuperior wealth, in the bufy fcenes of high **life,** could prefer the infipid charms **of lonely** Nature, were only fit **to** be the butt **of their** ridicule! It is probable

that the memory of thefe witticifms might not
have entirely faded before the early years of
the late Lord Orford, **who might have** caught
the mantle of thefe fpritely oracles, **and** have
pronounced **on** the poor Duchefs's character
and amufements in a fimilar tone.   ·

Still **I** muft not permit myfelf to be fo far
heated **by** my fubject, as to furrender the advantages **of a** juft but candid difcrimination.
Her **Grace** had, as **I** conceive, talents, as well
as virtues, which raifed her above the multi-
tude, much higher than her **rank. Her** powers,
with the aid of a little more arrangement, of
fomething more of fcholaftic polifh, and of **a**
moderate exertion of maturer judgment, might
have produced writings, which pofterity would
have efteemed both for their inftruction and
amufement. **But I** muft admit that fhe wanted
the primary qualities **of** genius.   She was
neither fublime nor pathetic.   She had not
the talent of feizing that *felection* of circum-
ftances, of touching by a few fingle ftrokes
thofe chords, which, through **the force of**
affociation in our ideas, calls **up at** once whole
pictures ! Imitators, and they whofe poetical

faculties **are not** genuine, multiply images, by which, while they think they are excelling their models, deſtroy the whole charm.

Her Grace wanted taſte ; ſhe knew not what to obtrude, and what to leave out. She **pours** forth every thing with an undiſtinguiſh-ing hand, and mixes **the** ſerious, **the** collo-quial, and even the **vulgar, in** a manner which cannot **be defended. In** the " *Life*," how-ever, now reprinted, this great **fault is leſs** apparent **than in any other of her** compoſi-tions.

But **we muſt not** compare **theſe** compoſi-tions with the more refined exactneſs **of later** times. In thoſe **days** what female writer was there, who could endure the critical acumen of the preſent period? Who now reads Mrs. Katharine Phillips, better known by her **poetical** name of *Orinda?* And Mrs. Behn, **who** lived ſomewhat later, is **more** remarkable **for** her licentiouſneſs than **for** any better quality. **Even** of Mrs. Killegrew, **the** encomium beſtowed by Dr. Johnſon[1] is

---

[1] In " The Life of Dryden."

generally thought to be undeferved. The Countefs of Pembroke, Lady Carew, Lady Wrothe, and a few others fucceeded; but their productions are now unnoticed, except by a few black-letter literati.

A True Relation of my Birth, Breeding, and Life.[1]

By Margaret, Duchess of Newcastle.

Y father was a Gentleman, which Title is grounded and given by Merit, not by princes; and 'tis the act of Time,[2] not Favour: and though my Father was not a

---

[1] [The notes are thofe of Sir Egerton Brydges, and I am not refponfible for them. The text of the Lee Priory Prefs reprint is full of typographical blunders, which, by careful collation with the rare copy in the Britifh Mufeum, have been corrected.]

[2] This remark, and fomething like this expreffion, had been already ufed by Lord Bacon, with regard to old nobility. If rank, ftation, or wealth, obtained by a low man, were commonly the refult of merit, the neweft honours would be the moft worthy of refpect; but as it

Peer of the Realm, yet there were few Peers who had much greater **Eſtates,** or lived more noble therewith : yet at that time great Titles were to be ſold,[1] and not at **ſo high** rates, but **that his Eſtate** might have eaſily purchaſed, **and was** preſt **for to** take ; but my Father did not eſteem Titles, **unleſs** they were gained by Heroick Aĉtions ; and **the** Kingdome being **in a happy Peace** with all other Nations, and **in itſelf** being governed **by a wife King, King James, there was** no Employments for heroick Spirits ; and **towards the latter** end of Queen Elizabeths reign, **as** ſoon as **he came** to Mans eſtate, he unfortunately fortunately killed **one** Mr. **Brooks** in a ſingle Duel ; for

---

is too often otherwiſe, **and** wealth is more apt **to** follow narrow cunning, **and** perhaps fraud, than generous in-duſtry or ſkill, and titles, inſtead **of** being the **recom-**penſe of generally-admitted worth or talents, too often flow **from an individual** aĉt **of** whim or intereſt by a corrupt Miniſter, the diſtinĉtions which have been created by Time, **are, on the** whole, more worthy of eſteem **and** admiration, than thoſe **which** favour has procured **to** the preſent poſſeſſor.

 [1] This relates **to the reign of** King **James.** The faĉt is a matter **of** general, **not ſecret** hiſtory, and may be found **even in** the pages **of** Hume, which are generally deficient in minute details.

my father by the Laws of Honour could do
no lefs then call him to the field, to queftion
him for an injury he did him, where their
Swords were to difpute, and one or both of
their lives to decide the argument, wherein
my Father had the better; and though my
Father by Honour challengd him, with
Valour fought him, and in Juftice killed him,
yet he fuffered more then any Perfon of
Quality ufually doth in cafes of Honour; for
though the Laws be rigorous, yet the prefent
Princes moft commonly are gratious in thofe
misfortunes, efpecially to the injured: but
my Father found it not, for his exile was
from the time of his misfortunes to Queen
Elizabeths death; for the Lord Cobham [1]
being then a great man with Queen Eliza-

---

[1] This was the Lord Cobham, whofe fubfequent mif-
fortunes, condemnation, lofs of eftate, long imprifon-
ment, and death in miferable poverty, as a Principal in
what is called *Raleigh's Plot,* have been too often related
to need repetition. See more efpecially " *Memoirs of
King James's Peers,*" 8vo. 1804. It feems aftonifhing,
though the fact ftands on various authorities, that Cobham, weak as he was both in head and heart, fhould
ever have been a favourite of the bold and magnanimous
Queen.

beth, and **this** Gentleman, Mr. Brooks, a kind of a Favourite, and as I take it Brother to the then L. Cobham, which made Queen Elizabeth fo fevere, not to pardon **him**: but King James of blefled memory gracioufly gave him his Pardon, and leave to return home to his Native Country, wherein he lived happily, and died peaceably, leaving a Wife and eight Children, three Sons, and five Daughters, I being the youngeft Child he had, and an Infant when he died.

As for my breeding, **it was** according to my Birth, and the Nature of my Sex; for my Birth was not loft in my Breeding, for as my Sifters was or had been bred, fo was I in Plenty, or rather with fuperfluity; Likewife we were bred Virtuoufly, Modeftly, Civilly, Honourably, and on honeft principles: as for plenty, we had not only, for Neceffity, Conveniency, **and** Decency, but for delight and pleafure **to a** fuperfluity; 'tis true we did not riot, but we lived orderly; **for** riot, **even in** Kings' Courts and Princes' Palaces, brings ruin without content or pleafure, when order **in lefs fortunes fhall live more** plentifully and **delicioufly then** Princes, that lives in a hurlie-

burlie, as I may terme it, in which they are
feldom well ferved, for diforder obftructs;
befides, it doth difguft life, diftract the appe-
tites, and yield no true relifh to the fences;
for Pleafure, Delight, Peace and Felicitie,
live in method and temperance.

As for our garments, my Mother did not
only delight to fee us neat and cleanly, fine
and gay, but rich and coftly; maintaining us
to the height of her eftate, but not beyond it;
for we were fo far from being in debt, before
thefe warrs, as we were rather beforehand
with the world; buying all with ready money,
not on the fcore; for although after my
fathers death the Eftate was divided between
my Mother and her Sonns, paying fuch a fum
of money for Portions to her Daughters,
either at the day of their marriage, or when
they fhould come to age; yet by reafon fhe
and her children agreed with a mutual confent, all their affairs were managed fo well,
as fhe lived not in a much lower condition
than when my father lived; 'tis true, my
mother might have increaft her daughters
Portions by a thrifty fparing, yet fhe chofe to
beftow it on our breeding, honeft pleafures,

and harmlefs delights, out of an opinion, that if fhe bred us with needy neceffitie, it might chance to create in us fharking quallities, mean thoughts, and bafe actions, which fhe knew my Father, as well as herfelf did abhor: likewife we were bred tenderly, for my Mother Naturally did ftrive, to pleafe and delight her children, not to crofs or torment them, terrifying them with threats, or lafhing them with flavifh whips, but inftead of threats, reafon was ufed to perfuade us, and inftead of lafhes, the deformities of vice was difcovered, and the graces and virtues were prefented unto us, alfo we were bred with refpectful attendance, every one being feverally waited upon, and all her fervants in generall ufed the fame refpect to her children, (even thofe that were very young) as they did to her felf; for fhe fufferd not her fervants, either to be rude before us, or to domineer over us, which all vulgar fervants are apt, and ofttimes which fome have leave to do; like-wife fhe never fuffered the vulgar Serving-men to be in the Nurfery among the Nurfe-Maids, left their rude love-making might do unfeemly actions, or fpeak unhandfome words

in the prefence of her children, **knowing that**
youth is apt to take **infection by** ill **examples,**
having not the reafon of diftinguifhing good
from bad, neither **were we** fufferd to have
any familiaritie with the vulgar fervants, or
converfation : yet caufed us to demean our
felves with an humble civillity towards them,
as they **with** a dutifull refpect to us, not becaufe they **were** fervants were we fo referved ;
for many Noble Perfons are forced to ferve
through neceffitie ; but by reafon the vulgar
fort of fervants, are as ill bred **as** meanly
born, giving children ill examples, and worfe
counfel.

As for tutors, although we had for all forts
of vertues,[1] as finging, dancing, playing on
mufick, reading, writing, working, and the
like, yet we were **not** kept ftrictly thereto,
they were rather for formality then benefit,
for my Mother cared not fo much for our
dancing **and** fidling, finging and prating of
feverall languages, as that we fhould be bred
virtuoufly, modeftly, **civilly,** honourably, and
on honeft principles.

---

[1] *Virtuofos,* accomplifhments.

As for my Brothers, of which I had three, I know not how they were bred, firft, they were bred when I was not capable to obferve, or before I was born; likewife the breeding of men were after different manner of ways from thofe of women: but this I know, that they loved Virtue, endeavoured Merit, prac-tic'd Juftice, and fpoke Truth; they were conftantly loyal, and truly Valiant; two of my three Brothers were excellent Soldiers, and Martial Difcipliners, being practifed therein, for though they might have lived upon their own Eftates very honourably, yet they rather chofe to ferve in the Wars under the States of Holland, than to live idly at home in Peace: my Brother, Sir Thomas Lucas, there having a Troop of Horfe; my brother, the youngeft Sir Charls Lucas ferving therein: but he ferved the States not long, for after he had been at the fiege and taking of fome Towns, he returned home again; and though he had the lefs experience, yet he was like to have proved the better Soldier, if better could have been, for naturally he had a practick Genius to the warlike arts, or Arts in War, as Natural Poets have to Poetry:

but his life was cut off before he could arrive
to the true perfection thereof; yet he writ
"A Treatife of the Arts in War," but by
reafon it was in characters, and the key thereof
loft, we cannot as yet underftand any thing
therein, at leaft not fo as to divulge it.[1] My
other Brother, the Lord Lucas, who was
Heir to my Fathers eftate, and as it were the
Father to take care of us all, is not lefs Valiant
then they were, although his fkill in the
Difcipline of War was not fo much, being
not bred therein, yet he had more fkill in the
ufe of the Sword, and is more learned in
other Arts and Sciences then they were, he
being a great Scholar, by reafon he is given
much to ftudious contemplation.[2]

Their practice was, when they met together, to exercife themfelves with fencing,
wreftling, fhooting, and fuch like exercifes,
for I obferved they did feldome hawk or hunt,
and very feldom or never dance, or play on

---

[1] See an account of Sir Charles Lucas, in "Lord
Clarendon's Hiftory."

[2] His defcendant and reprefentative, the only furviv-
ing daughter of the late Earl of Hardwicke, now enjoys
the *Barony of Lucas*, as heir to this brother.

mufick, faying it was too effeminate for Mafculine Spirits; neither had they fkill, or did
ufe to play, for ought **I could hear**, at Cards
or Dice, or the like Games, **nor given to any**
vice, as I **did** know, unlefs to love **a miftrefs**
were a crime, not that **I** know any they **had**,
but what **report** did fay, and ufually reports
are falfe, at leaft exceed the truth.

As for the paftimes of my Sifters when
they **were in the country**, **it** was to reade,
work, walk, and difcourfe **with** each other;
for though **two** of my three brothers[1] were

---

[1] Sir Thomas Lucas of St. John's, near Colchefter,
married Mary, daughter of Sir John Fermor of Efton-
Nefton, in Northamptonfhire, by whom he had Thomas
Lucas of St. John's, near Colchefter, Efq. who by
Elizabeth, daughter and coheir of John Leighton **of**
London, Gent. had three fons and five daughters, *viz.*

1. **John Lucas** of St. John's, near Colchefter, afterwards *Lord Lucas,* who married Anne, daughter of Sir
Chriftopher Neville, Kt., younger brother of the Lord
Abergavenny, by whom he had John, his fon and **heir**,
born about 1624.

2. Sir Thomas Lucas, **a** captain **in London**, who
married a daughter of Sir John Byron, **Kt.** by whom
he had a fon, Thomas.

3. Sir Charles Lucas.

4. Mary, wife of Sir Peter Killegrew, Kt.

5. Anne.

6. **Elizabeth**, wife of William Walter, Efq.

married, my Brother the Lord Lucas to a
virtuous and beautiful Lady, daughter to Sir
Chriftopher Nevil, fon to the Lord Abergavenny, and my brother Sir Thomas Lucas
to a virtuous lady of an ancient family, one Sir
John Byron's Daughter;[1] likewife, three of
my four fifters, one married Sir Peter Killegrew, the other Sir William Walter, the third
Sir Edmund Pye, the fourth as yet unmarried,
yet moft of them lived with my mother, efpecially when fhe was at her country-houfe,
living moft commonly at London half the
year, which is the Metropolitan city of England:[2] but when they were at London, they
were difperfed into feveral houfes of their
own, yet for the moft part they met every

---

7. Catherine, wife of Sir Edmund Pye of London, Kt.
8. Margaret, afterwards Duchefs of Newcaftle.*
Arms. Argent, a fefs between fix annulets, gules.

[1] Sifter to the anceftor of the prefent Lord Byron;
by which muft be corrected an error in the new Edition
of " *Collins's Peerage,*" which ftates the Duchefs to
have been the iffue of this marriage.

[2] A beautiful picture of family harmony and affection; and curious as fhewing the cuftom of the greater
gentry to pafs the winter in London even then.

---

* Harl. MSS. 1542, f. 59.

day, feafting **each** other like Job's Children.
But this unnatural **War came** like a whirl-
wind, which fell'd down their Houfes, where
fome in the Wars were crufht to death, as
my youngeft brother Sir Charls **Luças,** and
my Brother Sir Thomas Lucas; **and** though
my Brother **Sir** Thomas Lucas died not immediately of his wounds, yet a wound he received on his head in Ireland fhort'ned his
life.

But to rehearfe their Recreations.   Their
cuftoms were in Winter time to go fometimes
to Plays, **or to** ride in their Coaches about
the Streets to fee the concourfe and recourfe
of People; and in the Spring time to vifit the
Spring-garden, Hide-park, and the like places;
and fometimes they would have Mufick, and
fup in Barges **upon the Water;**[1] thefe harmlefs recreations they would pafs their time
away with; for I obferved, they did feldom
make **Vifits,** nor never went abroad with
Strangers in their Company, but onely themfelves **in a Flock** together agreeing **fo well,**
that there feemed **but one** Minde amongft

---

[1] **This is alfo a** very curious picture of manners.

them: And not onely my own Brothers and Sisters agreed fo, but my Brothers and Sisters in law, and their Children, although but young, had the like agreeable natures, and affectionable dispofitions; for to my best remembrance I do not know that ever they did fall out, or had any angry or unkind difputes. Likewife, I did obferve, that my Sifters were fo far from mingling themfelves with any other Company, that they had no familiar converfation or intimate aquaintance with the Families to which each other were linkt to by Marriage, the Family of the one being as great Strangers to the reft of my brothers and Sifters, as the Family of the other.

But fometime after this War began, I knew not how they lived; for though moft of them were in Oxford, wherein the King was, yet after the Queen went from Oxford, and fo out of England, I was parted from them; for when the Queen was in Oxford, I had a great defire to be one of her Maids of honour, hearing the Queen had not the fame number fhe was ufed to have, whereupon I wooed and won my Mother to let me go; for my Mother, being fond of all her Children, was

defirous to pleafe them, which made her confent to my requeft. But my Brothers and
Sifters feem'd not very well pleas'd, by reafon I had never been from home, nor feldome
out of their fight; for though they knew I
would not behave my felf to their, or my own
difhonour, yet they thought I might to my
difadvantage, being unexperienced in the
World, which indeed I did, for I was fo
bafhfull when I was out of my Mother's,
Brothers, and Sifters fight, whofe prefence
ufed to give me confidence, thinking I could
not do amifs whilft any one of them were by,
for I knew they would gently reform me if I
did; befides, I was ambitious they fhould
approve of my actions and behaviour, that
when I was gone from them, I was like one
that had no Foundation to ftand, or Guide to
direct me, which made me afraid, left I fhould
wander with Ignorance out of the waies of
Honour, fo that I knew not how to behave
myfelf. Befides, I had heard that the World
was apt to lay afperfions even on the innocent, for which I durft neither look up with
my eyes, nor fpeak, nor be any way fociable,
infomuch as I was thought a Natural Fool;

indeed I had not much Wit, yet I was not an Idiot, my wit was according to my years; and though I might have learnt more Wit, and advanced my Underſtanding by living in a Court, yet being dull, fearfull, and baſhfull, I neither heeded what was ſaid or practic'd, but juſt what belong'd to my loyal duty, and my own honeſt reputation; and, indeed, I was ſo afraid to diſhonour my Friends and Family by my indiſcreet actions, that I rather choſe to be accounted a Fool, then to be thought rude or wanton; in truth, my baſhfulneſs and fears made me repent my going from home to ſee the World abroad, and much I did deſire to return to my Mother again, or to my ſiſter Pye, with whom I often lived when ſhe was in London, and loved with a ſupernatural affection: but my Mother adviſed me there to ſtay, although I put her to more charges than if ſhe had kept me at home, and the more, by reaſon ſhe and my Brothers were ſequeſtered from their Eſtates, and plundered of all their Goods, yet ſhe maintained me ſo, that I was in a condition rather to lend then to borrow, which Courtiers uſually are not, being always neceſſitated by reafon of great expenfes Courts put them to. But my Mother faid, it would **be a dif**grace for **me** to return out of the Court fo foon after I was placed; fo I continued almoft two years, until fuch time as I was married from thence; for my Lord the Marquis of Newcaftle did approve of thofe bafhful fears which many condemn'd, and would choofe fuch **a** Wife **as he** might bring to his own humours, and not fuch an one **as was** wedded to felf-conceit, **or one that** had been **tem**per'd to the humours of another; for which he wooed me for his **Wife** ; and though **I did** dread Marriage, and fhunn'd mens companies **as** much as I could, yet I could not, nor had **not** the power to refufe him, by reafon my Affections were fix'd on him, and he was the onely Perfon **I** ever was in love with: Neither was I afhamed to own it, but gloried therein, for **it was** not Amorous Love, I never was infected therewith, it is a Difeafe, **or a** Paffion, or both, I only know by relation, not by experience ; neither could Title, Wealth, Power, or Perfon entice me to love ; **but my** Love was honeft and honourable, being **placed** upon Merit, which Affection joy'd at the fame of his Worth, pleas'd with delight in his Wit, proud of the refpects he ufed to me, and triumphing in the affections he profeft for me, which affections he hath confirmed to me by a deed of time, feal'd by conftancy, and affigned by an unalterable decree of his promife; which makes me happy in defpight of Fortune's frowns; for though Misfortunes may and do oft diffolve bafe, wilde, loofe, and ungrounded affections, yet fhe hath no power of thofe that are united either by Merit, Juftice, Gratitude, Duty, Fidelity, or the like; and though my Lord hath loft his Eftate, and banifh'd out of his Country for his Loyalty to his King and Country, yet neither defpifed Poverty, nor pinching Neceffity could make him break the Bonds of Friendfhip, or weaken his Loyal Duty to his King or Country.[1]

But not onely the family I am linkt to is ruin'd, but the Family from which I fprung, by thefe unhappy Wars; which ruine my

---

[1] The whole of this long paffage is in fentiment, and in the fpirit of the language, (though fome of the parts of it are awkwardly conftructed) highly amiable, eloquent, and affecting.

Mother lived to fee, and then died, having lived a Widow many years, for fhe never forgot my Father fo as to marry again ; indeed, he remain'd fo lively in her memory, and her grief was fo lafting, as fhe never mention'd his name, though fhe fpoke often of him, but love and grief caufed tears to flow, and tender fighs to rife, mourning in fad complaints ; fhe made her houfe her Cloyfter, inclofing herfelf, as it were therein, for fhe feldom went abroad, unlefs to Church ; but thefe unhappy Wars forc'd her out, by reafon fhe and her children were loyall to the King; for which they plundered her and my Brothers of all their Goods, Plate, Jewels, Money, Corn, Cattle, and the like, cut down their Woods, pull'd down their Houfes, and fequeftered them from their Lands and Livings ; but in fuch misfortunes my Mother was of an heroick fpirit, in fuffering patiently where there is no remedy, or to be induftrious where fhe thought fhe could help : She was of a grave Behaviour, and had fuch a Majeftic Grandeur, as it were continually hung about her, that it would ftrike a kind of an awe to the beholders, and command refpect from the

rudeſt ; I mean the rudeſt of civiliz'd people,
I mean not ſuch Barbarous people as plundered her, and uſed her cruelly, for they
would have pulled God out of Heaven, had
they had power, as they did Royaltie out of
his Throne : alſo her beauty was beyond the
ruin of time, for ſhe had a well favoured
lovelineſs in her face, a pleaſing ſweetneſs in
her countenance, and a well-temper'd complexion, as neither too red nor too pale, even
to her dying hour, although in years, and
by her dying, one might think death was
enamoured with her, for he imbraced her in
a ſleep, and ſo gently, as if he were afraid to
hurt her : alſo ſhe was an affectionate Mother,
breeding her children with a moſt induſtrious
care, and tender love, and having eight children, three ſons and five daughters, there
was not any one crooked, or any ways de-
formed, neither were they dwarfiſh, or of a
Giant-like ſtature, but every ways proportion-
able ; likewiſe well featured, cleer com-
plexions, brown haires, but ſome lighter than
others, ſound teeth, ſweet breaths, plain
ſpeeches, tunable voices, I mean not ſo much
to ſing as in ſpeaking, as not ſtuttering, nor

wharling in the throat, or fpeaking through
the nofe, or hoarfly, unlefs they had a cold, or
fqueakingly, which impediments many have :
neither were their voices of too low a ftrain,
or too high, but their notes and words were
tuneable and timely : I hope this Truth will
not offend my Readers, and left they fhould
think I am a partial Regifter, I dare not com-
mend my Sifters, as to fay they were handfome ; although many would fay they were
very handfome : but this I dare fay, their
Beautie, if any they had, was not fo lafting as
my Mothers, Time making fuddener ruin in
their faces than in hers ; likewife my Mother
was a good Miftrifs to her fervants, taking
care of her fervants in their ficknefs, not
fparing any coft fhe was able to beftow for
their recovery : neither did fhe exact more
from them in their health then what they with
eafe or rather like paftime could do : fhe
would freely pardon a fault, and forget an
injury, yet fometimes fhe would be angry ;
but never with her children, the fight of them
would pacify her, neither would fhe be angry
with others, but when fhe had caufe, as with
negligent or knavifh fervants, that would

lavifhly or **unneceffarily wafte, or** fubtily, and
thievifhly **fteal, and though** fhe would often
complain that **her** family **was** too great for
her weak Management, **and** often preft my
Brother to take it upon him, yet I obferve fhe
took a pleafure, and fome little pride, in the
governing thereof: fhe was very fkilful in
Leafes, and fetting of lands, and Court-keep-
ing, ordering of Stewards, and the like affairs:
alfo I obferved, that my mother, nor Brothers,
before thefe wars, had **ever** any Law-fuites,
but what an Attorney difpatched in **a** Term
with fmall **coft,** but if they had, **it was** more
than I knew **of, but, as I** faid, my Mother
lived to fee the **ruin of** her children, **in** which
was her ruin, and then dyed : **my** brother Sir
Thomas **Lucas** foon after, my brother Sir
Charles Lucas after him, being fhot to death
for his loyall Service, for he was moft conftantly Loyal and Courageoufly active, indeed
he had a fuperfluity **of** courage ; **My** eldeft
fifter died fometime **before** my Mother, her
death being, **as I believe,** haftned through
grief of her onely daughter, on which fhe
doted, being very pretty, fweet natured, and
had an extraordinary wit **for** her age, fhe

dying of a Confumption, my fifter, her Mother,
died fome half a year after of the fame difeafe,
and though time is apt to wafte remembrance
as a confumptive body, or to wear it out like
a garment into raggs, or to moulder it into
duft; yet I find the naturall affections I have
for my friends, are beyond the length, ftrength,
and power of time : for I fhall lament the
lofs fo long as I live, alfo the lofs of my Lords
noble Brother, which died not long after I returned from England, he being then fick of an
Ague, whofe favours and my thankfulnefs, ingratitude fhall never disjoyne; for I will build
his Monument of truth, though I cannot of
Marble, and hang my tears and Scutchions on
his Tombe.   He was nobly generous, wifely
valliant, naturally civill, honeftly kind, truly
loving, Virtuoufly temperate; his promife
was like a fixt decree, his words were deftiny,
his life was holy, his difpofition milde, his behaviour courteous, his difcourfe pleafing, he
had a ready wit and a fpacious knowledge, a
fettled judgment, a cleer underftanding, a
rationall infight; he was learned in all Arts
and Sciences, but efpecially in the Mathematicks, in which ftudy he fpent moft part of

his time ; and though his tongue preacht **not**
Moral Philofophy, yet **his** life taught **it,** indeed he was fuch a perfon, that he might have
been a pattern for all Mankind to take :[1] he
loved my Lord his brother with a doting affection, as my Lord did him, for whofe **fake I**
fuppofe he was fo nobly generous, carefully
kind, and refpectfull to me ; for I dare not
challenge his favours as to my **felf,** having
not merits to deferve them, he was **for a** time
the preferver of my life, **for** after **I was**
married fome two or three years, my **Lord**
travell'd out of France, from the City of
Paris, in which City he refided the time **he**
was there, fo **went into** Holland, **to a** Town
called Rotterdam, **in** which place he ftayed
fome fix months ; from thence he returned to
Brabant, unto the City of Antwerp, which
city **we** paft through, when we went into
Holland, **and** in that City my Lord fettled
himfelf and Family, choofing it for the moft
pleafanteft, and quieteft place to retire himfelf
and ruined fortunes in : but after we had re-

----

[1] Sir Charles Cavendifh's character is drawn in equally
glowing colours by Lord Clarendon.

main'd fome time therein, we grew extremely
neceffitated, Tradefmen being there not fo
rich as to truft my Lord **for** fo much, or fo
long, as thofe of France ; yet they were fo
civill, kind and charitable, as to truft him, for
as much as they were able ; but at laft neceffity inforced me **to** return into England to
feek for reliefe ; for I hearing my Lord's
Eftate, amongft the reft of many more eftates,
was to be fold, and that the wives of the
owners fhould have an allowance therefrom,
it gave me hopes I fhould receive **a** benefit
thereby ; fo being accompanied **with** my Lords
only brother Sir Charles Cavendifh, who was
commanded to return, to live therein, or to
lofe his Eftate, which Eftate he was forced to
buy with a great Compofition before he could
enjoy any part thereof ; fo over I went, but
when I came there I found their hearts as
hard as my fortunes, and their Natures as
cruel as my miferies, for they fold all my
Lords Eftate, which was a very great one,[1]
and gave me not any part thereof, or any al-

---

[1] I think fhe eftimates it in her " *Life of the Duke* "
at upwards of £22,000 **a year,** which is equal at leaft to
£150,000 a year at this time.

lowance thereout, which few or no other was
fo hardly **dealt withall**; indeed, **I did not**
ftand as a beggar **at the Parliament** doore, for
I never was at the **Parliamente** Houfe, nor
ftood **I ever** at the doore, as **I do know,** or
can remember, I am fure, not as a Petitioner,
neither did I haunt **the** Committees, for I
never was at any, as a Petitioner, but one **in**
my life, which was called Gold-fmith's-Hall,
but I received neither gold **nor filver** from
them, only an abfolute refufall, I fhould have
no fhare of my Lords Eftate; for my brother,
the Lord Lucas, did **claim in my** behalf fuch
a part **of** my **Lords** Eftate as wives had **al-**
lowed them, but **they told** him, that **by** reafon
I was married fince my Lord **was** made a
Delinquent, I could have nothing, nor fhould
have any thing, he being the greateft Traitor
to the State, which was to be the moft loyall
Subject **to his King and** Country: but I whif-
peringly fpoke to my brother **to conduct** me
out of that ungentlemanly place, **fo** without
fpeaking to them one word good **or** bad, I returned to my Lodgings, **& as** that Committee
was the firft, fo was it **the** laft, I ever was at
as a Petitioner; 'tis true I went fometimes to

Drury Houſe to inquire how the land was
ſold, but no other ways, although ſome reported I was at the Parliament Houſe, and at
this Committee and at that Committee, and
what I ſhould ſay, and how I was anſwered ;
but the Cuſtomes of England being changed
as well as the Laws, where Women become
Pleaders, Attornies, Petitioners and the like,
running about with their ſeverall Cauſes, complaining of their ſeverall grievances, exclaim-
ing againſt their ſeverall enemies, bragging of
their ſeverall favours they receive from the
powerfull ; thus Trafficing with idle words
bring in falſe reports and vain diſcourſe ; for
the truth is, our Sex doth nothing but juſtle
for the Preheminence of words, I mean not
for ſpeaking well, but ſpeaking much, as they
do for the preheminence of place, words
ruſhing againſt words, thwarting and croſſing
each other, and pulling with reproches, ſtriv-
ing to throw each other down with diſgrace,
thinking to advance themſelves thereby ; but
if our Sex would but well conſider, and rationally ponder, they will perceive and finde, that
it is neither words nor place that can advance
them, but worth and merit : nor can words

or place difgrace them, but inconftancy and boldnefs: for an honeft Heart, a noble Soul, a chafte Life, and a true fpeaking Tongue, is the Throne, Sceptre, Crown, and Footftoole, that advances them to an honourable renown, I mean not Noble, Virtuous, Difcreet, and worthy Perfons, whom neceffity did enforce to fubmit, comply, and follow their own fuites, but fuch as had nothing to lofe, but made it their trade to folicite; but I difpairing being pofitively denied at Goldfmiths Hall,—befides I had a firm faith, or ftrong opinion, that the pains was more than the gains, and being un-practifed in publick employments, unlearned in their uncouth Ways, ignorant of the Hu-mours and Difpofitions of thofe perfons to whom I was to addrefs my fuit, and not know-ing where the Power lay, and being not a good flatterer, I did not trouble myfelf or petition my enemies; befides I am naturally Bafhful, not that I am afhamed of my minde or body, my Birth or Breeding, my Actions or Fortunes, for my Bafhfulnefs is in my Nature, not for any crime, and though I have ftrived and reafoned with myfelf, yet that which is inbred, I find is difficult to root out,

but I do not find that my Bashfulnefs is concerned with the Qualities of the Perfons, but
the number, for were I enter amongft a company of Lazaroufes, I fhould be as much out
of countenance, as if they were all Cefars or
Alexanders, Cleopatras or Queen Didoes;
neither do I find my Bashfulnefs rifeth fo
often in Blufhes, as contracts my Spirits to a
chill palenefs, but the beft of it is, moft commonly it foon vanifheth away, and many times
before it can be perceived, and the more
foolifh, or unworthy, I conceive the company
to be, the worfe I am, and the beft remedy I
ever found was, is to perfuade myfelf that all
thofe Perfons I meet are wife and vertuous;
the reafon I take to be is, that the wife and
vertuous cenfure leaft, excufe moft, praife beft,
efteem rightly, judge juftly, behave themfelves
civilly, demeane themfelves refpectfully, and
fpeake modeftly, when fools or unworthy perfons are apt to commit abfurdities, as to be
bold, rude, uncivill both in words and actions,
forgetting or not well underftanding themfelves, or the company they are with; and
though I never met fuch forts of ill bred creatures, yet Naturally I have fuch an Averfion

to such kinde of people, as I am afraid to meet them, as children are afraid of spirits, or those that are afraid to see or meet Devills; which makes me think this Naturall defect in me, if it be a defect, is rather a fear than a bashfulness, but whatsoever it is, I find it troublesome, for it hath many times obstructed the passage of my speech, and perturbed my Naturall actions, forcing a constrainedness or unusual motions, but, however, since it is rather a fear of others than a bashfull distrust of my self, I despaire of a perfect cure, unless Nature as well as Human governments could be civilized and brought into a Methodicall order, ruling the words and actions with a supreme power of reason, and the authority of discretion: but a rude nature is worse than a brute nature, by so much more as man is better than beast, but those that are of civil natures and gentle dispositions, are as much nearer to celestiall creatures, as those that are of rude or cruell are to Devills: but in fine, after I had been in England, a year and a half, in which time I gave some half a score visits, and went with my Lords brother to hear Music

in one Mr. Lawes[1] his houfe, three or four
times, as alfo fome three or four times to
Hide Park with my fifters, to take the aire,
elfe I never ftirr'd out of my lodgings, unlefs
to fee my Brothers and Sifters, nor feldom
did I drefs my felf, as taking no delight to
adorn my felf, fince he I onely defired to
pleafe was abfent, although report did drefs
me in a hundred feverall fafhions : 'tis true
when I did drefs myfelf, I did endeavour to
do it to my beft becoming, both in refpect to
my felf and thofe I went to vifit, or chanc't
to meet, but after I had been in England a
year and a half, part of which time I writ a
Book of Poems, and a little Book called my
Philofophical Fancies, to which I have writ a
large addition, fince I returned out of England, befides this book and one other : as for
my book intitled *The Worlds Ollio*, I writ moft
part of it before I went into England, but
being not of a merry, although not of a froward
or peevifh difpofition, became very Melancholy, by reafon I was from my Lord, which

---

[1] Lawes was a celebrated mufical compofer, the friend
of Milton.

made my mind fo reftlefs, as it did break my
fleeps, and diftemper my health, with which
growing impatient of a longer delay, I refolved
to return, **although I** was grieved to leave Sir
Charles, my Lord's Brother, **he** being fick of
an ague, of which ficknefs he died : for though
his ague was cur'd, **his** life was decayed, he
being not of a ftrong conftitution could not, **as**
it did prove, recover his health, for the dreggs
of his Ague did put out the Lamp of his life,
yet Heaven knows **I** did not think his life was
fo near to an end, for his Doctor had great
hopes of his perfect recovery, and by reafon
he was to go into the Country for change of
aire, where I fhould have been a trouble,
rather than any ways ferviceable, befides, more
charge the longer I ftayd, for which I made
the more haft to return to my Lord, with
whom I had rather be as a poor begger, than
to be Miftrefs of **the** world abfented from
him ; yet, Heaven hitherto hath kept **us, and**
though Fortune hath been crofs, yet we do
fubmit, and are both content with what is,
and cannot be mended, and are fo prepared
that the worft of fortunes fhall not afflict our
minds, fo as **to** make us unhappy, howfoever

it doth pinch our lives with poverty ; for, if Tranquillity lives in an honeſt mind, the mind lives in Peace, although the body ſuffer : but Patience hath armed us, and Miſery hath tried us, and finds us Fortune-proof, for the truth is, my Lord is a perſon whoſe Humour is neither extravagantly merry, nor unneceſſarily ſad, his Mind is above his Fortune, as his Generoſity is above his purſe, his Courage above danger, his Juſtice above bribes, his Friendſhip above ſelf-intereſt, his Truth too firm for falſehood, his Temperance beyond temptation, his Converſation is pleaſing and affable, his Wit is quick, and his Judgment is ſtrong, diſtinguiſhing cleerly without clouds of miſtakes, diſſecting truth, ſo as it juſtly admits not of diſputes : his diſcourſe is always new upon the occaſion, without troubling the hearers with old Hiſtoricall relations, nor ſtuft with uſeleſs ſentences, his behaviour is manly without formallity, and free without conſtraint, and his minde hath the ſame freedom : his Nature is noble, and his Diſpoſition ſweet, his Loyaltie is proved by his publick ſervice for his King and Countrey, by his often hazard-ing of his life, by the loſſe of his Eſtate, and

the banifhment of his Perfon, by his neceffitated Condition, and his conftant and patient
fuffering ; but, howfoever our fortunes are,
we are both content, fpending our time harm-
lefsly, for my Lord pleafeth himfelf with the
Management of fome few Horfes, and exercifes himfelf with the ufe of the Sword; which
two Arts he hath brought by his ftudious
thoughts, rationall experience, and induftrious
practice, to an abfolute perfection: and though
he hath taken as much pains in thofe arts,
both by ftudy and practice, as Chimifts for
the Phylofopher's Stone, yet he hath this advantage of them, that he hath found the right
and the truth thereof and therein, which
Chimifts never found in their Art, and I
believe never will : alfo he recreates himfelf
with his pen, writing what his Wit dictates to
him, but I pafs my time rather with fcribling
than writing, with words than wit, not that I
fpeak much, becaufe I am addicted to contemplation, unlefs I am with my Lord, yet then
I rather attentively liften to what he fayes,
than impertinently fpeak, yet when I am
writing, and fad faind Stories, or ferious humours, or melancholy paffions, I am forc'd

many times to exprefs them with the tongue before I can **write them** with the pen, by reafon thofe thoughts **that are** fad, ferious, **and** melancholy, are apt **to contract and** to **draw** too much back, which oppreffion doth **as** it were overpower or fmother the concep- tion in the **brain,** but when fome of thofe **thoughts are fent** out in words, they give the reft more liberty **to place** themfelves in a more **methodicall order,** marching **more** regularly **with my pen, on the ground of white** paper, but my letters feem **rather as a** ragged rout, than a well armed body, **for the brain being** quicker **in creating** than **the hand in writing,** or **the memory in** retaining, **many fancies** are loft, **by reafon they ofttimes outrun the pen;** where **I, to** keep **fpeed in the Race, write** fo faft **as I ftay not fo long as to** write my letters plain, infomuch as fome have taken my hand- writing for fome ftrange character, & being accuftomed fo to do, I cannot now write very plain, when I ftrive **to write my** beft; indeed, my ordinary hand-writing **is** fo **bad as** few **can read it, fo as to** write it fair for the Prefs, **but however,** that little **wit I** have, it delights **me to fcribble it out,** and difperfe it about, for I being addicted from my childhood to contemplation rather than converſation, to ſolitarineſs rather than ſociety, to melancholy rather than mirth, to write with the pen than to work with a needle, paſſing my time with harmeleſs fancies, their company being pleaſing, their converſation innocent, in which I take ſuch pleaſure, as I neglect my health, for it is as great a grief to leave their ſociety, as a joy to be in their company, my only trouble is, leſt my brain ſhould grow barren, or that the root of my fancies ſhould become inſipid, withering into a dull ſtupidity for want of maturing ſubjects to write on : for I being of a lazy nature, and not of an active diſpoſition, as ſome are that love to journey from town to town, from place to place, from houſe to houſe, delighting in variety of company, making ſtill one where the greateſt number is ; likewiſe in playing at Cards, or any other Games, in which I neither have practiſed, nor have I any ſkill therein : as for Dancing, although it be a graceful art, and becometh unmarried perſons well, yet for thoſe that are married, it is too light an action, diſagreeing with the gravity thereof ; and for Revelling I am of too dull a nature, to make one in a merry fociety; as for Feafting, it would neither agree with my humour or conftitution, for my diet is for the moft part fparing, as a little boiled chickin, or the like, my drink moft commonly water, for though I have an indifferent good appetite, yet I do often faft, out of an opinion that if I fhould eat much, and exercife little, which I do, onely walking a flow pace in my chamber, whilft my thoughts run apace in my brain, fo that the motions of my minde hinders the active exercifes of my body : for fhould I Dance or Run, or Walk apace, I fhould Dance my Thoughts out of Meafure, Run my Fancies out of Breath, and tread out the Feet of my Numbers, but becaufe I would not bury myfelf quite from the fight of the world, I go fometimes abroad, feldome to vifit, but only in my Coach about the Town, or about fome of the ftreets, which we call here a Tour, where all the chief of the Town goe to fee and to be feen, likewife all ftrangers of what quallity foever, as all great Princes or Queens that make any fhort ftay : for this Town being a paffage or thorough-fare to moft parts, caufeth many

times perfons of great **quallity to be here,**
though not as inhabitants, yet to lodge for
fome fhort time ; and all fuch, as I faid, take
a delight, **or at left** goe to fee the cuftome
thereof, **which moft** Cities **of** note in Europe
for all I can **hear,** hath fuch like recreations
for the effeminate Sex, although for my part
I had rather fit at home and write, or walk,
as I faid, in my chamber and contemplate ;
but I hold neceffary fometimes **to** appear
abroad, befides I do find, that feverall objects
do bring new materialls for my thoughts and
fancies to build **upon, yet** I muft **fay** this in
the behalf of my thoughts, that **I** never found
them idle ; **for** if the fenfes brings no work in,
they will work of themfelves, like filk-wormes
that fpinns out of their own bowels ; Neither
can I fay I think the time tedious, when I am
alone, **fo I** be near **my** Lord, and know he **is**
well.

But now I have declared to my Readers,
my Birth, Breeding, **and** Actions, to this part
of my Life, I mean **the** material parts, for
fhould I write every particular, as my childifh
fports and **the like, it would** be ridiculous and
tedious ; but I have been honorably born and

Nobly match't; I have been bred to elevated thoughts, not to a dejected fpirit, my life hath been ruled with Honefty, attended by Modefty, and directed by Truth : but fince I have writ in generall thus far of my life, I think it fit, I fhould fpeak fomething of my Humour, particular Practice and Difpofition; as for my Humour, I was from my childhood given to contemplation, being more taken or delighted with thoughts then in converfation with a fociety, in fo much as I would walk two or three hours, and never reft, in a mufing, confidering, contemplating manner, reafoning with my felf of every thing my fenfes did prefent, but when I was in the company of my Naturall friends, I was very attentive of what they faid or did; but for ftrangers I regarded not much what they faid, but many times I did obferve their actions, whereupon my Reafon as Judge, and my Thoughts as Accufers, or excufers, or approvers and commenders, did plead, or appeal to accufe, or complain thereto ; alfo I never took delight in clofets, or cabinets of toys, but in the variety of fine clothes, and fuch toys as onely were to adorn my perfon : likewife I had a naturall ftupidity towards the learning of any other Language than my native tongue, for I could fooner and with more facility underftand the fenfe, then remember the words, and for want of fuch memory makes me fo unlearned in foreign Languages as I am : as for my practife, I was never very active, by reafon I was given fo much to contemplation; befides my brothers and fifters were for the moft part ferious, and ftaid in their actions, not given .to fport nor play, nor dance about, whofe company I keeping, made me fo too : but I obferved, that although their actions were ftay'd, yet they would be very merry amongft themfelves, delighting in each others company : alfo they would in their Difcourfe exprefs the generall actions of the world, judging, condemning, approving, commending, as they thought good, and with thofe that were innocently harmlefs, they would make themfelves merry therewith ; as for my ftudie of books it was little, yet I chofe rather to read, than to imploy my time in any other work, or practife, and when I read what I underftood not, I would afk my brother, the Lord Lucas, he being learned, the fenfe or meaning thereof, but my ferious ftudy could not be much, by reafon I took great delight in attiring, fine dreffing, and fafhions, efpecially fuch fafhions as I did invent myfelf, not taking that pleafure in fuch fafhions as was invented by others: alfo I did diflike any fhould follow my Fafhions, for I always took delight in a fingularity, even in accoutrements of habits, but whatfoever I was addicted to, either in fafhion of Cloths, contemplation of Thoughts, actions of Life, they were Lawful, Honeft, Honourable, and Modeft, of which I can avouch to the world with a great confidence, becaufe it is a pure Truth; as for my Difpofition, it is more inclining to be melancholy than merry, but not crabbed or peevifhly melancholy, but foft, melting, folitary, and contemplating melancholy; and I am apt to weep rather than laugh, not that I do often either of them; alfo I am tender natured, for it troubles my Confcience to kill a fly, and the groans of a dying Beaft ftrike my Soul: alfo where I place a particular affection, I love extraordinarily and conftantly, yet not fondly, but foberly and obfervingly; not to hang about them as a trouble, but to wait upon them as a fervant, but this affection will take no root, but where I think or find

merit, and have leave both from Divine and
Morall Laws; yet I find this paſſion ſo trouble-
ſome, as it is the only torment to my life, for
fear any evill misfortune or accident, or ſick-
neſs, or death, ſhould come unto them, inſomuch as I am never freely at reſt : Likewiſe
I am gratefull, for I never received a curteſie
but I am impatient, and troubled untill I can
return it; alſo I am Chaſte, both by Nature
and Education, inſomuch as I do abhorre
an unchaſt thought: likewiſe I am ſeldom
angry, as my ſervants may witneſs for me, for
I rather choſe to ſuffer ſome inconveniences
than diſturbe my thoughts, which makes me
winke many times at their faults; but when
I am angry, I am very angry, but yet it is
ſoon over, and I am eaſily pacified, if it be
not ſuch an injury as may create a hate;
neither am I apt to be exceptious or jealous;
but if I have the leſt ſymptome of this paſſion,
I declare it to thoſe it concerns, for I never
let it ly ſmothering in my breaſt to breed a
malignant diſeaſe in the minde, which might
break out into extravagant paſſions, or railing
ſpeeches, or indiſcreet actions; but I examin
moderately, reaſon ſoberly, and plead gently

x

in my own behalf, through a defire to keep thofe affections I had, or at leaft thought to have; and truly I am fo vain, as to be fo felf-conceited, or fo naturally partial, to think my friends have as much reafon to love me as another, fince none can love more fincerely than I, and it were an injuftice to prefer a fainter affection, or to efteem the Body more than the Minde; likewife I am neither fpitefull, envious, nor malicious; I repine not at the gifts that Nature, or Fortune beftows upon others, yet I am a great Emulator; for though I wifh none worfe than they are, yet it is lawful for me to wifh my felf the beft, and to do my honeft endeavour thereunto; for I think it no crime to wifh myfelf the exacteft of Natures works, my thred of life the longeft, my Chain of Deftinie the ftrongeft, my mind the peaceableft; my life the pleafanteft, my death the eafieft, and the greateft Saint in Heaven; alfo to do my endeavour, fo far as honour and honefty doth allow of, to be the higheft on Fortunes Wheele, and to hold the wheele, from turning, if I can, and if it be commendable to wifh anothers good, it were a fin not to wifh my own; for as Envie is a vice, fo Emulation is a Virtue, but Emulation is in the way to Ambition, or indeed it is a Noble Ambition, but I fear my Ambition inclines to vain-glory, for I am very ambitious; yet 'tis neither for **Beauty, Wit,** Titles, Wealth, or Power, **but** as they are fteps· **to** raife me to Fames Tower, which is **to** live by remembrance in after-ages: likewife I am, that the vulgar calls, proud, not out of a felf-conceit, or to flight or condemn any, but fcorning to do a bafe or mean act, and dif-daining rude or unworthy perfons; infomuch, that if I fhould find any **that were** rude, **or** too bold, I fhould be apt **to be fo** paffionate, as to affront them, **if** I can, **unlefs** difcretion fhould get betwixt my paffion and their bold-nefs, which fometimes perchance it might, if difcretion fhould croud hard for place; for though I am naturally bafhful, yet in fuch **a** caufe **my** fpirits would be all on fire, otherwife I am **fo well** bred, as to be civill to all perfons, of **all** degrees, or qualities: likewife **I** am fo proud, or rather juft to my Lord, as to abate nothing of the qualitie **of his** Wife, for if honour be the marke **of** Merit, and his Mafters royall favour, who will favour none

but thofe that have Merit to deferve, it were
a bafenefs for me to neglect the Ceremony
thereof: Alfo in fome cafes I am naturally a
Coward, and in other cafes very valiant; as
for example, if any of my neereft friends were
in danger, I fhould never confider my life in
ftriving to help them, though I were fure to
do them no good, and would willingly, nay
cheerfully, refign my life for their fakes : likewife I fhould not fpare my Life, if Honour
bids me dye; but in a danger where my Friends,
or my Honour is not concerned, or ingaged,
but only my Life to be unprofitably loft, I am
the verieft coward in Nature, as upon the Sea,
or any dangerous places, or of Thieves, or
fire, or the like; Nay the fhooting of a gun,
although but a Pot-gun, will make me ftart,
and ftop my hearing, much lefs have I courage
to difcharge one ; or if a fword fhould be held
againft me, although but in jeft, I am afraid :
alfo as I am not covetous, fo I am not prodigall,
but of the two I am inclining to be prodigall,
yet I cannot fay to a vain prodigallity, becaufe
I imagine it is to a profitable end; for perceiving the world is given, or apt to honour
the outfide more than the infide, worfhipping

fhow more then fubftance; and I am fo vain, if it be a **Vanity, as to endeavour to be** worfhip't, rather than **not** to be **regarded;** yet I fhall never be **fo** prodigall **as** to impoverifh my friends, or go beyond the limits or facilitie of our Eftate, and though I defire to appear **to the** beft advantage, whileft I live in the **view of** the public World, yet I could moft willingly exclude myfelf, fo as Never to fee the face of any creature, but my **Lord, as** long as I live, inclofing myfelf like an Anchoret, wearing a Frize gown, **tied** with a cord about my wafte: but I hope my readers will not think me **vain** for writing my **life,** fince **there** have been many **that** have done **the like, as** Cefar, Ovid, and many more, both men and women, and I know no reafon I may not do **it as** well as they: **but** I verily believe fome cen**fur**ing Readers **will** fcornfully fay, why hath this **Lady** writ her own Life? fince **none** cares **to** know whofe daughter fhe **was, or** whofe wife fhe is, **or** how fhe **was bred, or** **what** fortunes fhe **had,** or how **fhe** lived, **or** what humour or difpofition fhe **was** of? I anfwer that **it** is true, that 'tis **to** no purpofe to the Readers, but **it is** to the Authorefs, becaufe I write it for my own fake, not theirs; neither did I intend this **piece for to** delight, but to divulge; not to pleafe the **fancy,** but to **tell** the truth, left after-ages fhould miftake, in not knowing I was daughter to one Mafter Lucas of **St.** Johns, near Colchefter, in Effex, fecond wife to the Lord Marquifs of New-caftle; for my **Lord** having had two Wives, I might eafily **have been** miftaken, efpecially if I fhould dye and my Lord Marry **again.**[1]

---

[1] It is remarkable that this has, notwithftanding, been the cafe. See "The Lounger's Common-Place Book," vol. iii. p. 398.

FINIS.

CHISWICK PRESS:—PRINTED BY WHITTINGHAM AND WILKINS, TOOKS COURT, CHANCERY LANE.